"Why are you weeding in the dark, Rianne?"

"It soothes me when I feel hemmed in."

"Something happen at work today? The kids?"

She looked toward the hedge. Her shoulders drooped. She shook her head.

He didn't know why it hurt, but it did. He wanted her trust. Trust. Belief. Support. Yeah, he wanted the combo. He wanted to offer comfort. Which would mean touching more than her hands. *Not wise, Jon.* Except, wisdom and want were at a draw and he was all out of referees.

"Come here." He tugged her forward until her shoulder leaned into his chest. *For her comfort,* he told himself, and wrapped his arms around her. "Shh. We're okay," he murmured into the crown of her hair. Holding her loosely, waiting until the tension left by degrees.

She felt great in his arms. Small, warm, soft.

A surge to claim her rushed up, stunning him....

Dear Reader,

Well, we hope your New Year's resolutions included reading some fabulous new books—because we can provide the reading material! We begin with *Stranded with the Groom* by Christine Rimmer, part of our new MONTANA MAVERICKS: GOLD RUSH GROOMS miniseries. When a staged wedding reenactment turns into the real thing, can the actual honeymoon be far behind? Tune in next month for the next installment in this exciting new continuity.

Victoria Pade concludes her NORTHBRIDGE NUPTIALS miniseries with *Having the Bachelor's Baby,* in which a woman trying to push aside memories of her one night of passion with the town's former bad boy finds herself left with one little reminder of that encounter—she's pregnant with his child. Judy Duarte begins her new miniseries, BAYSIDE BACHELORS, with *Hailey's Hero,* featuring a cautious woman who finds herself losing her heart to a rugged rebel who might break it…. THE HATHAWAYS OF MORGAN CREEK by Patricia Kay continues with *His Best Friend,* in which a woman is torn between two men—the one she really wants, and the one to whom he owes his life. Mary J. Forbes's sophomore Special Edition is *A Father, Again,* featuring a grown-up reunion between a single mother and her teenaged crush. And a disabled child, an exhausted mother and a down-but-not-out rodeo hero all come together in a big way, in Christine Wenger's debut novel, *The Cowboy Way.*

So enjoy, and come back next month for six compelling new novels, from Silhouette Special Edition.

Happy New Year!

Gail Chasan
Senior Editor
Silhouette Special Edition

Please address questions and book requests to:
Silhouette Reader Service
U.S.: 3010 Walden Ave., P.O. Box 1325, Buffalo, NY 14269
Canadian: P.O. Box 609, Fort Erie, Ont. L2A 5X3

A Father, Again

MARY J. FORBES

Silhouette

SPECIAL EDITION

Published by Silhouette Books

America's Publisher of Contemporary Romance

To Karen, for loving Jon Tucker the way I did.

Thanks to Tom Lindmark for his descriptive e-mails
on the geography and history of the Clatskanie area.
Any errors are entirely mine, not his.

 SILHOUETTE BOOKS

ISBN 0-373-24661-7

A FATHER, AGAIN

Copyright © 2005 by Mary J. Forbes

This edition published by arrangement with Harlequin Books S.A.

® and TM are trademarks of Harlequin Books S.A., used under license.
Trademarks indicated with ® are registered in the United States Patent
and Trademark Office, the Canadian Trade Marks Office and in other
countries.

Visit Silhouette Books at www.eHarlequin.com

Printed in U.S.A.

Books by Mary J. Forbes

Silhouette Special Edition

A Forever Family #1625
A Father, Again #1661

MARY J. FORBES

grew up on a farm in Alberta amidst horses, cattle, crisp hay and broad blue skies. As a child, she drew and wrote about her surroundings, and in sixth grade composed her first story about a lame little pony. Years later, she was an accountant and worked as a reporter/photographer for a small-town newspaper and attained honors degrees in education. She has also written and published short fiction.

Today, Mary—a teacher by profession—lives in the Pacific Northwest with her husband and two children. A romantic by nature, she loves walking along the ocean shoreline, sitting by the fire on snowy or rainy evenings and two-stepping around the dance floor to a good country song—all with her own real-life hero, of course. Mary loves to hear from readers. You can contact her at www.maryjforbes.com.

May 4

Certain moments in life go beyond the casual flickering of memory in your mind's eye. I call these moments "crystals." They let your palm and fingers relearn the cool curve of the doorknob. They let your bare soles recall the comfort of the mat's ragged braids. They let your nose remember the difference between the oatmeal cookies in the oven behind you, and the sap in the trees across the yard. But above all, you see, again, how shadow and light stroke cheek and jaw. And you recognize the hurried cadence of your heart.

Today I embraced a crystal moment.

—Journal entry of Rianne Worth

Chapter One

Damn the woman and her cat.

Jon Tucker trotted down his back veranda steps and strode across his weed-blooming yard. Under his arm, the cardboard box rustled. It wasn't that he resented cats. He didn't like them touring his yard, was all. He didn't like *anyone* on his property.

What he did like—*prized*—was his solitary life.

That's why he'd bought this quiet, street-end property with its decrepit·Victorian and two acres of woods.

His brothers knew the score, even though they didn't relish it, even though they had tried to change his mind more than once. Heck, after his twenty-two-year absence, who could blame them?

He could forgive Luke and Seth.

He wouldn't forgive his neighbor.

The woman just didn't get it. Cats roamed. The orange lady

in the box was an expert. He'd chased her off his land time and again since moving back to Oregon's Columbia County two weeks ago. Now, she'd had the gall to birth three kittens on his shirt. His *favorite* shirt. The last of his police-academy attire, the last tangible link to the force that had been his life, his blood, for two decades.

The last link to his memories.

His nightmares.

The neighbor woman would pay. Damn straight she would.

He sidled through the narrow gap in the ten-foot juniper hedge dividing their backyards. Most likely, when it was planted years ago the owners had been on more friendly terms. Their kids, dogs—*and cats,* no doubt—had beat this path through it. Well. He'd call the local greenhouse the instant he dumped off the wailing felines and order another shrub to fill in the spot. What did it matter, his mounting costs?

Shifting the box, he climbed the three back steps of the cottage's porch. His boot heels rapped the slats of its deck. His knuckles rapped the door.

The place needed an overhaul. A big paint job. In contrast, the yard would scoop the blue ribbon at the local fair. Dethatched turf; daffodils and tulips nodding from borders; the apple tree blossoming in the May sunshine; bedding frames in a porch corner.

He knocked again.

Where was she? He'd seen her old red Toyota in the carport.

The door cracked open.

A woman stood in a rectangle of muted light.

He stood tongue-tied, impassioned rants gone.

She was tiny. Lower than his shoulder. Auburn hair. Ratty blue sweatshirt. Small, bare feet. Maroon-stained toenails.

"Yes?"

One word. It locked his gaze to her caution-filled, flax-brown eyes; an instant later, she blinked and sucked in a quick breath.

A small meow tore through his trance.

C'mon, Jon. You're here for a reason. Thrusting the box forward, he said, "Your cats."

She grabbed the unwieldy carton; the door swung wider and he saw a child, a girl a bit younger than Brittany, hovering near the kitchen table, big-eyed behind round lenses, pinky in her mouth.

"Cats?" The woman frowned. "We only have one. Sorry. We try to keep her in the house, but sometimes she slips out the door behind us."

"Now you have four," he said gruffly. "Kitty had a litter."

Her eyes widened. She peered under a flap. "Oohhh," she exclaimed softly. "Sweetpea… No *wonder* you were so fat."

Sweetpea?

His neighbor looked up. His throat tightened. Hers was an honest face, a gentle face. *Life's not honest,* he wanted to tell her. *It's cruel. Callous. Unjust.*

A shy half smile. "My daughter Emily—" she glanced back at the child "—found her in an old tub of dried sweetpea vines inside our garden shed a month ago, thin as a rail and shaky with hunger. I don't think she'd been fed in two weeks. We put ads in the paper, but so far no one's claimed her."

Jon stared at the woman. Green and gold dappled her irises. He turned on his heel.

"Wait—" She followed him across the porch. "Where did you find Sweetpea?"

"On my shirt." In the shadiest corner of his back deck, to be exact. Where he'd tossed his sweatshirt on the Adirondack chair when the temperature broke the eighty-degree mark while he'd been hammering in a new railing. He trotted down her steps and headed for the chink in the hedge without a backward look.

"Sweetpea," he muttered. *More like sourpuss.* The claw marks on his hands proved it.

He'd get that extra juniper in before the sun went down.

Rianne Worth watched the broad back of her visitor disappear.

Jon Tucker.

Heavens, when had she seen him last? More than twenty years ago, at least. She hadn't recognized him. Not until he'd looked directly at her, demanding she keep her cats off his land. Those eyes, oh, she'd remember them in any decade! Eyes she still saw every so often in her slumbering dreams. Inscrutable, more than a little perilous.

"Who was that man, Mommy?"

Rianne turned to the child at her side. Her shy angel-girl. One day—soon—Emily would shout and laugh and charge into rooms like any normal eight-year-old. *You will, Em. I promise.* "Our new neighbor, pooch."

"He looks mean."

Rianne couldn't deny it; he *had* looked mean. And angry. What had the years done to shroud him in that aura of arctic barrenness? The Jon Tucker of her youth flashed across her mind. Rough-and-tumble black hair, leather jacket, souped-up yellow pickup. Tough and grim. Kind in heart.

"Is he like Daddy?"

God forbid. "No, honey he's not like your father." At least not the Jon she remembered. "He doesn't like to be bothered, that's all," she said, trying as always to look for the good, the decent. She knelt and held open the box flaps. "Come see what he brought."

"Oh, Mom-*meee!*" Emily breathed reverently. "Sweetpea's got babies!" She reached in a tiny finger.

"Careful, honey. Don't touch the kitties for a week or so."

"I know. We learned that in science."

Rianne touched her daughter's hair. "Smart girl to remember."

"They're so *cute.*"

"They are," she agreed. Sort of. Three mouse-sized creatures with awkward heads, squashed ears and closed eyes clambered over one another to nurse.

Emily stroked Sweetpea's back. The cat yielded a purry meow, sniffed daintily at the girl's fingers. "When'd she have them?"

"Today, it seems."

Brown eyes centered on Rianne. "Did the man take her to the vet'narian?"

"No. She birthed her kittens at his house. Em, once the kittens are weaned, Sweetpea will have an operation so she can't have any more babies—"

"Is that why he talked so mad?"

"Who?"

"The man."

"He wasn't mad, honey. Just a little concerned." All right, prickly as a chained dog. When she'd opened the door, his big, strong body had blocked out the day—similar to another muscled body—and her heart had stumbled.

Then she'd seen his eyes, his beautiful, ink-blue eyes.

Since the sold sign had disappeared next door, she'd seen him off and on, laboring on that century-aged house. He hadn't waved, nodded, said hello. But, then, neither had she.

And now?

He hadn't recognized her, nor was he inclined to friendliness, and he seemed to dislike animals. She would need to keep close tabs on Sweetpea, plus make a spaying appointment with the veterinarian ASAP.

Hoisting up the carton, she stood. "Let's take the kittens

inside, Em. Sweetpea's probably hungry and needs a clean bed for her babies."

Rianne carried the box into the kitchen and positioned it beside the cat's food dish. Sweetpea lifted herself away from her wriggling offspring, then hopped out of the box to lap at the fresh water Rianne brought.

"She's thirsty, Mom." Emily squatted inches from the little family. "Hungry, too," she added when the mother cat meowed her gratitude for the canned food.

The back door slammed. "I'm starving, Mom! What's to eat?"

Sam, Rianne's thirteen-year-old son, flung himself into the kitchen, cheeks red, brown hair mussed from the bike ride home.

"Hey, suhweeet!" Slinging off his backpack, he dropped to his knees beside his sister. "Sweetpea had kittens? That's so cool."

Rianne's heart swelled. Every moment of joy was like a gift; she vowed to keep them coming.

"Whose shirt?" Sam eyed the faded, navy-blue cotton bunched in the bottom of the box.

"It belongs to our neighbor. Jon Tucker."

"The biker guy? The one with the long hair and the tattoo here?" He patted his left forearm.

"Yes."

"Oh, man, this is *major* cool. Now that you've met him, maybe I can go over and see his Harley."

"Don't, Sammy," Emily piped up. "He talks really mean."

Sam's grin vanished. "Mean?"

Okay, Rianne thought, *let's iron this out right now.* "Mr. Tucker isn't accustomed to having animals around, Sam. It seems Sweetpea's been visiting regularly."

"But she's just a cat!"

"Some people are afraid of cats. They may've had a bad experience with them as a child or they might have allergies. Like Em with pumpkins. You know how she breaks out in a rash whenever she eats pumpkin pie?"

Emily nodded; Sam simply stared.

She went on. "As you know, people can have reactions to cats and other animals. Sometimes," she paused for effect, "they get upset. Em cries because the rash itches and hurts. But a man like Mr. Tucker doesn't cry. Instead, he may get worried or anxious."

"Why doesn't he cry?" Emily asked.

Sam rolled his eyes. "Haven't you learned anything? Men don't cry."

Rianne crouched between her children. "Some men do cry. It depends on the person and the circumstances."

She didn't believe it of Jon. Not with his flat voice. His ice eyes.

"Dad never cried," Sam spat. "He just…just…"

"As I said, it depends on the person, honey. Either way, it isn't a fault. Just because you don't see someone cry, doesn't mean they don't hurt inside."

"Is our neighbor hurting?" Emily asked.

"I think he had a bad day." She gave both kids a quick hug. "We need to put Sweetpea and her family into her basket."

They replaced the shirt with an old blanket and decided to transfer the basket to Rianne's sewing room where it was quieter, where southern sunshine warmed the small space for most of the day. Safe and snug, the mother cat stretched beside her brood. Her rough, pink tongue reassured each mewling kit.

Sitting back on her heels, with Jon's shirt in her lap, Rianne watched the new family. And her own.

Sam stroked Sweetpea with the back of his right hand, his deformed hand. He'd been born with a normal left hand, but a finger and thumb were its right counterpart. Her son had learned early in life to hide his handicap. His father hadn't wanted to see it, to admit it existed. In the fifteen months since Duane Kirby's car crashed and killed him, Sam was slowly transforming. Rianne encouraged him; his school counselor coached him. At home, using his right hand had become second nature.

Around strangers he remained shy about his handicap.

Soon that, too, would change.

Nothing would keep her from giving her children what they deserved: a loving, happy home. *With friends and fun and all things normal.* Everything she'd grown up with, here in Misty River.

"Are you taking the man's shirt back to his house, Mom?" Emily asked.

"I need to wash it first."

Sam reached over, tapped the slim, curved edge of a capital S. "What's the logo?"

Rianne pressed back the folds of the material, careful to hide any bloody smears. An oval seal came into view, its gold letters arcing above a shield. Seattle Police. Jon was a cop?

Sam leaned over. "What's it say?"

Rianne bundled the shirt into a ball and climbed to her feet. "It's a bit messy from the birth. Could you take out those brownies I baked yesterday, Sam?"

"Can I have two? I'm starving."

"Me, too." Emily got up.

"Fine, two each and pour some milk. I'll be back as soon as I get the washing machine going."

She went down the basement stairs, headed for the cramped laundry room. Maybe Jon wasn't a cop. Maybe he'd received an SPD sweatshirt from a friend.

And if he was?

If he is, it's got nothing to do with you.

It simply meant that tough, bad-boy Jon Tucker of Misty River, Oregon, had become an officer of the law dressed in blue, with thirty pounds of weaponry strapped to his body. If there was irony in that, so be it.

The Jon Tucker today is not the man you remember.

No. At fourteen, she'd been enthralled. A little in love. And, unable to make sense of her English class. Who cared that Robert Browning wrote love sonnets to his wife, Elizabeth? That Alfred Lord Tennyson saw "a flower in a crannied wall"?

Twenty-year-old Jon Tucker had.

Sitting on the worn vinyl seat of his old Ford pickup, Rianne had listened while he interpreted the rich beauty of poetry and the classics. That year, she got her first A in English. And Jon, treating her with the ease of a big brother, got her heart. He'd left Misty River a year later, and she'd tucked him into a quiet corner of her soul where he hovered like a tiny, bright spot all through high school.

All through her marriage.

"Mom?" called Sam.

"Be right there!"

She eyed the sweatshirt in her hands.

Water under the bridge.

She shoved the garment into the washer's barrel. Several socks, another shirt, softener, and the lid clunked down.

What was he doing back in Misty River?

And what had he, standing on her porch in faded jeans and white T-shirt, thought of *her?*

Doesn't matter.

Your tummy is doing little spins.

It is not.

Of course it is. You know why, don't you?

Oh, yes, she knew why.

Jon Tucker lived next door. And she was no longer a child-ish fourteen-year-old with braces on her teeth.

"You figure June is the earliest we can dig up this mess, put in new brick?" Jon asked. He and his brother sat on Jon's porch steps surveying his ragged driveway in the evening light.

Seth lifted his cap, raked back his shaggy hair and gave the lane another thoughtful study. Tall weeds sprouted at its edges. Grass tufted through spider-web cracks in the concrete. "Wish I could fit you in before, J.T., but you know how it is."

"Yeah." Jon did know. Seth and his crew had been booked nearly six weeks ahead since March. Seemed everybody and his dog wanted some type of contracting work done this spring.

Jon figured the driveway would take a week or so. Situ-ated last on the narrow tree-lined street, his parcel of land was the biggest. And the shabbiest. Great for the price, not great for renovations.

Checking the sky, Seth commented, "Looks like we'll be held up another day as it is."

Over the Coast Range mountains, rain made a dull approach into the valley. Terrific. Another day's delay to the house's ex-terior changes. Jon wanted them done by mid-June when he could concentrate on the inside—and Brittany's bedroom.

"Well," he said and grinned. "Considering the price you're charging me, I suppose I can wait for the driveway." Besides, it wouldn't do for his brother to bump a paying cus-tomer because his long-lost kin had hit town and wanted in-stant curb appeal.

The red, dented Toyota rolled up next door. His neighbor, Ms. Kitty Litter. The one he'd dubbed Ms. Sex Kitten in the past twenty-four hours.

"You talked to her yet?" Seth drawled, watching what Jon watched—slim, black-hosed legs swinging from the car. Gold skirt above feminine knees. Clingy black sweater. Small shapely curves.

"Yesterday. For about sixty seconds. Seems like a nice enough woman." It didn't matter one way or the other; he wasn't into congeniality, especially with the neighbors.

"She's single again."

"Huh." Jon figured as much. Mr. Kitty Litter had been visibly absent since Jon had moved into the vicinity. "Didn't get around to the small talk."

The woman held a brown bag. Her eyes found his across ninety feet of ratty grass. She didn't move, didn't open her mouth, just stood and looked back at him.

A dark-haired boy, about twelve, entered the carport from their backyard. She slammed shut the car door, the sound hollow in the quiet dusk.

"Hi, sweetie." Her smile could liquefy a steel girder.

The kid hauled up the mountain bike propped against the house. "Can I go over to Joey's for a half hour?"

"Where's Emily?"

"With the kittens. Can I go?"

Lightning crinkled the navy sky and thunder growled, closer now. She looked west, past Jon and Seth, as if they were transparent. "Not tonight, Sam."

"Aw, Mom… I'll pedal real fast," he added eagerly.

"No, Sammy. It's after eight and I don't want you coming home in a downpour."

"Pleeease."

She veered another look Jon's way. "I said no."

Without a word, the kid shoved the bike back into place, spun toward the rear of the house and vanished behind the junipers. Shoulders squared, she skipped a third look their way. Jon almost smiled. She had grit, this woman.

With her son. With him and Seth as an audience.

She hadn't run off. That point alone was enough to jack up his admiration about two hundred notches. Offering the slightest of nods, he conveyed what he felt. Deference in the slant of her chin, she returned the gesture and walked out of sight.

Sparse drops of rain fell. Seth set down his empty soda can. "Well. This town hasn't seen anything that pretty in a while."

"That a fact?"

"Uh-huh." A measured look at Jon. "You really don't remember her, do you?"

"Should I?"

"Hell, I thought every guy from sixth grade up, living to a hundred, would remember the way that red hair used to hang past her— Hell," he said again, clearly disconcerted about the direction of his musings.

Jon stared at the carport. "She's…*Rianne Worth?*"

"Bingo."

Clueless fool. She knew you. He took in the weathered little house. "Husband?"

"Dead, what I heard. She showed up one day early last summer from California somewhere, rented a motel for a week, then moved in there. She's a part-time librarian or some such at Chinook Elementary. Hallie knows her. Says she subs now and then at the high school as well."

Jon kept silent. He wondered what Seth's daughter thought of Rianne Worth as a teacher. Jon knew what *he* used to think of her, as a teenager.

Too many years ago, way too many years.

The rain increased. Drops mottled the driveway. Seth got to his feet and pulled the bill of his cap low. "Okay, I'm off."

"Yep." Jon rose. "Talk to you tomorrow."

Shoulders hunched against the rain, his brother headed for his green pickup. Moments later, Jon stood alone.

A steady drizzle pelted the earth like buckshot. Thunder

tussled in the heavy, dismal sky. He made no move to go inside, instead allowed the storm to soak him. Harder, faster it came, collecting in puddles where the aged concrete had sunk over time. The budding trees fronting his yard glistened in a tangle of shiny, black prongs.

Since he was a kid, he'd enjoyed rain, would walk hours in it when his mother was on an extrarotten binge. When her drunken cursing defiled their home, and his father escaped out back to the shed and his brothers hid in their bedrooms or the basement.

Listening to the rain, feeling its blunt, wet needles cool his skin, helped him forget some of life's uglies. Of course, no matter how hard it rained, how far he walked, one of those uglies would *never* fade.

A sound to the left drew him. Rianne Worth, still in heels, skirt and clingy top, was piloting a giant purple umbrella while lifting two bags of groceries from the trunk of her car. Success evaded her; the trunk was loaded. She, on the other hand, kept dodging a sheet of rain baling through the tattered roof of the carport directly above the bumper. She had to move the car forward another two feet, which was impossible, or back it up, which would put her smack into the rain.

He could help.

Don't get involved.

She struggled another minute, gave up and carried a lone bag around back.

Ah, damn it.

Crossing his soggy mess of lawn, Jon stepped over the pruned shrub roses edging her drive. Behind the car, the cold stream from the roof caught him full across the neck and shoulders, drenching his ponytail and T-shirt. Five plastic bags in one hand, six in the other, he shook his head, blinked water from his eyes and rounded the rear bumper.

She stood ten feet away. A petite gold and black silhouette under a purple mushroom. *Rianne.*

Twenty-two years, and what could he say?

You've grown up damn pretty?

You're someone I don't recognize?

Hell, most days he barely knew himself.

"Shut the trunk," he ordered, shouldering past her and heading for the back of the cottage. He bowed his head to the striking rain while her shoes clicked behind him.

Under the porch overhang, she flipped the umbrella closed, parked it against the wall, then held open the door, waiting for him to proceed into the warm house.

In a minuscule entryway, he stopped. "Where?"

"To the left."

A whiff of her scent mingled with the damp air.

Rain on woman.

He turned into a kitchen about the size of his bedroom closet and set the bags in front of the stove and refrigerator. When he straightened, she stood near the door, hands clasped in front of her, little-girl fashion.

"Thank you," she said in that same soft tone he remembered.

"You're welcome." He looked at his grubby harness boots. Sprigs of dead grass clung to the toes. "I've dirtied your kitchen."

"Don't worry about it. Would you like some coffee?"

He ran a hand down his dripping cheeks, scraped back his soggy hair. He could stay, get to know her as a neighbor—the five second Hi-how's-it-going? type—or he could leave.

Seth's comments pitched both options. "You remember me."

Her eyes didn't waver. "Yes. I do."

He flinched. She would. Two decades ago, every kid from first grade up knew the Tuckers. Not hard in a town of a thousand souls. Not hard when, on any given day, the mother of those Tuckers stumbled down the sidewalk, drunk.

"Well," he said, disgruntled she undoubtedly recalled those days. "I'll go then."

"Jon." His name was a touch. "I'd really like you to stay for coffee. You were kind enough to help, and…" The half smile from yesterday returned. "I feel responsible for what Sweetpea did to your shirt."

"Forget it. Cat needed a spot, shirt fit the bill."

"I've washed it. Wait a second." She disappeared down a short hallway.

He took a breath. Fine. He'd stay for a cup. He went to the door, took off his boots, set them on the outside mat with its white scripted Welcome to Our Home.

Her footsteps returned. "Jon?"

"Here."

"Good. You stayed." She smiled and placed his neatly folded shirt on the table, then began scooping coffee into a maker. He approached the end of the counter where she worked.

Abruptly, she faced him. "Are you a cop?"

"I was. I quit a month ago."

He'd been asked to take stress leave and had opted for retirement. After Nicky's death, his work had suffered. Hell, after the loss of his son life became an abyss—where he still floundered.

Rianne set the coffee on.

"Where are your kids?" he asked. *The boy with the bike?*

"Downstairs, watching TV." She checked a sunflower clock on the wall above the stove. "It'll be Emily's bedtime in fifteen minutes. We'll have time for one cup before the nightly whining begins." She sported another of those sweet smiles. He sported fantasies that were way out of line.

Not wanting to hear about kids, tooth-brushing or bedtime rituals, he asked, "That decaf?"

"I'd be wide-eyed as an owl with the real stuff. Please. Sit." She motioned to the table with four ladder-back chairs, then opened a tiny pantry to shelve the groceries.

He stepped beside her and placed three cans of spaghetti sauce on an upper shelf. Before he could reach for another tin, she said, "Would you please sit at the table?"

"I don't mind a little kitchen duty."

She took the tin from his hand. "I'd rather you sat."

It took two seconds for irritation to plant itself. Good enough to play pack mule and carry groceries, but apparently lacking the aptitude to see where they belonged.

Just like Colleen. *"Go do your man thing and stay out of my kitchen. I don't need you here."*

In the end, had she needed him anywhere? As her husband? As the father of their kids?

"Thanks, but I really don't have time for coffee," he said, stepping over three bags. "Got a ton of work that needs doing." Grabbing the shirt she'd laundered, he headed for the door and his boots. *So much for neighborly ways.*

"Jon. Don't go. It's…"

A sitcom's cackle drifted up from below. Rain drummed on the roof above.

"It's not you," she went on, throat closing. "It's me. I…" Her heart thrummed. *Men in general make me edgy.* Logically she knew Jon was not "men in general." Still… He defeated her own height of five-four by almost a foot. And in that soaked navy T-shirt his chest appeared unforgiving.

She avoided looking at his arms, his hands. She'd seen them lift the groceries like a spoonful of granola. Powerful. Dusted with dark, masculine hair, right to the knuckles on his work-toughened fingers. A wolf tattoo prowled along rain-damp skin above his left wrist. Once the town rebel, now a man of dark secrets and possible danger.

But look at him, she did. Straight into eyes as indifferent as a tundra windchill. "I'm not used to having company." Purposely, she kept her hands loose. "You took me off guard." Because she hadn't expected to see him again for at least another week or two, except maybe across the distance of their yards.

Then out of the wet, dark weather he'd loomed…black ponytail plastered to his neck…frown honing every determined angle of his face… And her breath…

She hadn't breathed calmly since.

He said nothing, but neither did he leave. Just looked at her. Waiting.

"I'm sorry," she offered finally.

"For what?"

"For how I must sound. As I said—"

"You're not used to company or want it. That makes two of us." The words were sensitive as winterkill.

He turned and stepped out onto the deck, pushing wool-socked feet into his boots. Without bothering with the laces, he walked down the steps, into the rain.

She wanted to call out. Invite him back. Wanted to explain it wasn't him, but another that had her fluttering worse than a nervous house wren. Silent, she went to the edge of the porch. Self-control was difficult to teach, arduous to learn. At the moment, she needed strength. If it looked cowardly, she didn't care. She clasped her hands in front of her.

Halfway across her lawn, he stopped. Rain lashed his heavy shoulders and skimmed from an implacable chin.

"Good-bye, Rianne."

Securing the laundered shirt under an arm, he shoved his hands into his pockets and disappeared through the hole in the juniper hedge. He *had* known who she was. Why hadn't he acknowledged her yesterday? Or had Seth sitting on those steps confirmed it today?

"You remember me."

She'd never forgotten.

She listened to the downpour on the roof. Heard it gush in the eaves. Watched a mini waterfall at the side of the porch.

Chilled, she went back into the house, where she finished the groceries, working efficiently, rolling up the plastic bags and tucking them into a drawer. From the skinny broom closet, she hauled out the mop. After wetting the sponge under the tub tap in the bathroom down the hall, she set about tidying up puddles left by big, work-battered boots. *He means nothing to me. Nothing.*

Then why did you put him in your journal?

She clenched her jaw to an aching point.

God help me, I'll erase it tonight.

But she heard again her name, submerged in a deep quiet timbre.

Chapter Two

Phone to his ear, Jon propped a hip on the counter in his spacious kitchen and stared absently at his reflection in the dark glass shielding the wet night. Three rings.

"Come on," he muttered. "Pick up."

Five rings. "Hi," said a familiar, breathless voice.

"Hey, Colleen."

A pause. "It's you."

Who were you expecting? "It's me," he acknowledged. "Brittany around?"

"She's busy watching TV."

He tamped down a flash of ire. "Could you get her please? I'd like to talk to my daughter."

Muffled tones told him his ex-wife had covered the mouthpiece. Then, "Brittany would rather not tonight. She's not feeling well."

To hell with it. "Just get her, Colleen. If she doesn't wanna talk she can tell me herself. Or should I drive up this minute and see what the problem really is?"

"You wouldn't."

"Try me."

Again silence, again the muffled conversation. "Fine, I'll get her."

He winced as the receiver slammed the light-green counter he knew so well. In the background, he heard a male voice comment, "Don't let him hassle you, Col." Jon pinched the bridge of his nose and counted to two hundred by fives. Finally footsteps, running ones, came closer. The phone scraped off the counter.

"Daddy?"

"Hey, peanut. How ya doing?"

"Okay, I guess."

"Not feeling so hot, huh?"

"No."

"Got a cold or a tummy-ache?"

"Uh-uh."

Pause.

"You can tell me, sweetheart."

"Mom said I shouldn't talk to you."

Anger leapt, a fresh flame. He curbed the urge to bellow through the phone for his ex-wife. "Why not, Brit?"

"I dunno." He imagined her tracing patterns along the countertop. "Mom said it gets me mixed up. Especially now that she's gonna marry Allan."

With effort Jon pulled in a calming breath. He didn't give a flying fig who his ex married, but to play on Brittany's feelings made his blood pump. He forced his fingers loose on the receiver. "Do you want me to stop phoning, honey?"

He felt her hesitate. His heart disintegrated.

"When I'm with you—" her voice was tiny "—I don't

want to come home. But I don't want Mom to be alone either."

"Aw, peanut…"

He heard her sniff. God, he wished he had Harry Potter's broom to zip himself there. But what good would that do? Right or wrong, good or bad, he and Colleen were divorced. End of story.

"Dad?"

"Yeah, love."

"I don't like Allan," she whispered.

Jon's inner antennae shot up. "Why, Brit?"

"I dunno. Just that he pretends he's you, and I don't like that."

He emitted a relieved sigh. If that was all—

"And Allan says things about Nicky."

A chill spiked Jon's skin. His son. His beautiful, dark-haired, blue-eyed son. Who at fifteen had attracted girls, gloried in the attention, but still found time to read his sister a bedtime story. Who would have grown into a fine, upstanding young man had his father been there to guide him.

He swallowed the burl in his throat. "What things, Brit?"

"Mean stuff. Like, if we'd had him for a father Nicky would still be alive. Stuff like that."

Jon squeezed his eyes shut and pressed his lips together. The SOB was right. If they'd had anyone but Jon as a father, his son might very well still be kicking a football or slam-dunking baskets with his high school buddies. But then, if they'd had anyone else, Nick wouldn't have been his son, and Brittany—with her little freckled nose and long, pale hair—wouldn't be his daughter. The proverbial catch-22.

One totally unfair to play on his baby girl.

He opened his eyes and pushed a rough-padded finger above his right eyebrow where a headache festered. That Brittany wasn't in some psychiatrist's office with the mumbo crap being fed her by Colleen and the esteemed twit, Allan, was a wonder. "Sweetheart, I want you to listen real careful, okay?"

"Okay."

"When Allan, and even Mom," he added with a wince, "start saying things about Nicky that you don't like, I want you to get up and walk out of the room."

"But what if we're in the car going somewhere?"

Ah, hell. "Ask them to not discuss Nick in front of you and if they continue, sing to yourself. Try to block it out as best you can. All right?"

"I'll try."

"You know I love you with all my heart."

"I love you, too."

"I'll see you soon, all right?"

"When?"

"Summer…in a couple of months, like we talked about."

"Allan says I should stay here for the summer."

Jon bounced a fist on the counter. How he kept his voice from shaking, his emotions from screaming, was a miracle. "Peanut, that's not going to happen. Now, I'm going to say good-night because I still need to talk to Mom before I hang up."

"Okay. She's in the foyer saying goodbye to Allan." There was a shuffle on the line. "Gross. They're kissing and I can see Allan's tongue. Yuck!"

Damn you, Colleen. Not in front of my daughter. "Brit, honey, tell her I need to talk to her, pronto."

"Right. Bye, Dad."

"Bye, peanut."

The phone met Formica a second before he heard her yell for Colleen. It took almost six minutes of long-distance time for his ex to pick up. She got right to the point.

"Just so you know, I don't like being yanked away from an important matter."

"The next time you want to do the tongue tango with your lover, do it without *my* daughter around."

"How dare you. Al and I were discussing our wedding."

"I won't beat around the bush, Colleen. Brittany is staying with me when school's out whether your boyfriend likes it or not. It's what we decided on paper, and no one's going to keep my daughter from being with her daddy. Understand?"

"Perfectly. Why should I expect anything different?" she said bitterly. "It's always been *you*, hasn't it? Whatever's good for *you*. The kids and I were always last on your list."

Pain lanced through him. "I can't help what happened in the past. But I sure as hell can help what's happening right now. If Brittany wants to be with me for two months, then she can. Neither you nor that jackass you're marrying has a right to take that away from her. And—" his voice turned dark "—if you do, we'll revisit this in court. Oh, and another thing. Brittany doesn't like Allan playing dad around her. Tell him to lay off."

"He does *not* play anything around her. He just wants to be a good father figure. Which is a lot more than her real daddy's been over the last ten years."

That stung. "Look, I'm sorry I've hurt you, but dredging up the past is useless. We can't change it."

"Tell that to your daughter when she cries at night for her brother." The phone clicked off.

Jon had no idea how long he stood there with the receiver humming before he finally set it back in the cradle.

Blindly, he looked at the oak cupboards housing his few cracked dishes. He should go upstairs, take a long, hot shower. His clothes were sticky and cold on his skin from the rain, his hair knotted and damp. If he wasn't careful, he'd be down with a bug and where would that get his plans to finish this house?

In a daze he looked around the room. *Like you really need a place this size, Jon.*

Where had his mind been when he'd bought it? Brittany was ten years old, a sprite with his blue eyes and her mom's fair hair. A sprite who'd visit three times a year. Who required one bedroom, not five.

And when she went back to Seattle?

Here he'd be.

Lone wolf prowling inside four dozen tall walls.

Evenings, he'd sit out back. Sip a cool one as the sun dwindled. Day after day, year after year. He'd watch the grass grow, the trees spread wider, the hedge reach another ten feet toward the sky. All for what? Brittany?

In three, four years Seattle would be prime pickings for a teenager doing all the things young girls do at that age.

Misty River, Oregon, with its conservatism, offered piddly.

He didn't fool himself into thinking she'd want to spend even a weekend with him when that time came.

Then why not let Allan-the-Great take over? Be the father figure she needs? A man home every evening, staying till morning. A family man. A man who could give Colleen another baby.

Another brother for Brittany.

Jon spun around and cursed. Stalking to the door, he yanked it open and stepped onto the back deck. The rain had quit and the moist night air struck like a frigid fist. Let him come down with SARS. Everything that mattered was lost already.

Job.

Marriage.

Family.

Nick.

The floorboards thundered under his socked heels as he paced from one side to the other.

Stopping abruptly, he gripped the new wood railing he had hammered into place two days ago. The rain slackened into a fine mist. He let it bathe his face, easing the pain. When he could think again, he hauled in a long breath and found himself staring across the dripping hedge. From behind frilly curtains, amber light glowed in the windows of the small house next door. A woman's shape hovered in the closest window, then was gone.

Rianne.

Getting ready for bed? He checked the big, luminous digital on his wrist. Nine-forty-three. He fancied her changing into some cotton affair, cool for the upcoming warmer nights, but unadorned, unsexy, wholly feminine, wholly *her.*

He pictured himself there…her skin warm, soft like the down of the bed's duvet…

He turned and strode into his barren house.

"Yo, Joe! Hang on a sec, man," Sam called as his best bud passed him in the corridor of milling students and clanging lockers. They had five minutes before Friday's last afternoon class started and Joey Fraser, Sam knew, was on his way to the upper level.

Slamming shut his locker, he turned and pushed through the crowd to where Joey waited near the outside doors. "What up, man? Aren't you going to math?"

"Me'n a couple guys're skipping," Joey said.

"Skipping?"

Joey sniffed. "No big deal. I can catch up. Wanna come?"

Brown fuzz grew along his friend's upper lip and on his pointy chin, and Sam had to raise his eyes an extra couple of inches to meet Joey's. "Can't, man. Gotta test. Old lady Pearson'll have my butt if I don't show."

"Tell her you're sick."

Sam snorted. "Yeah, like that's gonna work. She just saw me two minutes ago in the library."

"So?"

"So, if I don't pass this lab, the witch is gonna phone my mom. I've already failed the last two." He hadn't really, but he might as well have. The marks barely skimmed sixty. Lately, his concentration was the pits. Studying was the pits.

He knew why. It was Joey. His pal. His best bud.

Who looked at Sam as if he had two heads. The way he was right now. *What's the matter, Joe?*

His pal turned toward the doors.

"Want to do something after school?" Sam asked. Almost too eagerly, he realized, when Joey shrugged and looked away. Sam pressed on. "I have to baby-sit Emily till four. We can dunk some balls at my house."

The week they'd moved in, Sam's mom had bought a basketball stand for the driveway. Last summer, he and Joey had done a lot of one-on-ones and hung out at each other's houses, watching movies, playing computer games, roller-blading.

Joey never saw Sam's deformity as untouchable. In fact, the first time they met, Joe had given Sam's hand its highest praise ever with his cool "suhweet."

This last month, though, Joey acted squirmy whenever Sam suggested they do stuff together. When he called Joey's house, Sam often heard other guys in the background. Twice he'd recognized Cody Huller's voice. Cody with earrings, nose-ring and orange, half-shaved hair. What Joey saw in Cody was beyond Sam.

Joey said, "After school me'n the guys are hanging on Main."

The guys. Did he mean Huller? Sam hitched a careless shoulder. "Sure, whatever."

"Gotta go," Joey said. "Later, okay?"

"Yeah." Sam watched his friend push through the doors, toward the warm afternoon sunshine. "Later."

Walking to class, Sam knew something had changed between them. He couldn't name it, couldn't describe it. Joey still looked like Joey, still walked like Joey, still talked like Joey. But there was a difference.

Like Sam was a big waste of time to his friend.

The cranky sputter of a lawnmower unwilling to catch grated on Jon. Tossing the crowbar he'd been using to rip apart the front veranda steps this particular Saturday morning, he considered his options. He could walk into Rianne's yard and see about the problem, or he could jam in a pair of earplugs and pretend she didn't exist.

Neither option appealed to his good sense.

But then, good sense had taken a hundred-year hike, so what the hell?

Scowling, he yanked off his battered leather gloves, shoved them into his right hip pocket and headed once more into her backyard. Four days and this would be his third visit. Soon, they'd be attached at the hip.

Was that as good as attracted to her hip—among other things? He scowled harder. "You're depraved, Tucker."

Adjusting the brim of his Seahawks cap over his brow, he rounded her road-weary car.

She was in pink cutoffs, bent over the machine.

Jon stopped. Shook his head. Blew a weighted breath. Hightailing it back to his house—or the Pacific—loomed like one grand invitation. The farther from this woman the better.

"Dang thing," she grumbled, oblivious to all but the mean red machine squatting idle at her feet.

"Troubles?"

Her head jerked up. "Jon." His name, a silken thread on the warm, sunny air.

He walked over, focused on the mower. "Did you prime it?"

"Yes, and probably flooded it."

Hunkering beside the mower, he checked the carburetor. The Columbia River was in better condition. "Yup, flooded."

She expelled air. "The thing's been acting up ever since I started cutting the grass a couple of weeks ago."

Grunting in response, he inspected the wire to the ignition. While the machine appeared adequate enough to work, it could do with a cleaning. A second scan and he found the problem. "The spark-plug cap is off."

"It is?" Her shoulder came level with his chin as she peered at the tiny cup between his fingers. If he leaned sideways a little, he could bury his face in her hair.

"When's the last time this thing had a tune-up?" he grumped.

"Don't know. I bought it from a friend. It worked fine until..." She turned her head. Their eyes caught. "Now."

She had brown lashes. Straight and thick as a baby's toothbrush.

He shoved the cap on to the spark plug then climbed to his feet.

She moved to the opposite side of the mower.

Okay. You want the machine between us? Well, baby, so do I. He said, "It'll need to sit ten minutes for the primer to drain before you can try it again."

Checking the plain-banded watch at her wrist, she frowned. "Running late?"

"No. Yes." Exasperated fingers checked the green bandanna around her ponytail. "I had a number of things I wanted to get done this morning, that's all." She looked around her small yard. "This could wait, I suppose." Her brown eyes found his. "Thank you. Again."

He shifted, awkward with how the softness in her voice, her look, affected him. "Mower isn't running yet."

"It will be."

Once more their eyes held. He looked away, zeroing in on the apple tree covered in white flowers. "If you need a hand, I'm working on my front steps."

"Jon," she said when he turned to go. "About the other night—"

"Past."

Undaunted by his tough tone, she went on. "Nevertheless, I want to explain. When I said I wasn't used to having company, I meant male company. Since my husband died, I haven't been much into developing…friendships."

"Understood."

"Especially with men."

Considering his own choice about women and involvements, he accepted her avowal. "I know the feeling. I'm divorced.".

"Oh."

For several long seconds, the morning held its quiet. A yellow butterfly flitted over the mower, bent on reaching the apple tree.

Then, because the thought had bugged him for two days he said, "You recognized me that first day on the porch with the cats."

She smiled. "Yes. Ninth-grade English, how could I forget?"

"Ahh." He'd wondered if she recalled sitting on her mother's back step, him explaining Wordsworth and Whitman.

She went on, "And you used to hang with these guys. Once after school, one of them stopped me. He said things…and started handling my hair. It was very long at the time." She looked to the hedge between their properties. Sunshine fueled flames into that hair now. "He scared me." Her eyes were steady. "You told him to leave me alone."

"Gene Hyde."

"Yes, Gene Hyde."

Misty River High's class-A idiot. The guy had wrapped a strand of her hair around his hand—with lewd innuendoes.

"I remember. It was beside the gym and you were…" *Wide-eyed and skittish as an alley cat.* "Very young."

"Barely fourteen."

She'd been Seth's age. A kid.

And Jon had wondered after all those trips he'd driven her and his little brother home from school—he wondered what she'd be like one day as a woman.

Now, he knew.

Except, now he no longer cared. Or so he told himself. Of course, his conscience wouldn't allow him to veto his four-day fantasies. She was female—an alluring female—after all.

He bent, checked the primer. Free of gas. Taking hold of the starter cord, he yanked. The engine roared to life.

Rianne grabbed the handle. Her shoulder brushed his arm; her woman's smell beguiled his nose. "Thank you," she mouthed over the buzzing motor. A quick smile and she pushed forward, hips swaying with each determined step of her dusty sneakers, following the cutter's path toward the edge of the yard.

He still had her image, her scent swirling in his head when he rounded the corner of the house and almost bumped into a tall, gangly kid chasing a runaway basketball. The same kid he'd seen the night he'd carried in her groceries.

In one swoop Jon anchored the ball against his body with an elbow. "You Rianne's boy?"

The kid gave him a cautious look. "Yeah."

"How old are you?"

"Thirteen."

"Shouldn't you be helping your mother instead of playing?"

The teenager had the decency to scan the backyard. "You mean like mow the lawn?"

"That'd be a start."

"Yeah, well, Mom doesn't want me operating machines."

"Why not?"

"She's scared I might hurt myself."

"Do you think you'll hurt yourself?"

The boy looked as if Jon had broken a raw egg on his head. "No way. I can handle a stupid mower."

Jon released a mild snort. Kid had guts, he'd give him that. "Lesson one. No machine is stupid. If you don't respect it, it won't respect you. Got it?"

The boy nodded.

"Good. Lesson two. Mothers tend to think their kids stay babies forever." Jon lifted his eyebrows. "Up to you to choose."

"Geez. Like that's hard."

"Thought so." Jon handed him the ball. "Sam, right?"

The boy nodded.

"Think you can handle those two lessons, Sam?"

Something shifted in his dark eyes. "I can handle 'em, sir."

Jon shook his head. "Not sir. Just Jon. Nothing more, nothing less. Now, go help your mother."

The last thing she wanted, marching out of her house, was to confront Jon Tucker. Brutally masculine, with those polar eyes icing a person in a heartbeat, she suspected he wasn't a man who would give one hoot about what she had to say.

But say it, she would.

Just as she had, in the end, to Duane.

No one—not now or ever again—would castigate her children or berate her mothering skills. Duane had discovered it the court-induced way. Jon Tucker would learn it in plain jargon.

He worked on a plank supported by a pair of sawhorses several feet from his front steps, marking out a distance with a thick carpenter's pencil and tape measure. Clad in the same frayed jeans, blue plaid shirt and cumbersome work boots of an hour ago, he had her heart taking another boisterous tumble.

In the last sixty minutes he had rolled his sleeves to his biceps. Bread-brown muscles strained in the sun.

The wolf tattoo glistened within dark hair.

She chanced a furtive study of the man who had kept her spinning silly girlish dreams as a teenager. The harsh-crafted angles of his face, profiled against the bright day, showed an assertive nose, a bold ridge of brow. He'd switched the cap so its visor hid the five-inch bracket of ponytail. Pale skin peeked above the plastic band across his forehead. A silver ear stud flaunted wickedness.

She pressed down a corner of excitement. And guilt because of her mission.

After all, he'd taken time from his work to fix her beat-up, old mower.

At her approach, his long, powerful body unfolded with calm ease. Slowly she was acclimating to the way he didn't smile, didn't speak, simply looked at her with that impenetrable, intelligent expression. Acknowledging the latter, she took heart and stepped close enough to speak in a normal tone. "Can we talk?"

He shot a look toward her house. "The mower again?"

"No. My son."

Those eyes conveyed nothing. Not curiosity, not amusement, not compassion. Two decades ago, a dozen expressions would have skimmed his rebel teenage features in mere seconds.

Why are you so empty, Jon?

She towed in a nourishing breath. She was here for Sam. "Please don't persuade my son to do things against my will."

His black brows sprang. "How'd I do that?"

"By telling him to mow the grass."

Silence. In the woods a bird trilled a minimusical.

She pressed on. "You probably think he's old enough, that he should be a man. Well, I'll decide when the time is right and until then I don't want my son handling machinery."

He gave her another long look, picked up a compact saw, flicked a switch and notched one end of the plank. When it was done, he carried the wood to the steps.

It wasn't so much a dismissal as disinterest.

Jon Tucker simply did not care one way or another.

In all her years with Duane, she couldn't recollect feeling as detached as Jon looked. Alone, yes. Despondent, yes. But never detached to the point where life constituted meaningless mechanical movement from one day to the next.

She drew closer, watching as he fit the board in place. "Sam's not like other boys."

Would he quit working and look at her? Discuss this rationally? Or—the thought nipped her mind—was he like Duane after all, harboring an inner explosive rage while on the outside he appeared calm?

Ludicrous. Jon was nothing like her dead husband. She didn't know how or why, but she sensed a deep, agonizing pain in the man working on his house.

She started back to her yard, weighing her suspicions.

"Rianne."

She hesitated. "Yes?"

"What's the real reason?"

"He has a deformed hand." *Lobster claw.* An informal medical label for the fusing of all fingers into one, separate from the thumb. A hideous label. But a label, nonetheless.

Something stirred in his eyes. Interest? "I hadn't noticed."

"He usually hides his right hand in his pocket." *When he's around strangers.*

"Do you want him to be like other boys?"

"What kind of question is that? Of course I want him to be like other boys."

"Then let him mow the lawn."

"That has nothing to do with—"

"It has everything to do with it. Let him be normal. He doesn't have a disease. He has an individual hand, is all."

An individual hand. Such an unfeigned term. Her annoyance evaporated.

He came toward her, the hammer in his tool belt softly bumping one strong thigh. Stopping within her space, he reached out and stroked her cheek with a heavy knuckle. The touch shot heat clean to her toes.

She wanted to lean toward it.

Toward him.

His hand dropped and she stood, heart thrumming, unable to move. His lips were masculine, the bottom one more supple. A corner of his mouth hitched—a smile?—then vanished.

"Boy has your eyes."

"He looks like his father." Abashed by her outburst, she glanced away. She didn't want Jon Tucker assuming Duane Kirby meant anything. Anything at all.

"Still has your eyes. Same color."

"I thought you..." What? Had no interest? Didn't care?

"Don't give a damn?"

Her cheeks burned.

He moved closer.

The warm morning and the heat of his body drifted over her. She wanted to scurry under the shrubbery, hide from those intense blue eyes.

"What are you really afraid of, Rianne?"

She stared at him. "Who said I was afraid?"

His eyes darkened. Without a word, he returned, lax-limbed and indifferent, to his tools and wood.

Chapter Three

"Nope."

"Just like that—no?" Luke Tucker set down his early-morning coffee, fresh from the pot of Kat's Kitchen. "This town needs a new police chief, Jon. Pat Willard's let the department corrode for years. You going to sit there and take the chance one of his *prodigies,*" the word edged on acidic, "will slide into his shoes in September?"

Jon paused, knife and fork hovering over his open Denver sandwich, Kat's dawn-riser special, and looked across the booth at his eldest brother. "Police work and I don't mix."

"Aren't you taking this a little out of context?"

"Not as I see it."

Luke's mouth relaxed. "You've got to let go, man."

Jon stared at his plate. The hunger grumbling in his gut dissipated. Damn. He looked forward to eating breakfast with Luke and Seth. Since he'd moved back, this was one ritual he relished, meeting with his brothers every Wednesday—hump day—for an early bite. It had started because Jon's kitchen was a shambles. The second week they'd come because he'd needed their company. All those years away…he'd missed his brothers.

And today… Today, Seth couldn't make the six-fifteen meet because of a job. Or, had it been a setup? Luke charming Jon into taking up the feeble torch Pat Willard would pass on?

No, Seth had too soft a heart. Especially when it involved his brothers or their alcoholic mother who still lived in the same 1920s house on the outskirts of town where they had grown up. Seth wouldn't know an ulterior motive if it knocked him in the nose.

Nor would his little brother interfere in how Jon handled his pain.

Not like Luke. Who never wasted words or time. *Good lawyer.*

Jon swallowed the bite he'd been chewing before taking a sip of coffee. "I don't need you giving me a quickie psych review on how to deal with my kid."

"If you're talking about your daughter, I wouldn't dream of it. If you mean Nicky… That's another story."

"And none of your business."

Hurt flickered in Luke's eyes before he concentrated on scraping up the last of his scrambled eggs.

Jon set down his utensils with a clatter. "Look, I know what you're trying to do, and I appreciate it. But I've got to find my own way with this."

"You need to talk to somebody." Luke held up a hand. "I know. I haven't forgotten Seth and those school counselors. But this thing… You're not responsible for what happened to your son, J.T."

"Yes, I am, dammit." At the rise of Jon's voice, several

nearby customers glanced their way. He gave them a hard look. Facing his brother, he said quietly, "Bottom line? I wasn't there for my family. Colleen had to handle Nick's re-belliousness alone. When I realized there were problems, I should've gotten off Drug Squad. But I didn't. I liked busting down doors and grabbing bad guys too much. I wanted the rush too damn much." He shook his head, miserable. *Should've been there for you, Nicky.*

"More coffee, boys?" a grandmotherly waitress asked. Kat, owner of the café, held a steaming carafe.

Jon shook his head, caught up in his brother's inquisition. Caught up in memories of Nicky.

"Thanks, Kat," Luke said and held out his cup.

Jon studied his brother. Eleven months older, he had the same rangy build as his siblings—a feature they'd inherited from their father. While Jon stood tallest at six-five, Luke didn't seem any shorter at six-two. The man had shoulders wider than a toolshed and arms that could put a wood-framer to test. While all three brothers had received a variation of their father's dark coloring, Luke was the only one who'd been blessed with their mother's aesthetic, straight nose and gray eyes.

Those same eyes settled on Jon. "What?"

"How come you never married again?"

Luke looked away. "Never found the right woman."

Ginny Keegan had been the right woman. Once. She and Luke had married in college. And divorced eight years later. Three Tuckers, three divorces. Not good odds.

"Okay," Jon said. "Here's the deal. I don't ask you ques-tions, and you butt out of my problems."

"Circumstances are entirely different. I didn't lose a son and blame it on my job."

"*Your* job wouldn't lose you a son," Jon said testily.

"You think defense lawyers don't work long hours? However, if I'd *had* a son—" Luke stared into his cup "—he might've rebelled just as well to make a point against what *I* stand for."

Touché. Teenagers of men in Luke's position were known to buckle under peer pressure. Hell, teenagers in general were considered a rebellious lot. Hadn't he, Luke and Seth done the same once? Done whatever it took to be accepted by their pals, despite their deplorable home life?

"Look. You were a good cop, J.T.," Luke went on. "The best. I've checked. You can be again."

Jon set down his half-finished coffee, dug out some bills and tossed them on the table. "Not gonna happen. I'm setting up to make furniture for the next thirty years."

Luke's mouth tightened and Jon quelled a chuckle. No mistaking they were brothers. Both were face pullers when the chips toppled.

He shoved out of the booth. His house waited. "Same time next week?"

"Yeah, sure."

He gave his brother's shoulder an affectionate squeeze. "Take care, bud."

Outside, he took a long breath of warm, sunny air. Living in Misty River felt damn good. It had to. Where else could he go?

Rianne turned the ignition of her Toyota again. *Click.*

Of course. The old thing would have the nerve to die when she was running late for the first day of work this week. Well, bemoaning the fact wouldn't start the car either. Thank goodness Sam had gone ahead on his bike.

"What's the matter with the car, Mom?"

Emily wasn't so lucky. Wednesday, Thursday and Friday, the three days Rianne taught in Chinook Elementary's library, they rode to school together. A comforting ritual after they'd moved to Misty River a year ago, when her children hadn't established friendships yet. Then Sam met Joey Fraser who lived up the street and, for her son, going with Mom became "uncool." But Emily still rode with Rianne.

"The battery's probably dead, Em." Rianne sighed. *Darned old car. There goes another chunk of budget. Laughing yet, Duane?*

"I thought gas made the car go," Emily said.

Rianne patted the child's hand, hoping to ease the disquiet she knew churned inside her daughter when things went slightly off kilter. "They both do, pooch."

"Can you get a new one?"

"Yes, but I need to go to the Garage Center for that."

Emily followed Rianne out of the vehicle, dark eyes big behind her glasses. "Are we gonna be late? Can I take my bike? Please? I don't want to be late, Mom."

"Hang on, honey." Rianne popped the hood. "Maybe it's something else." *Something simpler.* She could hope.

Other than caked-on grime and grease, the engine appeared the same as the last time she'd seen it. Were the battery terminals more corroded? She couldn't remember. The car was thirteen years old and, during their marriage, Duane had looked after its mechanics. How long did a battery last? Five years? Ten? The life of the car?

Why hadn't she asked the mechanic when she'd bought new rear tires last fall?

Because you didn't want to admit a lack of car sense to a man. Now, look where it's got you. Late for work and Emily late for school.

She checked her watch. Eight-forty. Fifteen minutes before first bell. If they walked fast they'd make it just in time. "Get our lunches out of the car, Em. We're walking."

"But Mo-om, we'll be *way* late."

Rianne surveyed the engine again. "I'll call Mrs. Sheers and tell her our problem." Cleo Sheers was the secretary. She'd pass the message on to the principal and Beth Baker, Em's teacher.

Emily tugged Rianne's sleeve. "Mom," she whispered.

"Hmm?" Looking at this mess, she knew she needed a whole new car.

"Troubles?" a low, rusty voice said.

Rianne jackknifed up, almost batting her head on the hood.

He stood by the driver's door, hands jammed in hip pockets. She should have guessed by Em's behavior that her big, moody neighbor hovered nearby. What did he do, keep her under surveillance?

"Good morning." Ungrateful thoughts weren't her style, although *hot stuff* appeared to be his in those worn black jeans and that snowy T-shirt. She couldn't take her eyes off his damp hair caught in a loose tail. *Like a settler, traveling the Oregon Trail in a prairie schooner.*

Clipping a nod, he stepped forward and closed the hood with a flick of the wrist.

"What are you doing?"

"Driving you and your daughter to school. The battery's done for." He pointed his chin at the front seat. "Why don't you get your things and I'll start the truck."

Not a question, a subtle command. Cops, she knew, issued directives to maintain order and stability. She, however, was not a felon nor an obnoxious bystander nor, for that matter, a wife whose independence and self-worth had been boxed into the dirt.

She was a woman standing securely on her own two feet.

About to say as much, she opened her mouth—except he was already striding for the black truck in his driveway.

"Are we going with him, Mommy?" Emily asked, pinky disappearing into the corner of her mouth.

Rianne squelched the urge to raise a fist to her dead husband. "It's okay, sweets." Carefully, she adjusted the girl's glasses on her freckled nose. "We won't be late now. Come on." Hand in hand they stepped between the barren rose bushes and headed for the grumbling diesel truck.

Jon leaned across the seat and shoved open the door. "Give me your bag, Bo Peep."

A timid smile crept along Emily's mouth. In that instant, Rianne forgot her woman's right to independence. A warmth spread from her heart outward. Jon Tucker, man of few words, had baited a smile from her little girl.

A precious, rare smile.

Emily climbed onto the high seat. While Jon strapped her in, Rianne climbed beside her. Why hadn't she chosen slacks today or one of her loose, ankle-length skirts? No, silly woman that she was, she'd selected her favorite: black, slim and short.

The truck smelled of tools. And Jon. Over Emily's head, Rianne caught his regard—flame-blue and intense. Her heart pinged. She faced the windshield and worked on her seat belt.

Calm down.

Five minutes of speed and silence got them to Chinook Elementary. He parked near the entrance. Children hung in clusters up and down the sidewalk. Across the playground smaller ones dashed between older students, chasing balls, playing tag. A group of boys, a few years younger than Sam, roughhoused near the gym exit.

Rianne climbed from the cab. Emily slid to the ground with a "'Bye, Mom" and drifted toward some girls skipping rope.

Jon rounded the nose of the idling truck. "Got a minute?" His gaze lingered on the skin below her hemline.

She looked toward the school doors. "If it's quick."

"What time are you finished?"

"I'll get one of my colleagues to drive us home."

"What time?"

Another take-charge man.

He's different.

How so?

She relented. "Three, but I usually don't get out of here until four."

"Your daughter stays with you?"

"Yes."

"I'll be here at four." He started for the driver's side.

She went after him. "It's not necessary. We can get home on our own."

He stepped from the curb. Even with the added height of the sidewalk, she still had to tilt her head.

"It's not a contest, Rianne. I'd like to pick you up after school, okay?"

His quiet "like" did it, had her tongue powerless. "Fine."

A softness she hadn't seen before touched his eyes. "See you then," he said.

Without another word she walked into the school. She would not watch him drive away. Not with this warmth in her cheeks.

The day crawled. Although four different classes came into the library throughout the morning, the clock was glued to one spot for endless, interminable minutes at a time.

Midmorning she made a call to the Garage Center and requested an attendant put a new battery in her car. The house call would be an added expense but she'd manage it.

Shortly after one she received a call that her battery had been looked after—not by the attendant. By a neighbor.

She didn't need to ask which neighbor.

The rest of the afternoon Rianne fumed.

At quarter to four, she looked through the library's tall, wide windows. Luckily, the room took up the better portion of one corner facing the street, where she could watch who entered the grounds and who parked along the curb.

Jon arrived at five to the hour, stopping the pickup exactly where he'd dropped her off. Rianne held her breath. Would he come into the building?

He elected to wait outside his truck, leaning against it the way he had for Seth over at the high school twenty-two years ago. Long, strong legs braced, hiney affixed to the front fender, arms folded over that chest. Dark glasses masking those blue, blue eyes.

Tingles clustered deep in her belly.

Pull yourself together. The last thing you need is another man in your life—especially one who's used to taking charge.

But he's a good man, one you've never forgotten.

He's also changed.

She didn't know if she liked the change. Unfortunately, no matter what she told herself while she typed up a staff memo about new book arrivals, her breathing quickened and her palms dampened. Finished, she stuck the memo in tomorrow's agenda and rose from her chair.

"Ready?" she called to Emily who was seated at a work center.

Pushing at her glasses, her daughter tossed several pencil crayons into a shoe box. "Are we riding with that guy again?"

"Mr. Tucker, Em. He does have a name."

No comment. Emily set the shoe box on a shelf Rianne had designated specifically for student accessories. "Do you like my science title page?" her daughter asked.

Beth Baker, Em's third-grade teacher, was doing a unit on the water cycle. Studying Emily's work—a wreathed shape of earth, water and sky in various co-existing forms—Rianne smiled, "Great stuff, Em. Did you think this—" she traced the circle "—up yourself?"

"Uh-huh. I still have to color the rivers and lakes. See?"

"Yes, I see, and the sky, too. And the border. Don't want any white space left."

"No, and Mrs. Baker said we can hand it in soon's we're all done with the unit." The picture went carefully into a Duotang.

Rianne shut off the library's lights. "Let's go home, love."

The moment they stepped through the entrance doors, Jon came away from the truck in an expeditious move.

"Hi," he said, voice low, quiet. The sunglasses went into a shirt pocket.

Catching his look, Rianne had the odd feeling that, conditions permitting, he might have set an intimate hand at the back of her waist. But then, he was opening the door, taking Emily's bag. "Hey, Bo Peep. How was your day?"

"Fine."

"No nasty ole boys snitchin' a kiss or two?"

A tiny giggle erupted. "No-ooo! That's *yucky*."

"Good," he said. He took Rianne's bag as well and set both on the floorboard of the crew cab. "Wouldn't want you running off and getting married."

"Mr. Tucker!" Emily covered her mouth in shock, but her eyes danced behind the round-rimmed glasses.

Oh, Jon, Rianne thought. She was blindsided by his kindness, his goodness. *Do you know what you've done?*

In less than eight hours big, beard-shadowed Jon Tucker had Emily smiling. Giggling. *Laughing.* Emily who never tittered with a grown man. Duane had seen to that. *"Can't you read yet, Emily Rose? Can't you add? Come on, get with the program."*

Rianne shuddered. Why hadn't she left years ago? *Because you were afraid. Afraid you'd lose custody of the kids.*

No matter. She should have found the fortitude, the courage. For Em and Sam she should have—

Jon cupped her elbow with a work-roughened palm. "Rianne?"

"I can manage the step, thank you."

"Hurry, Mom. I'm starving."

"Hang on, short stuff. Your mom doesn't want to rip her stockings getting in."

"I can manage," Rianne repeated and held his gaze until he stepped back.

Another quick, silent trip home. Jon pulled in behind her Toyota. Rianne and Emily climbed from the truck.

"'Bye, Mr. Tucker." Her daughter ambled toward the backyard, book pack swinging from her skinny little arm.

"See you, Bo Peep." Shoving the sunglasses onto his head, he slammed the truck's door, then came around to Rianne, scowling.

Now what? His moods changed quick as the weather.

She said, "Bill Martins at the Garage Center said you were responsible for fixing my battery. Thank you. And for the rides."

"That why you were ticked at the school? Because I fixed your car?"

"No." She wasn't about to explain Duane. "It's been a long day, that's all." She dug into her purse, began writing out a check on the hood of the truck.

"What're you doing?"

"Paying you what I would've paid Bill."

Her heart fluttered when he snatched the pen out of her hand. "Forget the damned money. I didn't do it for a reward. The battery was one I had lying around."

Slowly, carefully, Rianne turned. "If you won't take payment for the battery I still owe you the cost of installing it."

"I don't want your money, Rianne."

For a long moment his eyes pinned her. Her heart thumped like a drum. She took back the pen. "How much?"

"Two hundred dollars."

She choked. "Two hundred—"

Not a muscle moved in his hard face. "Take it or leave it."

She studied her car. A used base model, bought the year she married Duane, the year she'd had Sam. Dented, decrepit, dying.

Jon remained motionless, thumbs hooked in his front pockets, feet planted. *Let your eyes warm a little. Just a tad, like they did with Emily.* They continued their cool scrutiny.

"Fine," she snapped. "Two hundred."

Where she'd get the money, she didn't know. But she would. As sure as God made apples and pears, she would prove to Jon Tucker and every man like him that she could navigate life's bites with the best of them.

Finished, she held out the check.

Without a glance, he stashed it in a pocket. Tilting up her chin with a knuckle, he said, "There's nothing wrong with being a woman, Rianne. Remember that next time a man wants to help you into a vehicle."

They'd never been this close, inches close. Black rings surrounded his irises, pools of wishes and dreams and fantasies into which she could dip her heart.

Her mouth moved, as if to speak, as if to—

He strode to the driver's door and leapt into the cab. Full-throttle, the truck backed out of the lane. He didn't go home. Instead, he gunned it all the way down the street.

She didn't move. Couldn't.

Around her silence dropped like a shackle.

Chapter Four

After school, Sam headed for the bike racks at the east door of Misty River High. Unlocking the safety chain from the front tire of his Schwinn, he contemplated asking Joey to sleep over Friday night. With a couple of sleeping bags downstairs, they could watch videos, eat popcorn, talk girls.

Ashley Lorenzo was kind of pretty. He'd caught her looking at him a few times. Once, in study hall, she had even given him a smile. And she never looked at his hand.

Pulling his bike from its stall, Sam saw his friend walk through the doors. "Hey, Joe-man. You riding today?"

"Nah. Bikes're for little snots."

"You rode yesterday," Sam pointed out.

"Yeah, well, yesterday's history. 'Sides, walking's better. You get to talk to girls."

Sam considered that. Across the street he saw Ashley, bag

on her shoulder, strolling off with a couple other junior-high girls. Tomorrow he'd leave his bike at home.

"Wanna double anyway?" Sam asked.

Joey debated. Shrugging, he ambled over and perched himself between the handlebars.

Sam peddled out of the school yard. It was tricky balancing a guy twenty pounds heavier on the bike, but Sam wanted muscles and muscles came when you worked up a sweat. "Got much homework?" he asked, peering around Joey's sturdy frame.

"Nah."

"Want to do something after?"

"Dunno."

They were coming up to the intersection leading away from school property. Sam brought the bike to a crawl, checking both ways before striking off across the pavement.

"Hey, Joe!" a thick voice called.

"Code-myster. What's up, man?" Joey jumped from the handlebars, forcing Sam to stop midway in the street. Cody Huller swaggered up with Mick Lessing. Sam avoided both boys when possible.

A car, waiting for them to cross, honked at the idle group.

"Yeah, yeah," Huller grumbled with an arrogant glance. "Don't get your tail in a knot."

A woman poked her head from the driver's window. "Come on, you guys, I'm late for an appointment."

"Hey!" Huller barked. "Chill, okay? This *is* a school zone." He ducked his head and flung out his arms in a sarcastic winging of the entire surroundings. With a salute Sam wouldn't have dared offer in a hundred years, Huller moved toward the opposite curb. Joey snickered. Sam hoped the woman didn't recognize *him*.

Huller said, "Claw-man, let Lessing here see your hand. He's never had a close-up of a cripple before."

Both laughed. Three girls walking by made tsking noises. Red splashed Joey's cheeks. His effort to grin failed.

Sam's chest tangled with a snake. *Claw-man.* He looked at Joey. His friend looked away. *O-kay. Thanks, dude.*

Readjusting his bookpack, Sam pushed his bike back to the street and hopped on the seat. "See ya around, Joe."

"Yeah."

"Running, wimp?" Huller singsonged. "Can't take the heat?"

Sam skidded to a stop. A year older than Sam, Huller stood six inches taller and reminded him of a weed his mother yanked from her flower beds last year. Skinny and ugly. "I'm not afraid of you, loser."

Joey's jaw dropped. Lessing hooted.

Huller stepped into Sam's face. "Yeah?"

"Yeah."

With one hand, the kid shoved Sam back against his bike. Hard. He stumbled, went down, the bike twisting clumsily under him on the pavement. The rear wheel axle caught him in the lower part of his spine, arrowed pain straight up to his skull and down to his toes. Tears pricked his eyes.

Lessing giggled.

Joey stepped forward. "Hey, Cody, take it easy, man."

The bigger boy swung around. "Who's side you on, Fraser?"

Joey backed off, flashing a what-can-I-do? look at Sam.

Ignoring the sting in his back, Sam scrambled to his feet, left fist clenched at his side. A hot ball of rage coiled in his stomach. "You sonuva—"

Huller leaned forward. "Say it, cripple. I dare ya."

Sam spat on the ground between them. Fury blinded him. Through the red haze he saw his father sneering at him. He saw his mother cowering on the floor. He hauled back and rammed his fist into Cody Huller's gut.

The older boy staggered, surprise glittering in his slitty eyes. He rushed Sam. Together they hit the pavement. No time to consider pain or bruises. Huller slammed a fist into Sam's face and his left cheekbone sang with pain. Then all he could do was cover his head while Cody Huller had his way.

To Sam it felt like hours, though it probably lasted no more than five seconds. Suddenly, Huller was snatched away.

"What's going on here?" Mr. Kosky boomed. "You boys got nothing better to do?"

The high school principal helped Sam off the pavement. Dirt ground between his molars. He touched his tongue to a lip split like an over-ripe grape. His left eye dripped water worse than the leaky tap in the bathroom at home. Around them students gathered, gawked. Street traffic slowed to a crawl.

"He started it." Huller pointed at Sam. "He punched first."

"That right?" Kosky asked.

Sam looked away. Right or wrong, he wasn't saying. Let the principal think what he wanted.

Trouble was, the man had the body of a compact engine. Muscled forearms, solid thighs, a barrel chest. Hard to ignore a guy like that training his hawk eyes on Sam. "You need to get some antiseptic on that cut, son."

To the other three standing on the sidewalk, gazes shifting everywhere, Kosky ordered, "Cody, Joey, Mick. I want you all in my office. Immediately. You, too, Sam."

"I didn't do nothing!" Huller cried. "It was his fault!"

"We'll deal with it in the office, Cody." The principal scanned the crowd. "The rest of you go home."

The crowd of students began splitting up. By suppertime, the whole school would know. By tomorrow, half of Chinook

Elementary would have heard from their older brothers and sisters.

Shame washed over Sam. *Emily.* He imagined her big eyes brimming with panic again. He'd bet every cent he had in the meager savings account his mom had opened for him that tonight his sister would sleep with her blankey and for the next week gnaw her pinky until it resembled a raw breakfast sausage.

As for his mother's reaction...forget it.

Rianne unlocked the back door and waited for Sam and Emily to proceed into the house. Barely half over, the week was turning into a spiel to rival CNN news. First, her car battery, then Jon and his outrageous installation fee, and now Sam played action hero and reaped a two-day school suspension.

Pointing to the kitchen table, she said, "Sit, both of you. We have some things to discuss."

Sam dropped his bag and threw himself onto a chair. "What for? Everything was said in Mr. Kosky's office."

Hugging her bookpack, Emily sat across the table, myopic eyes on her brother.

"What I need to say is private." Rianne leaned against the counter. She couldn't sit, not while anger churned her blood. Sam's eye looked awful. Beneath it, puffy half moons pushed the lids to a slit. Yellow antiseptic—which Greg Kosky had applied—colored the boy's thin cheekbone.

A ringing quiet fell. Sam jiggled the toe of one dusty sneaker. He refused to look at Rianne.

Emily stuck her little finger into the corner of her mouth.

On the floor by the corner window, Sweetpea lounged on a small flowered mat with her two-week-old offspring tumbling playfully around her. The animal gave Rianne a squint-eyed look, licked the face of Squeak, a scruffy-tailed, dappled kitten that walked with its hips to one side.

Rianne took a deep breath. "Sam, I understand why you hit Cody. He said some cruel things."

Sam looked out the window. "He called me a cripple."

"Yes, he did," she conceded, wondering if her heart could shred further. In Greg Kosky's office, with students and parents present, the Huller boy had admitted to the fact.

"Just like Dad used to." A tear dripped from Sam's wounded eye. He swiped it with the heel of his hand and winced.

"Yes, just like your father," she echoed, wanting to hold her son, shield him, protect him from all abhorrences in the world.

Sam lifted his head, fighting not to cry. "When Cody pushed me all I could see was Dad and—and you. I had to stop him."

Without delay, Rianne knelt in front of her child and clasped his dirt-stained hands. "Sam, don't let your father's behavior influence your emotions when someone hurts you verbally. It isn't right."

"What Dad did wasn't right either, but you let him do it."

She squelched a cry. Oh, Lord, she had to make him see. She had to show him that fists, foul words and rages were not the way to solve problems or get what he wanted, when he wanted it.

"Do you think I'm proud of that? I kept forgiving your father, hoping he'd change, hoping *I* could change him. It took me a long time—years, in fact—to realize he never would, that what he did was not a demonstration of love, but a weakness of spirit." She squeezed Sam's hands. "Honey, you are not weak of spirit. You're strong, good, beautiful. Inside and out. If someone can't see that, it's their loss, not yours."

He jumped up. "I hate who I am! I hate that I don't have normal hands like every other kid! Why was I born this way?"

Battling tears, he ran down the hall. Seconds later, his bedroom door slammed hard enough to slip the pictures on the walls. The kittens wrestling with the mat wobbled hurriedly to their mother's comforting body.

"Mommy?"

Emily slid from her chair and came around the table. Wrapping her arms around Rianne's neck, she straddled her lap and hugged her close.

"It's okay, honey." Rianne stroked the child's hair. "Sam's just upset about what happened today."

"Will we have to move away?"

Her heart constricted. "No. Sam likes it here, and so do you. This is only a little bump in the road." She hoped.

"Then why did he say those things about his hand?"

"Because he's hurting right now."

"That boy wasn't nice," Emily murmured.

"Some people aren't." Life fact number one.

A hush fell. Sweetpea purred reassuringly to her family. Emily snuggled closer. "Mr. Tucker wouldn't say those things."

"He doesn't have a disease. He has an individual hand, is all." No, Jon would never hurt Sam. Jon was a *man*. Not a coward.

A good man.

A decent man.

A man—two hundred dollars be damned—she could fall for. If she was interested. *Which I'm not.*

She kissed Emily's hair. "Let's scrounge up some supper."

"Mom?"

"Yes, sweets?"

"I think Mr. Tucker would beat that kid up, don't you?"

Rianne cupped her child's face and willed the kink in her stomach to loosen. "Emily, Jon would not lay a finger on Cody Huller. Ever." Perhaps her certainty had to do with what had happened more than twenty years ago with Gene Hyde.

The corners of Emily's mouth lifted. "Me, either. Not really." She settled a cheek against Rianne. "I like it when he calls me Bo Peep," she said shyly.

Rianne gave her a hard hug. "I do, too, sweetheart."

"He's nice."

"Mmm." And handsome. And kindhearted. And... *Oh, Rianne, do not go there.*

The flashlight beam flickered a third time on the other side of the juniper border. Edging along the wall of his unlit kitchen, Jon felt the hair at the back of his neck climb.

Someone was in Rianne's backyard.

He checked his wristwatch. Ten fifty-four. Who the hell was skulking around on a night swarthier than sin? On a Wednesday night, no less. *A school night.* Except for the dim wash of yellow in her kitchen window—the stove light he guessed—Rianne's house had been dark since ten o'clock. Again, he checked the time. Two minutes.

Three.

He waited. Peered through the black pane. Five minutes.

Whoever it was hadn't moved more than four feet, or lifted the flashlight higher than six inches off the ground.

Twenty years on the force spurred him into action. Silently, he went through his dark house to the front door. He'd ambush the bastard from her carport. Face to face.

Slipping into a pair of chewed-up sneakers, he went out the door, crept down the veranda steps. The day had closed with a bank of dirty, gray clouds; night prevailed in starless slumber.

A sudden breeze, cool for mid-May, cavorted with his hair, nipped through his T-shirt. The thick hedge and leafing trees ringing the properties sighed gustily. Earth and sap scents plied his lungs. Easing over the rosebushes, he slunk to the Toyota, inched along the cottage wall.

Whoever the offender was, he stayed put.

Digging and scraping in the soft, spring dirt.

Jon smiled grimly. His colleagues hadn't called him Wolf for nothing. He could sneak up on a bad guy and have him in a half Nelson in seconds—without raising so much as a bead of sweat.

He waited. Watching. Listening.

A sniff. Again, the flashlight flicked on, arced toward the plants bordering the lawn. Another sniff. Before the light snapped off, Jon saw a slim arm swipe across a pale face. What the—? Stepping away from the wall, he started across the backyard. "Rianne?" he called softly, not wanting to alarm her.

The beam of light zapped into his eyes, full on. He stopped, allowing her time to recognize him. The light died.

Continuing forward he asked, "What're you doing out here?"

"Weeding." Her voice sounded thick, watery.

Crouching on the balls of his feet beside her, he chided, "You always weed your flowers in the middle of the night?"

She took up the flashlight, centered its beam on several low-growing plants, troweled up a balky dandelion. Her gloved hands worked steadily, lifting the odor of earth into the night. "Why are you here?" she asked.

"I saw the light and wondered who was in your yard."

"Well, now you know."

His eyes adjusted to the obscurity. The soft glow from the kitchen stove penetrated the dark like a beacon. Her cheek and jawline were pale as paper. Picking up the flashlight, he cupped her chin. "Close your eyes," he said, lifting the light enough to catch what he suspected. "You've been crying."

She plucked the flashlight from his hand. "Go home, Jon. I appreciate you checking out the premises, but everything's fine, so please, go back to your house."

"Not until you tell me what's wrong."

"It doesn't concern you."

"If it's the two hundred dollars, I—"

"It's not."

He should leave. Get up and walk away. Women had no place in his life. *Families* had no place in his life. He'd been there, done that two-step and messed up the dance big-time. But he'd never been one to shun another's pain. And Rianne's pain struck him like the butt end of a hammer to the chest. Sharper and harder than anything had in a long while.

He stilled her restless hands. "I'm a good listener."

"I can't talk about it. Not with you."

"Why?"

"Because you're my…my…"

"Neighbor?" He removed the trowel and her gloves.

"What're you doing?"

"Holding your hands." He enfolded her small, slim fingers in his own.

"Why?"

"It grounds me."

"Since when do you need grounding, Jon Tucker?" she asked, and the edges of her mouth lifted briefly.

"When I see a woman cry."

"I'm not."

"No?" He touched a fingerpad to the satin of her cheek to catch a willful tear.

"I'm not crying," she insisted.

Jon studied her. His thumbs caressed the backs of her chilled hands. "Why are you weeding in the dark, Rianne?"

"It soothes me when I feel hemmed in."

"Something happen at work today? The kids?"

She looked toward the silhouette of the hedge. Her shoulders drooped. She shook her head.

He didn't know why it hurt, but it did. Oddly, he wanted her trust. He wanted what he'd lost from Colleen all those years ago. Trust. Belief. Support. Yeah, he wanted the combo.

Most significantly, he wanted to offer comfort. Which would mean touching more than her hands. *Not wise, Jon.* Except, wisdom and want were at a draw and he was all out of referees.

"Come here." He tugged her forward until her shoulder leaned into his chest. *For her comfort,* he told himself and wrapped his arms around her, shifted into a more favorable position, though her spine remained rigid, her shoulders stiff. "Shhh. We're okay," he murmured into the crown of her hair. Holding her loosely, waiting until the tension left by degrees.

She felt great in his arms. Small, warm, soft. A surge to claim her rushed up, stunning him. He hadn't felt this kind of need since his first years with Colleen.

Beating back the assault, he closed his eyes, content to merely sit and hold her. "What if your kids wake up? Won't they be scared you're not in the house?"

"I'll hear them through the screen door."

"Do you usually do this kind of thing—night gardening?"

A long moment passed before she answered. "I did before we moved here. This is the first time in—over a year and a half."

"Since your husband's death."

"Yes." Voice barely audible.

He wanted to ask how the man died. Had it been sudden? An accident? Slow while disease ate him away? Was the reason she'd returned to Misty River because memories elsewhere were too painful? Seth said she had no family here; her mother had passed away years ago. *What made you return, Rianne? What made you cry? Loneliness? Wishes for what could never be? A man you still love?*

He had no right to probe into her life. No business shouldering her troubles, letting the steel wall he'd forged around his heart melt or letting the high tide of her emotions sweep him under. No business at all.

He ran his mouth across her forehead, angled along her cheek. *Careful, Jon. Kissing her is dangerous.*

Boycotting his conscience, he found the corner of her mouth. One taste. One small taste, then he would leave.

Her head tilted a fraction. Their lips touched.

He brushed her softness.

Rianne, he thought dazedly. *Sweet Rianne.*

Lips clinging. Sinking deep. His heart took a thick, languid roll. His groin tightened. Up her back went his hands. Into the tumble of her hair. She was brandy after a long day's work.

"Rianne," he whispered against her mouth, "I want ..." *So much more than I can give.*

Kisses.

Kisses better than anything he'd ever experienced.

Kisses, until he was woozy with need. Need for her.

Then—her hands, flat on his chest. Pushing. "I can't do this, Jon." An uneven rasp of air. "It's a mistake."

Mistake? For a minute she'd been right there with him.

The faint light from her kitchen door deepened the flush on her cheeks. She shook her head. "I can't."

"Why?"

"I'm not... You don't know me."

"I know this much. I'm attracted to you. Have been for quite a while." *Teenage woolgathering come to roost.*

Again, that head shake. "I—I need to go."

Grabbing up the flashlight, she scrambled to her feet and rushed to the house. On the porch, she looked back through the obscurity, a last look at him. An instant later, the door closed.

Slowly, Jon stood. His knees groaned, age in the night. His breath hissed between his teeth. What the hell was he doing with a woman like Rianne? A woman who tasted of family and forever?

"Go home, Jon," he muttered. "Take a shower."

* * *

She leaned against her bedroom door and touched a shaky finger to her hot, tingling lips. Jon Tucker had kissed her. And she him. Kissed like a pair of lost souls after a ten-year desert trek. When had she set her mouth to a man's like that? Never. Not even with Duane while they dated.

She stared at her country quilt, its colors muted by the bedside lamp. How would it be to lie with Jon on that bed? Have his rough, callused fingers on her hidden flesh? His body on hers? Would he be gentle? Or would lust feed frenzy and fury as it had with Duane?

She observed the bed. *Her* bed. Not a man's bed. Not a marriage bed. Hers.

Alone.

The word filled the room and, suddenly, the years loomed ahead. Her, growing old and gray, never sharing intimacies within the confines of this space. A heaviness settled around her heart. Her eyes blurred and she closed them. Would Jon enter her room one night? Stand naked within its walls? Would the mattress dip with his weight? The springs creak in the hushed dark?

She blinked open her eyes.

He'll never cross this threshold.

For all Jon's big, rough-hewn exterior and cool, detached eyes, she'd experienced—for the first time in her life—reassurance and safety within a man's arms. And that scared her. She, whose confidence, whose independence was fresh as a newly scribed song.

Was she ready for a man in her life again? For Jon?

And when he discovers your past? The woman you were?

Sighing, she pushed off the door.

For that to happen, they would need to be in a relationship, something she wasn't planning for another decade. At least.

* * *

Slipping into one of four easy chairs facing a desk congested with books, files, stacks of papers, bins of folders, a jar of pens and pencils—a typical teacher's desk—Rianne waited for Eva Zeglen, Misty River's high school counselor, to finish her telephone call.

Last night the woman had phoned and suggested this early-morning meeting. Suspensions warranted school counselors contacting parents. Strangely enough, with all that had happened in her life, not once did Rianne imagine the topic to be a dark side to her son. Over the past eight months he'd made great strides with Eva, to the point where the counselor had spaced updates at two-month intervals.

Rianne forced evenness into her breathing. The confidence, the self-esteem Sam had gained… Gone with punches and bruises.

Out in the hallway a locker clanged, announcing the arrival of an early student. Another standard day.

"Fine," Eva told the caller. "I'll see you and your husband then." Setting the receiver in its cradle, she stood and smiled. "Sorry. An unexpected call." Pulling Sam's file from the Today basket, she came around the desk and lowered herself into the chair facing Rianne. "All right, then," she said, opening the file. "I'll be frank. I wanted to call you in last week, but I thought I'd give Sam the benefit of the doubt."

"Last week?" Rianne had seen Eva exactly three weeks ago. The next consultation was the end of June. In six weeks.

The counselor tugged on an earring below her gray hair. "Sam hasn't attended his last two sessions."

"I don't understand."

The woman sighed. "I didn't think you knew. The first time it happened he said he had to run an errand for you after school. Then, when he missed last Tuesday, I knew there was a problem."

Tension regrouped at the base of Rianne's skull. "Sam had no reason to miss those sessions. What are his teachers saying?"

"Nothing. Sam hasn't shown any overt changes. He's still polite and willing to listen and discuss things. As I mentioned at the last update, he's talking more freely about you and Emily. He's gained a great deal of confidence around his peers. Mike Sloane, his math teacher, said Sam's offered to buddy up with one of the slower kids for their geometry unit."

Rianne stared at the thick file on Eva's lap. "Do you think his absences might have something to do with Joey Fraser and Cody Huller?"

"They might." Eva flipped back a page, scanned some notes. She stopped midway, frowned. "Has he mentioned Joey?"

"Joey's his best friend, but I'm at a loss as to how…how Sam…" She couldn't finish. Sam's violence toward Cody Huller had her blinking hard. If he was following his father's path… She looked away. "Sorry. This hasn't been a good week."

"I know," she said quietly. "However, because of what's happened I will tell you this. Joey's important to Sam, but something's bugging him. Hopefully, he'll open up and talk about it—either to you or to me." She sent a warm smile. "With two of us on his side, we'll build a strong, open communication channel."

Rianne thought back to last night when Sam had run from the room. *I hate who I am!* The words still ripped through her heart. She straightened, mastered the hurt. "According to Mr. Kosky, Joey didn't stand up for Sam when the Huller boy called him names. Has Joey befriended that boy?"

"I've seen them together a few times, talking to some of the girls. I wouldn't say they're friends. Or enemies. Cody,

however—and I'm telling you this because we're teachers—
Cody has a bullying attitude. It wouldn't surprise me if Joey
is a tad afraid of him. Then again, I've noticed Joey becoming impressed with macho stuff, that's par for Cody."

"How do you mean?"

"Oh, the usual…mouthing off to staff. Skipping class.
Pushing younger kids in the halls. That sort of thing."

Was that happening to Sam? Not two weeks ago, he'd
stomped away from her when she had refused to let him go
to Joey's house in a thunderstorm. If Joey was easily influ-
enced by the Huller boy, what impact would he have on Sam?
And what could she do? Keep Joey and Sam apart, knowing
they were best friends? Proactive action? Intervention for
prevention?

Would Sam defy her—despite the fight and the name-call-
ing?

He hadn't allowed her into his room last night. Instead,
he'd growled at her to leave him alone when she'd knocked
on his door at mealtime and bedtime. Unwilling to let him fall
asleep hungry, she'd made a cold-cut sandwich—a truce
token—and sent Emily in as her messenger. This morning,
things hadn't altered but the plate lay empty on his nightstand,
and he had spoken pleasantly enough to Emily—even teased
her about picking favorites among the kittens. Rianne, he'd
barely acknowledged.

She focused on the counselor. "I know this is a lot to ask,
Eva, but would you talk to him today? I'll have him here after
school, three-thirty sharp."

"Sure, and I'll forewarn admin so they don't send Sam
packing if they spot him in the hallways."

"Thanks. I really appreciate this." Rianne hung her purse
strap over her shoulder, ready to rise. "Also…"

"Yes?"

She hesitated. "Could you ask him how he feels about his handicap? Last night he questioned why he'd been born with…a…"

Lobster claw.

No! Individual hand.

Rianne locked her fingers on her purse. "He hasn't spoken to me since." Her eyes lifted to this woman she'd come to respect. "He's just a little boy trying hard to fit in. Clichéd as it sounds, I want him to have what every mother wants for her kids. The absolute best."

Eva stood, set a hand on Rianne's shoulder. "As teacher to teacher, mother to mother, we'll get to the bottom of this. All right?"

She nodded. If she had to select anyone in the world who might succeed with Sam, it would be Eva Zeglen. "Okay."

"Good girl." Eva passed over a tissue. "Now, stop worrying," she ordered gently. "Sam loves you, I guarantee it."

Rianne gathered the words to her heart as she walked the block back to Chinook Elementary.

Chapter Five

From under the bill of his cap, Jon watched the kid toss the basketball heel to hand and fumble it one more time. For the better part of an hour while Jon worked his pry bar on the front exterior of the house, Rianne's son lollygagged in her driveway.

The boy wasn't sick; it wasn't a school holiday. Rianne, tote shouldered, daughter in tow, had left for work nearly three hours ago in that red rattletrap.

So why was the kid goofing off when he should be in class?

None of your business.

Jon hooked the claw under another deck board. Its nails complained mournfully as they left the bracing beam.

The kid spun the ball on the end of a finger.

Not your problem.

Rianne had cried last night. He had held her in his arms. Kissed her tears.

Don't get involved.

Except he was.

"Smart guys quit while they're ahead," he grumbled, whacking the nails out of the board.

After spending half a night kicking covers off his bed, how could he quit? He wanted her in his hands again, and...

He tossed the board; it clattered to the deck.

The kid kicked the ball high, soaring it over the budding shrub roses, dropping it on Jon's driveway where it bounced and rolled among potholes and weeds. As if he had all day, the boy sauntered over to retrieve the ball.

Jon set down the pry bar, lifted his cap, pushed a palm across his hot brow. Resettling the bill squarely over his eyes, he asked, "You playing hooky, Sam?"

"No."

"Ah. Your mom lets you stay home whenever you want."

A scowl. "No-o."

Wandering toward the boy, Jon mopped his nape with a bandanna from his hip pocket. Casually, he asked, "What happened to your face?"

"Ran into a door."

"Uh-huh." Jon returned the cloth to its pocket. "What's the other kid look like?"

Attention. "I, um, got him in the nose."

"Bleed some?"

"Yeah."

Jon nodded and strolled closer.

The kid shifted foot to foot, eyeing him sideways. "You're not, like, disgusted?"

"Should I be?"

Sam jerked up his chin. "I don't care. I'm not. I'm glad."

"Huh. I can see that."

The boy examined the ball between his hands.

Had Nicky ever tossed one? Probably. But not much with

him. He'd been too busy working. "Figure walking away is uncool, Sam?"

"No."

"Me either."

The kid's Adam's apple bobbed. "My mom said so, too."

Ah. That's why she'd cried. A vice squeezed Jon's chest. "Best listen to her then, son. She's right. Fists are emergency weapons only." He crooked a finger under the boy's bony chin, turned his face into the sunlight. The left eye resembled a mix of seasoned plum and pear. Purple and yellow. A mean, half-inch gash crusted on the kid's ballooned lower lip. "Must've had good reason to want to get your face this mashed."

"Huller's a jerk."

"That all?"

"He called me a cripple, a—a claw man."

Jon set his hands at his belt. "Yep. Huller's a jerk, all right. Be a shame to walk away from him."

Sam's eyes flamed. "The dorkhead called me a wuss. I'm never gonna be like my mom. I'm never gonna let anyone call me names or beat me—" His mouth snapped shut.

The hair on Jon's nape rose. "*What* did you say, boy?"

Sam stepped back, brown eyes round as walnuts in his bleak, battered face. "Nothing. I—I shouldn't I gotta go."

"Not so fast." Jon caught his arm, twig-thin under the shirt's fabric. "Who hit your mother?"

Sam stood docile, head bowed. Arm raised at an awkward angle in Jon's hand. "I'm sorry," he mumbled. "Honest. I didn't mean those things. I'm sorry." A tear slipped from his mangled eye.

Merciful God. The boy thought he was about to get a working over. A lump the size of Oregon squeezed into Jon's belly as he studied the teenager. Slim nose, splash of freckles.

Like his mother.

Rianne. Sweet Rianne with arms no bigger than her son's and hair soft as morning mist.

With a little half smile and a lot of guts.

With spunk and sadness mixed in her eyes. Sadness Jon had believed was for her dead husband. Sonuva… An alien rage swept through him. To steady himself, he set his hand on the boy's shoulder. "Look at me, Sam," he ordered quietly and waited until the boy raised his bruised face. "I'd never physically hurt you. Never. And on my own father's grave, I swear I'd never, *never* harm your mother." He let the words sink. "But I need to know if your dad did."

Sam stared at his worn sneakers. His silence spun volumes. Jon's gut did a hollow reel.

Some no-good bastard had hit Rianne.

Fury leapt. One finger at a time, he released the teenager's shoulder.

Sam's knee trembled. Against his milk-white face the bruise was a patch of blotted ink. "I don't—" he croaked, swallowed. "I don't want to talk about my dad."

"All right. We won't talk about him."

"You won't tell my mom? She doesn't like people knowing."

"I won't tell her."

"Promise?"

Jon held out his hand, palm up. "Lay it there." He received a surprisingly sound slap. "You've got my word." *For the moment.* "Now, want to tell me why you're home and not at school?"

"Are you kidding?" Sam regained his moxie. "Principal suspended us for the rest of the week. Sucks, man. I'm going to get so far behind."

"They're called consequences."

"Yeah, but it still sucks." He picked at a seam on the ball.

Jon contemplated the boy's reedy frame. "Want to put on a sweat for a couple days?"

Sam raised his head. "How?"

Jon affected a thoughtful examination of the weathered cottage. "Maybe fix up your back porch."

The boy checked out his home. His eyes were round when they returned to Jon. "You mean like paint it?"

"Not to start."

Again the once-over. Stunned, the boy asked, "You want me to scrape off all the old paint *first?*"

Jon grinned.

"Mom'll have a cow."

"Probably. Some women tend to get a little agitated when they think a man's infringing on their terrain."

Bingo. Define *man* and the kid balanced his bony shoulders.

"That's Mom." Sam snorted. "She never wants me doing anything dan-ger-ous. Thinks it might hurt me."

"She might be right."

"Nah." Sam examined his handicap as if seeing it for the first time. "She's just kinda protective."

"A mom's prerogative. So, what do you say? Wanna help her or not?" Jon nodded at the house.

Sam flexed his shoulders and grinned. "Yep. I do."

"Good boy." He cupped Sam's thin neck, turned his battered-puppy face toward the metal toolbox in his truck. "Let's see if we can find you a sturdy scraper."

Rianne walked across the deck and jabbed off the blaring radio.

"Hey!" Sam whipped around. "Oh. Mom. What're you doing home?"

"I came to have lunch with you." She surveyed the scraper in his hand, the scene around him. Paint shavings littered the deck. Some clung to his gray sweats and to the tops of his sneakers. A broom and dustpan lay haphazardly next to a galvanized bucket she recognized from the garden shed. Her eyes narrowed as she took in the backward cap on his head. "What are you doing, Sam?"

"Getting the veranda ready for a new coat." He checked out his work, beamed. "Whaddya think? Is it great or what?"

"I don't recall discussing this with you."

"I got the idea from Jon."

"From Jon." She should have known.

"Come on, Mom." Defensiveness crept into Sam's tone. "The place looks cruddy and, well, revolting the way it is."

"Is that what Jon said?"

"Not exactly."

She walked over and picked up his right hand. Two small scratches laced the finger, a blister was forming on his thumb. "Why aren't you wearing gloves?"

Sam pulled free, stepped past her, picked up the broom. "I'm not helpless, y'know. Geez. I thought you'd be happy I'm doing something useful instead of surfing the Net all day."

Her irritation abated. After his outburst last night and the cold-shoulder treatment this morning, Sam was eager to mend fences. More, she suspected, to prove he could make constructive, helpful decisions and follow through. Her drill sergeant approach wasn't what he needed. "Sorry, honey. You caught me by surprise."

"Yeah, well," he mumbled glumly, swiping at the shavings with a stroke of the broom. "You could at least act pleased."

"I am, Sam."

A wary glance.

"I am," she repeated, wishing she could ruffle his hair as she had a few years ago. Opening the door, she said, "Hungry? I have forty minutes before afternoon classes start."

Tossing the broom into a corner, he went in ahead. His mood lifted marginally when she set his favorite, an egg salad sandwich, in front of him.

She took a bite of her own before asking, "When did you talk to Jon?"

"This morning."

"Did you go over there or did he come here?"

"The basketball went into his yard." Sam's eyes lit up. "I think his house's going to look great after he gets all that junk off. He's fixing up the inside, too."

"You went into his house? Sam, you shouldn't be bothering—"

"No, it's okay, Mom. He told me about it while he got the scraper and stuff from his truck."

She sipped her juice. "Did you tell him why you were home?"

"Yeah."

Ho-kay. Not only had Jon carried her groceries, fixed her lawnmower, driven her to school, charged her two hundred dollars for a Mickey Mouse car repair and befriended her children, but now he knew about their family troubles. What did she know of him? Virtually nothing. Except…he was divorced and disliked cats.

And that he could kiss. Oh, yes, he definitely could kiss.

"Sam, I'd rather you didn't go to Mr. Tucker's."

"Why not?"

Indeed, why not. "Because," she began slowly, "he's a very busy man. He's trying to fix his house and—"

"He told me to come over any time."

"He was just trying to be nice."

"He *is* nice, Mom."

"Polite, I mean. He was trying to be polite."

Temper slashed Sam's cheeks. "Why don't you come out and say it? You just don't want me talking to him."

"No, Sam, I don't."

"Why?"

She picked up their plates and took them to the sink. How to explain to a teenaged boy—who was also your son—that a man like Jon Tucker made his mom toss half the night and lose concentration in daylight hours? Forming a bond with Jon meant repercussions. Hadn't he alluded to as much last night? A kiss among the plants wasn't where it would end with him.

You need to end it here and now.

Rinsing the plates, she tried for a more overt slant. "Jon is a private man." At least he appeared to be. "In the weeks he's been our neighbor, how many friends have you seen visiting him?"

Sam hesitated. "That doesn't mean anything. Maybe he goes and visits them. His truck's gone sometimes after supper. Anyways, he hasn't been here that long. Who would he know?"

Rianne set the dishes in the drying tray, reached for a towel. "A lot of people. He grew up here."

"How do you know?"

"This is my hometown, too, remember?"

She realized her mistake the instant Sam's eyes widened. "You knew him as a kid? Cool."

"It wasn't quite like that. He was older. We didn't run with the same crowd." To put it mildly.

"But you knew him," he insisted.

"He graduated from school long before I did."

"But you sorta knew him," Sam persisted. "Wow, I can't believe we're living next door to somebody you went to school with. Does he remember you?"

"In a way."

Sam's eyes lighted. "Was he a biker or in a gang?"

"No." *But he was fearless.*

"Then why don't you like him?"

Exasperated, Rianne set the dishes in the cupboard. "I like Jon fine, Sam." *Too fine.* "I just think we should give him some time to get used to us as neighbors before we start infringing on his privacy." She directed a meaningful look at him. "Understand?"

"Yeah, I guess."

"Good. Now, I have to get back to school." She set a kiss on his hair and left the kitchen.

"Want me to finish scraping the veranda?" Sam called as she reached the bathroom at the end of the hallway.

"Yes, but wear some gloves this time. There's a pair in the garden shed that should fit." The right-handed one he could cut to his specifications; he knew that.

"I like working without them."

"Sam…"

"No! Gloves are for babies."

She returned to the hallway so she could see him at the table in the kitchen. "Who told you that? I wear gloves all the time."

"You're a woman."

"Excuse me?"

Sam got up, shoved in his chair harder than necessary. "Jon doesn't wear gloves and he works with tons more dangerous tools than a paint scraper."

Rianne counted backward from a hundred—she reached ninety-six. "I'm not responsible for Jon. I am for you. Wear gloves, Sam."

"No." His mouth turned down. "Why do you have to ruin the only fun I've had all day?"

"Fun?" She stalked toward him. "You're on a two-day suspension, young man, not vacation time. If you want to keep working on that deck, you'll do it my way."

Suddenly he shrugged his shoulders. "Fine. I don't wanna

scrape the deck. I got better things to do, anyway." Brushing past her, he ran down the stairs. To the TV and computer.

Rianne leaned against the wall and sighed. What was happening to her family? What was happening to her? In the last two weeks she'd had three confrontations with Sam and several with her sexy neighbor. Last night Emily had gnawed her pinky, then hauled out her old, ragged blankey at bedtime.

At school, things weren't any better. This morning, four sixth graders requested an extension on their novel study reports due today, while one of the fifth-grade teachers wanted Rianne's help researching a science lesson—for tomorrow. Add to that, Eva Zeglen had called and said she'd gotten nowhere with Sam at yesterday's session.

Now this.

If she let Sam scrape the veranda, how would she pay for two or three gallons of paint she hadn't budgeted for? Her three-day work week gave her barely enough to keep the household in running order. Then there was Jon's battery bill.

Her life was scattering at every turn. She needed to get it back under control, dammit, and Sam would just have to…

Toe the line.

Duane's favorite words. *You'll toe the line around here and do exactly as I say. God forbid.*

She went to the stairs. "Sam. Come up here, will you?"

"What?" More growl than answer.

"If you promise to be extra careful, I won't make a fuss about the gloves."

A moment's silence. "I'm doing other stuff now."

"Terrific," she mumbled and grabbed her purse off the table. *Jon Tucker, you'll have some tall explaining to do later.*

Friday morning a howl punctured the hushed air. Jon's heart nearly pole-vaulted out of his chest. What the hell?

Dropping his hammer, he sprinted across two yards and flew around the back of Rianne's cottage. In a leap, he took the steps. His stomach plummeted.

Sam lay curled on his side, gripping his knee. A raw, bloody strip lay exposed on his thigh. Pain scrunched his thin face—a face whose wicked, yellow mending still tore at Jon's heart.

"Jon," he rasped. "I…"

"Easy, son." Immediately, he unplugged the small, droning machine spinning in a circle and stripped off his sweat-shirt. Bare-chested he knelt beside Sam. "I'm putting a tourniquet on your leg, okay?" Gently, he lifted the injured limb and knotted the cotton above the wound, stanching the oozing blood.

Sam bit his lip. "Hurts."

"I know." Amazing, he could speak with his insides thrashing like white-water rafts. "Where's Mom keep the medical supplies?"

"In her bathroom. It's—"

"I'll find it. Don't move."

He flung open the door, paced through the house to Ri-anne's bedroom. He barely glanced at the neat, country-style bed where tonight her sleep would be unsettled. Because of him. Because he'd gone against her wishes. Let her son borrow a heavy-duty belt sander—*an unwieldy power tool*—when the kid grumbled about the job going too slowly. In that, Sam was as impatient as Nicky.

"Hell," he grumped, hauling open drawers in the dwarf-sized bathroom that smelled of peach blossoms.

He knew better than to bend an ear to a whiney kid—es-pecially one dressed in a pair of shorts, for Pete's sake. Trou-ble was, in the past twenty-four hours that gaunt, battered face—never mind the family's obscene history—hell, the whole mess had nabbed his heart and hung on. And then there was Sam, reminding Jon too much—too damn much—of his own stubborn son.

From a lower drawer, he grabbed mercurochrome and first-aid supplies. Boot heels thundering, he paced back to the deck.

Squatting beside the boy, he gently dabbed the seeping edges of sliced skin with a clump of antiseptic-soaked gauze. "How'd it happen, Sam?" *Talk. Help the kid focus.*

"I—I tried to sand the bottom half of the corner post. Then—ahh!—the sander slipped."

Jon pictured it. Sam crouching, legs braced, the heavy, vibrating power tool flipping out of control in his scrawny hands. Swinging down onto his leg. Paring naked, susceptible flesh like bark from a willow. Flesh that now dyed the virginal gauze scarlet. "I'm taking you to the hospital."

"No!" Sam protested. "Mom'll shoot me."

Jon lifted the boy into his arms. Kid weighed less than a sack of sugar. "Don't worry," he said humorlessly. "I'm bigger. Bullet will get me first."

On the truck's floorboards he found a mangy green T-shirt, threw it on, and drove like the devil and ten shrill women were after him. *Why* had he let Sam use the sander? Why had he listened to the kid go on and on about needing to impress his mother?

A car honked when he narrowly cut around it. He shot a look at Sam. A trickle of blood oozed from the broken scab on the boy's lower lip where his teeth clamped it.

On a distant hill, the hospital loomed. Fear jolted through him at the sight of its red-lettered Emergency. *We called 911 right away. They couldn't help—couldn't help—couldn't help— Nicky!*

"How you feeling?" Jon asked, mouth sand-dry.

"Okay."

"We're almost there."

"Will I need stitches?"

"I don't know. You've scraped some skin, Sam." A lot of skin. "The least they'll do is bandage it."

"Will it leave a scar?"

"Can't say." God, he hoped not. But what did he know?

Downshifting at the hospital's entrance, he sneaked another look at the shirt-bandaged leg. Why hadn't Sam changed into jeans? Stubborn little cuss. Ah, hell, if he hadn't tried to play Papa Bear yesterday, Sam wouldn't have dreamed up deck-scraping in the first place. *You and your big dumbass mouth.*

Rianne. After today, she'd demand he stay as far from her family as possible. Like Colleen. Could he blame either woman?

Grimly, he drove to Emergency on the west side of the hospital, shut off the engine and threw open the truck door. "Hang on. I'll come around and get you."

"Jon?"

He glanced over. "Yeah?" Slumped in the corner, Sam resembled an urchin with that dirt smear on his chin.

"I should've wore jeans like you said," he whispered.

"Don't sweat it, son. Accidents happen."

"I would've changed, but they were in the laundry."

"It's okay, Sam. No one's blaming you."

"But I told Mom yesterday I wouldn't do the deck no more." The boy picked at a hangnail. "We got…well, into this argument and…and…." He glanced across the cab, remorse and tears in his Rianne-eyes.

Jon breathed deep. "You wanted to right a wrong."

Sam bowed his head. "Yeah. I guess. "

"She'll understand, Sam. One thing about your mom. She listens real well."

He helped the boy from the truck and through the electronic entryway. The twenty-bed hospital seemed deserted. A lone nurse stood at the station. Pleasant face, nice eyes. Her name tag read Heidi. Had there been a Heidi when the ambulance raced Nicky to Seattle's University Hospital?

The memory of that night barreled stark panic into Jon's heart. What if infection set into Sam's leg? *You're overreacting, Jon.*

Heidi helped Sam into a curtained cubicle and set about untying the shirt and removing the gauze. For a moment, the boy's eyes squeezed shut; his mouth pruned. Jon took the shirt, dropped it into a wastebasket. His stomach looped. Twice in two weeks Worth blood had stained his clothes. First their cat, now Sam.

He couldn't leave. Couldn't stop staring at the offense on that runty little leg dusted with brown fuzz. Nicky had been two years older. Dark like himself. With stronger legs.

Heidi shooed him toward the door. "Dr. Sterns will be right with him, Mr. Tucker. Why don't you get a coffee?"

"Jon?" Sam called before he got through the curtain. The poor kid looked the way a disaster survivor might. Battered eye, cut lip, ripped-up leg. "Can you call my mom?"

"On it right now, buddy."

Twenty feet from the waiting room he found a pay phone. A wall clock read 10:45. Rianne would be in class.

In less than two minutes her soft words were in his ear. "Rianne Worth speaking."

"It's Jon. Sam's had an accident with a belt sander." No use wasting time or words. He'd learned that as a cop. "Some of the skin on his left leg got scraped off. We're at the hospital."

She didn't exclaim or cry out, she simply said, "I'll be right there," then hung up.

* * *

She rushed into Emergency. Jon stood at the far end of the hall from the nurse's desk. She didn't wave, instead she hurried to the woman who could explain about Sam.

"The doctor is attending him at the moment, Mrs. Worth," the nurse told her after she introduced herself. "He'll be finished in a few minutes."

"I want to see my son."

"I'll take you in as soon as Dr. Sterns is done." The nurse smiled. "Your son is lucky Mr. Tucker was there."

"Lucky?"

"He cleaned and bandaged Sam's leg before bringing him in."

Of course. Jon the cop, certified in first aid, would have given Sam immediate treatment. A stab of anger. He had ignored her specific directions.

Frustrated, Rianne wheeled around—and almost collided with Jon. His eyes fixed on her. She wanted to be glad to see him, except the horde of questions bombarding her on the half-crazed drive from the school—all hingeing on the man who loaned hazardous power tools to kids—rose to the fore.

"He's going to be okay, Rianne." His baritone voice was ragged. "I swear."

For privacy, she moved to the side of the nurse's station. "Why was Sam using that sander, Jon?"

A heavy sigh. "He wanted to catch up on what he left yesterday."

"So you let a thirteen-year-old boy who's never handled machinery in his life, and who has a handicap to boot, con you into something you *knew* I'd be against?"

He looked shaken. "Sam was so damned determined. Like he had to prove something. I told him to use the hand scraper, but he begged and begged and…aw, hell." He threw back his head, blew a breath. His hair hung ruler-straight. Rebellious.

"And you gave in and let him use it." She wanted to scream.

"Yes." Jon regarded the examination area. The accustomed indifference stamping his face was gone. He looked at her. "I gave him directions and lectured him, *lectured* him on caution."

"Sam doesn't listen well to commands," she said, rubbing warmth into her arms.

"I wasn't commanding him, I was trying to teach him something." Under the day's new stubble, his skin appeared pallid. Again, he glanced down the corridor toward Sam's door. "God, I hate hospitals. If I only—"

"Forget the if-onlys," Rianne said. "What's done is done. We can't change the past."

"No," he agreed, "we sure as hell can't." His restless eyes scanned the nurse's area. "How long before that doctor finishes?"

Rianne strode down the hall. A man and a woman stood talking to a nurse. The woman clutched her tummy. Two people sat reading in the waiting room.

To heck with policy. She wanted to see her son. Now.

Pushing through the door of the examining room, she saw another nurse cleaning the raw wound on her son's leg.

"You can't come in here—" the woman, a sharp-eyed, bespeckled matron began.

"I'm his mother, and I can," Rianne interrupted. "Oh, Sammy," she cried softly, rushing to his side, catching his hand. Kissing his forehead and the cowlick he fought each morning.

His face was pale as birch bark. "I'm okay, Mom." A sheepish grin. "Just a little scratch."

Tears stung her eyes. "A little scratch, huh?" She stroked his hair. "Jon told me what happened."

Sam looked worried. "Don't blame him, Mom. It wasn't his fault. I should've been more careful—like you said."

"No one's to blame. Accidents happen. I'm just glad you're okay." She scanned his thin, angular face. *Sam.*

"I wore the gloves," he whispered.

"Oh, honey." She could barely speak through the emotion.

She stayed until he began to squirm with her hovering. Taking the cue, she said, "I'll be right outside."

In the corridor again, Rianne found Jon standing on the sun-splashed waxed floor of the waiting room, staring out its wide windows. She touched his arm. "He's fine."

"Good." Stabbing fingers through his hair, he held it back from his face. Sweat glistened along his nose, stained the fabric under his raised arm. She caught the musky odor of man and work.

His demeanor bothered her. Jon—cool, detached Jon—was fussing like a caged tiger. Was there something about Sam's accident he hadn't told her? "What is it?" she asked.

"Nothing. Just that with my memories, I'm not remarkably fond of hospitals."

She could see that. His mouth was a line of pain. His hands shook when he scraped back his hair a second time. Worried as she was about Sam, the turmoil in Jon suddenly seized her in a way she couldn't explain. *Something's wrong.*

She caught his biceps below the shirt's sleeve, where minuscule wood slivers clung. Dimly, her fingers registered warm, damp skin and solid, tough muscle. She looked around. "Let's go outside." Through the glass they could see Sam's door.

In the morning air, away from the redolence of disinfectant and sickness, Jon closed his eyes and breathed in visible relief. "Last time I was in one of these places was with my son."

He had a son? Of course. Why not? He'd left Misty River

over two decades ago. Plenty of time to marry, have children. Hadn't she? She now understood his ease with Emily and Sam.

"Where is he now?" she asked softly. Obviously, the family remained with his ex.

A mask fell over his face. Those indigo eyes dulled, flattened. He stared at some point past her shoulder. The lines bracketing his mouth sharpened. "He's dead."

Her jaw dropped. Dead? His son was dead?

"Oh, *Jon.* Oh, God, no."

Heartsick, she reached out to him, in comfort, in regret.

He jutted his chin toward the door. "Sam's released."

They went inside. She didn't know what to think or say. Her heart knocked about her chest, a wounded creature. A terrible shame washed through her.

She'd treated him like a criminal, grilling him about what he should or shouldn't have done with Sam, when all along he'd been cloaked in memories so grievous she couldn't begin to fathom their impact on the human psyche.

To have lost a child... *A child...*

It couldn't bear thinking about.

Yet, he endured it.

Every day. Every hour. Every minute. *Now.*

Sam's face lit up the instant he saw them. She tried not to gape at the fat, white bundle of cotton taped to his thigh. She wanted to cling to him. Breath in his unique child scent forever. Her son was alive, so very alive. For that, she held an eternity of gratitude.

Before making a fool of herself—worse, embarrassing Sam further—Rianne cupped his precious face in her hands. "You're okay."

"Yeah. The doctor says I'll probably have a scar, though."

She gave him a smile. "It'll show character."

He huffed a tiny laugh. "I guess."

A young man in a white lab coat, stethoscope around his neck, walked toward them. "Mrs. Kirby?"

"Actually it's Worth. Rianne Worth. I'm Sam's mother."

He held out a hand. "Ronan Sterns."

They shook politely. Smiling, he turned to Sam and clasped his shoulder. "You've got a brave guy here. He's going to be fine. Have him check back with me in a few days to ensure everything is proceeding as it should." He turned to Sam. "Change the dressing daily and apply the ointment. Okay?"

Sam nodded.

"Good, I'll see you later." Dr. Sterns left.

Outside, they headed for the Toyota. "You going back to work, Mom?" Sam asked, favoring his leg as he walked.

"I called in a sub for the rest of the day." She turned to speak to Jon, but he was heading for his truck. His strong, broad shoulders carried that horrendous burden of loss. Every step emphasized his aloneness.

She couldn't let him go. Not knowing about his son, not knowing he'd agonized as much as she—*more*—over Sam. "Jon!"

He turned. Her breath caught. T-shirt, jeans, boots—chevrons of his big, strong body. Sunshine dipped cobalt into his hair. Beneath its shadow the silver ear-stud flickered.

A plethora of details crowded her mind, things she suddenly wanted to examine, to say, to ask.

"I make a mean roast beef sandwich. Join us at the house?"

"I have to run to the hardware store."

"Will you be long? We can wait."

"I'll be all afternoon."

"Supper then. Main course, sloppy joes."

A crooked smile. "Sounds great, but I'm meeting Seth."

"Oh." Oddly, she felt deflated, silly. "Well, can't beat that. Some other time then."

"Yeah. Some other time."

She watched him get in his truck and pull away.

Her heart went with him.

Chapter Six

"Hi, peanut."

"Daddy!"

"Whatcha doing?"

"Dumb ole fractions."

"Good girl." Smiling, Jon imagined Brittany at her desk, bare feet tucked up yoga-style. Socks, shoes lost somewhere in the house. For years, Colleen had fought the habit, worrying bacteria or whatever equally vile fungus would infect the soles of her daughter's feet. Unbelievable, considering his ex-wife cleaned the floors every single, solitary day. "Getting ready to come here for the summer?"

"Uh-huh. I'm X-ing off every week. Six more, right?"

"Right, sweetheart. I can't wait either." A sudden surge of helpless yearning had him squeezing his eyes shut. He'd drive to Seattle June thirtieth and bring her back that night.

"Is your house nice?"

"It will be," he said, breathing easier. "Your room's next."

"Is it big? Can I bring Phooey?"

The little toy dog he'd bought two hours after Brittany's birth. The fuzzy, yellow creature seldom left her bed. During the day it guarded her frilly pillow; at night it cuddled in her small arms. Jon smiled. "You bet. Bring Phooey. We'll give him the best spot in the house."

"*Her,* Dad." Ten-year-old exasperation. "Phooey's a *girl.*"

He grinned, ear to ear. "Ahh. Right. I should remember, shouldn't I?" He hauled himself up on the kitchen counter, ready to settle in for a while.

"Yes, you should," Brittany reprimanded primly. "What colors are you painting my room?"

"What color would you like?"

"I don't want paint. I want wallpaper. Alison Bonnley's got wallpaper in her room and it's *awesome.* I want the kind with little suns and clouds on it. Do they have that there?"

Jon shuddered at the thought of tangling with a bunch of petite smiling suns and fat, puffy-faced clouds dancing across the walls of the bedroom he planned for his baby girl. He favored paint. Clean, fast, easy. But this was Brittany.

"I'll see what they have, honey. But if they don't—"

"Then I want flowers. *Little* flowers. *Pretty* little ones."

Flowers he could handle. Flowers were normal. "All right. I'll go down to the store first thing in the morning."

They talked for another fifteen minutes before he said good-night and blew her a kiss.

He missed her. Missed her like crazy. He looked down at the telephone, the only link to his daughter these past weeks. For the gazillionth time he questioned the logic of returning to Oregon. He should have stayed in the apartment he'd moved to following the divorce. Or found a house in Puyallup or Tacoma. An hour's drive, max, to his little peanut-girl.

Instead, he'd come here, back to his roots. Back to where he believed he could forget. *Fool. As if you could forget your son.*

Even now, ten hours later, this morning's incident made his heart thunder. Seeing Sam was seeing Nicky all over again. Lying on that gurney. Cold. Still. Not his son at all.

He forced himself to think of the wallpaper Brittany wanted. He'd get those damn suns and clouds if it killed him. He couldn't wait to hold his sweet punkin again. Have her little arms wrapped around his neck as he carried her off to bed to read stories—*Pippi Longstocking* had been a favorite—and whisper prayers. *There is no God, Brittany. God doesn't take fifteen-year old boys from their families.*

He'd say the prayers. For her.

Since her first steps, it had been their ritual whenever he was home, the reading, the prayers. Nicky's was a roustabout ride: hanging upside down over Jon's shoulder, under his arm like a football, wrapped around his waist like a belt. And giggling. How his son could shriek giggles.

Then one day Nicky became Nick and the rides ceased. Jon couldn't remember when it happened. One morning Nicky was a boy, the next he was using Jon's shaver and underarm deodorant.

He pressed a thumb and index finger into his eyes. His heart leaked pain. *Aw, Nicky...I love you, son.*

How long he sat on the counter, he didn't know. Seconds turned into minutes. Minutes into twenty.

A scraping sound came from beyond the back door. He looked around, dazed. The house groaned softly. Through the pane behind him, night encroached. Probably raccoons searching out a scrap of the lunch he'd eaten out on the veranda yesterday.

He dropped off the counter, massaged his neck. A soak in the tub couldn't hurt. His shoulders ached. Not from work—

that kept his body honed—but from his old, familiar nemesis: tension.

Thanks to the hospital.

A light knock had him scanning the rear entry. Who'd visit at nine-fifteen when they should be getting ready for bed? He pulled open the door.

She stood in a soft wash of kitchen light. Her dark eyes held his for three slow beats. He let himself look his fill. The green blouse of this morning was gone, exchanged for a snug striated sweater. The black skirt had traded places with tight, white jeans. Red-tipped toes peeked from the hems.

She looked sinful as the Friday-night express at the corner of Walk and Don't Walk.

"Hi." Her voice broke through his trance. "Hope I didn't interrupt anything."

"No, I was just—" *Going to take a bath. Wanna join me?* He swung the door wider. "Come in."

"I brought you some of our dessert." Her hands cupped a small cellophane-sealed bowl. "It's a mixture of strawberries, mangoes, cantaloupe, watermelon, bananas and grapes. The kids call it Looty Fruity." Amusement in her eyes, her voice. "Don't ask."

"Looty Fruity, huh? Looks good. How's Sam?"

"Doing his homework." She held out the dish. "Please accept my apology. For being such a shrew at the hospital this morning."

He took the fruit. "Your boy was hurting."

"If I hadn't argued with him yesterday about blisters, he wouldn't have asked you for that sander."

The point was moot. He stepped back. "Come in for a minute."

She glanced through the darkness, toward her property. "I can't. Emily's asleep and Sam's—"

"Doing homework." He tugged her inside, closed the door. "They know where you are, Rianne. And I need your advice on something." He strode to the refrigerator, set the fruit inside. "This way." He led her through the living room, to the stairs.

"Jon, I…"

He caught her hand. "It'll take five minutes, tops."

As they went up, he didn't let go. Her fingers curled small, warm and very feminine around his. Everything about her felt feminine. He wished the cur she'd married still lived. For the past day and half he'd had the impulse to maim.

Reaching the second level, he turned left, toward one of the four rooms taking up the west section of the floor.

The east section held the master bedroom, but for Rianne to see it now was too soon. *One day, maybe.* When she did, it would not be for the purpose of choosing wallpaper.

He shook his head as if to clear it. What the hell was the matter with him, thinking of her as some Saturday-night bar hop?

He flicked on the light in the one of the farthest rooms.

"My daughter's bedroom."

"You have a daughter, too?"

"Ten last February. She's with my ex in Seattle."

Pride had him towing Rianne over the threshold, into a room with two large windows and a spacious closet. Reluctantly, he released her hand, walked to one of the windows, parked his seat on its ledge and crossed his arms. "Brittany wants wallpaper. I like paint, but she's set on these—" he stifled a shiver "—suns and clouds. Personally, I can't imagine having fifty thousand skies bouncing at me from every angle, but…"

She laughed softly. "Be thankful it isn't cats and dogs."

Jon rolled his eyes. "Her second choice is flowers."

Rianne surveyed the room. Her pale penny-colored hair hung in a smooth sweep to her shoulders. "And in case they don't have the sunny skies, you'd like me to help pick flowers."

"Would you?"

"When do you want to go?"

"Tomorrow morning?"

She chewed her lip, thoughtful. He imagined her rearranging her schedule, her children to fit him.

"All right," she said. "After I mow the lawn. I might have to bring Emily, though."

"All the better. She can help select."

Her eyes tracked the room one last time before she turned into the hallway. Sighing, he unfolded himself and followed. Time to go. Except he didn't want her to leave. Not yet.

They went down the stairs. Her small fanny swayed in front of him. A whiff of peaches lured his nostrils.

Before stepping onto the darkened veranda, she said, "Don't rush the dessert. We can live without the bowl for a few days."

He followed her outside, closed the door and went to where she waited at the edge of the steps, hugging her arms against the chill night air. Beside her, he slid his hands into his back pockets and looked up at a spray of stars. Among the junipers, a frog serenaded his mate.

"Thanks in advance, from Brit and me."

"It's the least I can do after today. Sam thinks you're a hero." She smiled that little Rianne smile. "So do I."

Their eyes held for a long, long time. He wished he could see what she was thinking. He wanted to ask about the bastard she'd married. He wanted to tell her about Nicky.

He wanted to kiss her again.

He chose the last and lowered his head. She didn't draw away. His mouth grazed hers, a whispered union. Still, she didn't move. Lifting his head a fraction, he watched her eyes close. His hands stayed in their pockets; hers remained hidden under her arms.

He touched her lips again. Fruit, woman. *Ah, Rianne.*

The kiss deepened, clung. The sexiest thing, this tenderness, this sensuality.

Reluctantly he lifted away, set his forehead to her hair. "You need to go." His voice was thick.

"I know," she whispered.

"I watch your bedroom late at night."

"I think about you."

"Too many nights I can't sleep."

"Jon…"

"You shouldn't have come here tonight."

"I had to."

"Did you?"

"Yes."

He let the word echo. "There's something between us."

"I know. It worries me."

"Does it? Why?"

"Because it's a strange feeling."

"Strange?"

"New, unfamiliar. It makes me want to do things I've never thought about."

He raised his head. Her breath wisped against his jaw. Her dark eyes tempted his soul. "You shouldn't say things like that to a man. Especially in the dark." With his thumb, he outlined her lips. Her full, supple lips. Opening his hand, he cupped her cheek. "Good night, Rianne," he whispered.

Several seconds passed. She moved out of his reach, down the steps. A flash of those white, white jeans, then night closed in.

He remained rooted in place long after she'd gone into her house. Long after her light went out. Long after he assumed she slept.

Sam couldn't believe it. His mother was actually leaving the lawn-mowing to him. It had taken nearly all morning to convince her. Now, he watched Jon help her climb into the big, black truck before the vehicle slowly headed down the street.

Too bad he had to baby-sit Emily. Okay, that was a mean thing to think. Mostly, Emily minded her own business. Not like Joey's two sisters who always wanted to know what he was doing, who he was hanging with and where. If Emily did that to him, Sam would lock her in the bathroom. Well, not really, but he'd want to.

He moved out from behind the giant rubber plant near the window. One of the kittens, Dude, biggest of the litter, scampered on wobbly legs across the carpet toward him.

"Hey, guy," he said picking up the black ball of fur, holding it up to his face. "Like having the run of the house, do you?" The kitten mewled. "Thought so." Grinning, Sam gently set down the little creature. "Better not get into any trouble. Old Sweetpea's gonna put a curfew on you." He went to the top of the basement stairs, called down to his sister. "Em?"

"Yeah?"

"I'm mowing the lawn now, 'kay?"

For a moment, silence. She appeared at the bottom step, looking up with big eyes. "Y'are? Did Mom say so?"

"'Course she did." Man, even his sister took him for some kind of wimp. "Why wouldn't she? I'm old enough."

"Yeah, but, after yesterday—"

"Yesterday was an accident. She knows that." Disgusted that Emily, like their mom, would doubt his capabilities, Sam thrust his feet into his size-ten sneakers.

"Can I watch?" Emily climbed the stairs. Arms extended, hands gripping the railings on each side, she lifted herself off the top step, hung suspended a few seconds.

"Watch it," he warned, tugging at a knot in one lace. "You'll fall backward." Little sisters could be such a pain.

"I won't." But her toes settled again. "Can I come out and watch you cut the lawn?"

He made a face. "What for?" The lace snapped.

"There's nothing on TV."

"Then work on your science project or something." He didn't want his sister out there watching. What if he screwed up and the mower wouldn't start or, worse, ended up busted? The thing had probably been built in his great-grandpa's day.

"I'm all caught up on my project." Emily pouted as he threaded the frayed lace a second time. "I wanna go outside."

"All right!" *Stupid lace. Stupid sneaker.* "Fine." He tied off the tattered ends. "Just don't get in the way."

"I won't."

Slapping open the screen, he barged outside. "Why didn't you go with Mom? You would've had fun."

His sister was on his heels. "Didn't feel like it."

"Well, you should've."

"Well, I didn't want to, so there."

"No, you just wanted to stay home and bug *me.*"

"I am not bugging you. I'm trying to be nice." Her voice sounded small. Sam refused to look up. So what if she was little? So what if she adored him the way no one else did? He hauled the mower from the shed, uncapped the gas tank. He wasn't feeling sorry, no way. Not this time. Stubbornly, he kept his head down.

"Whatcha doing?"

"Checking to make sure it's got enough gas."

"Do you know how?"

He took it all back about Joey's sisters. Em could be a mega, major pest. "I know how," he retorted. After all, he'd seen his mother do it a thousand times.

His leg hurt. Under the bandage the skin burned. He should've been more careful yesterday. Way more careful.

He'd nearly wrecked it for himself with his mother. She didn't like him using power tools. Any kind of power tools. But he had to prove to her he was as normal as any other kid his age. Heck, most guys were doing neighborhood jobs already! Okay, so he didn't have the greatest coordination in his right hand. Big deal. He survived. Had since he was a baby, reaching for whatever.

Well, he wasn't a baby anymore. His mom and Emily better get that through their heads because things were going to change around here. He was darn near a man, didn't they know?

Across the cab, Rianne sneaked a peek at Jon. Since leaving his house, he hadn't said a word. Maybe she should have knocked on his door closer to noon rather than at eight-fifty. Maybe she should have called first. After all, weekends were for sleeping in. *As if you could have, thinking half the night about his son, his daughter. Him.*

He had a family.

Kissed her as no man had.

Did he still love his ex-wife? Did he have a good relationship with her and Brittany? Did that add to the log of pain he lugged around on his big shoulders? She wouldn't lie to herself. She wanted to be the one lessening the sorrow in his eyes about Sam's injury.

Sam.

Another male with too much disquiet in his eyes. Often of late, it mutated to belligerence. She wondered how Jon had handled his son's teenaged years. One day she might ask him. When the wound on his heart had a stronger scar.

Over breakfast she and Sam had had a small quarrel about his ability to operate the lawnmower. Given the incident with the sander, Rianne's arms goose-bumped at the thought of Sam and whirring blades. But his eyes, begging trust, caved

her resolve. Small penitence to pay after his unhappy words
about his birth. And so, she'd rushed away. Straight to Jon....

"Am I too early?" she had asked when he'd opened his
front door, overnight stubble dusting his jaw. He'd looked
tired, grumpy. Sexy. She couldn't believe she'd kissed him
twice, this man who'd invaded her dreams for more than
twenty years. He was right. Something stirred between them.

He dropped his hand from the door jamb. "I've been up a
while. Come in."

Stepping into the foyer, she chided herself for wearing a
dress rather than slacks. She felt as showy as the overgrown
majesty fern — its feathery leaves stretching on slim stalks toward the vaulted ceiling—in his living room. Jon headed for
the stairs. "Sorry for the lack of furniture. I live pretty much
in the den or in there." A nod at the kitchen. "Coffee's fresh."

"Emily's not coming."

He paused. "Would you rather do this another time?"

"And miss out on that it's-a-beautiful-day-in-the-neigh-
borhood wallpaper?" She grinned. "Not on your life."

Damp from a shower, his linear, black hair was accented
by the rills of impatient fingers. A silver F-18 thundered across
the fore of his navy sweatshirt. Pushed back, its sleeves re-
vealed ropy muscles. The wolf's prowess.

He said, "You're a captivating woman."

She bloomed and caught herself wanting to touch her hair
in that abashed female way.

A corner of his mouth scooted up. "I'll be back in three
minutes." And he was. Shaven. Leather binding his hair. Skin
humming with the freshness of soap.

This time, she waited until he opened the truck door and
helped her into the cab. She was beginning to favor its Jon-
essence to her own car....

Now, watching businesses flip up their shades and remove

Closed signs from windows and doors, she wondered who most needed the distractions of an adventurous morning—she or Sam.

"Here it is." Jon pulled up to a small, brick-fronted store called Waltzin' Paper and shut off the engine. "Ready to do the great grab-happy sky hunt?"

"Whenever you are."

He gave her a slow look. Her heart cheered.

A tiny chime tinkled against the door as they entered the building. Old, but clean and well organized, it exuded a welcoming atmosphere Rianne had liked the first time she'd come to the store. Cool air circulated from an overhead fan, sunlight poured through tall narrow windows.

A woman dressed in a long peasant dress crossed the uneven hardwood. "Hey, Rianne."

"How are you, Abby?"

"Getting there. Each day's a little better."

"I'm glad. Jon, have you met Abby Paris?"

Around Rianne's shoulder, he took the store owner's hand. "Jon Tucker."

Abby nodded. "Related to Seth Tucker, by chance?"

"My brother."

"Luke, too?"

"Luke, too."

Her eyes smiled. "How can I help you this morning?"

Jon looked around. "We need wallpaper," he said drily.

The counters were littered with catalogs and samples.

"Seems you've hit the jackpot," she said, equally dry. "Specifics or browsing?"

"Ten-year-old's bedroom."

She motioned to a corner in the rear of the store. "Try there." Embroidered pictures and portraits suited for children decorated the wall in a friendly clutter. Some were childish—

inclined for babies and toddlers—others favored designs for school-aged children.

"Friend?" Jon asked when he and Rianne were alone. He stood behind her. Their bodies shared warmth.

"I bought wallpaper for the bathroom here last summer."

"She married?"

Rianne shot him a look. Her stomach flip-flopped.

"What?" His mouth twitched. "I'm just making conversation."

She returned to the catalog. "Recently widowed."

He made a noncommittal sound. His biceps brushed her shoulder as he reached for a second book. She studied an assortment of patterns—balloons, clowns, dalmatians, Little Bo Peeps, elves crouched atop and under toadstools, fairies, butterflies—and tried to keep her mind on the task of choosing an appropriate selection for a little girl. Jon's forearm lay inches from her own. Why had he asked about Abby?

Because he's a man and he's single.

Jealous?

Of course not.

Hello, Pinocchio.

She slapped the catalog shut, grabbed the next.

"Not finding anything worthwhile?"

"No. Are you planning to ask her out?" Stupid words. What he did and who he did it with were off limits. Because they'd shared a couple of kisses didn't make him hers.

"Ask who out?"

"Abby."

He stopped flipping pages, his eyes blue as torch lights. "Why would I do that?"

"I thought…you were interested, that's all." Her upper body warmed. She bowed her head, looked over more pages. Patterns networked into a maze.

Jon turned a catalog page, traced a design. He had large, broad hands; the fingers were long and nicked with scars. Unlike Duane's short, slim, deceptively benign fingers.

"I've got interests," he said. "But not in her."

Rianne's heart kicked. "Oh."

"Oh? Just oh?" He closed his book, turned subtly, pressed closer. Heat, hers and his, penetrated areas of her bare skin. "You trying to ask me something here, Rianne?"

She flipped the pages faster. "Not at all. You're your own man. It's not for me to say who—" His hand stopped her motion.

"Look at me," he commanded softly.

She did. His irises were navy.

"Two-timing isn't my gig. Not before my marriage, not during and not now."

She looked down at their hands and couldn't deflect the tingle tripping low in her belly.

"I'd never hurt you, Rianne."

Her head snapped up. His eyes pierced her, and she knew he no longer spoke of Abby. *He knows. He knows about Duane.* Had Sam said something? No. No, Duane shamed Sam. Not even Eva Zeglen had procured the gist of her son's emotions on that issue.

"I never…" she began.

Gently, oh so gently, he curled her palm into his. Soothing. Like his voice. Soothing her. "Trust me."

Nerves traveled her spine. Could she tell him? Tell him about Duane? Officer Duane Kirby of the LAPD? Who protected and served all but his family?

As a former law officer, who would Jon side with? Her? Or the force—the way Duane's cronies had?

The circling thumb entranced her. She lifted her head, words on her tongue.

He said, "Know how slinky you look in this little green number?"

Slinky? Joy burst from her heart. A new description. She let it melt, a smoothie of slow, sweet delight, and sent a quick thank-you that the "little green number" had been the grab-and-run decision during her debate with Sam.

Jon fingered the hem of one short sleeve. "Soft. Like you."

She lowered her head, a furnace in her cheeks. He wasn't like Duane—or any man, for that matter. "It's jersey knit."

"Rianne? When we go out the first time? Wear it." Straightening, he moved away and opened another catalog.

"Are you asking me on a date?"

"Suppose I am. I'd like to repay your help today."

A thank-you date.

She focused on her job. Who was she to feel disappointed? Priority one was getting her family back to normal.

"Got some garters?" he murmured.

"What?" Her head shot up. His eyes held her in place.

"How about tall heels?"

A flame ignited under her skin. She ducked her head. "Yes to both." Goodness, they were staring at wallpaper and discussing undergarments. Did he realize how unparalleled this…this foreplay was to her?

"Rianne?"

"Yes?" Her voice had all but disappeared.

"You're incredibly sexy when you're shy."

She couldn't think. Or speak. And if she wasn't careful, she'd cry.

Chapter Seven

"I like this one best," she told him twenty minutes later.

Over her shoulder he studied curls of vines dotted with little purple and cream flowers. The pattern left space and air among leaves and blossoms and offered room for a ten-year-old to grow into sixteen without too much preamble. "Let's buy it."

"Don't you want to take a test sample home first?"

What he wanted was to go home and test her—taste her...in bed. Cooped up in this tight corner, inhaling her skin, listening to her soft "oooh"s and "ahhh"s as she turned page after page, had taxed his limitations. "I trust your judgment."

There, that half smile that slung a curve in his gut. "Get enough for two walls," she told him.

"Not the whole room?"

"You don't want claustrophobia."

"Good point." He searched out the store owner.

The moment they were in the truck, he said, "Want to grab a coffee at Kat's Kitchen?" The thought of dropping her off, returning to his empty house—in the middle of a Saturday—hollowed him the way it had last night standing on his deck after she'd gone.

"All right, but we do it Dutch."

He snorted and reached for the ignition.

She stayed his hand. "I mean it, Jon. We split the cost."

"You're fluffing those independent feathers again."

"Yes, I suppose I am."

He started the truck, but couldn't contain the pique he felt. "This is ridiculous. Can't you accept a token of appreciation?"

She said nothing until he'd driven the two blocks to Kat's and parked the truck. She faced the side window. "It's something I have to do. Can you understand that?"

Shame washed through him. Of course he could. He'd been to enough abused women's shelters during his years on the force to know independence pointed toward a road of victory. Her victory.

Still, he wanted her to lean on him—even for a moment.

The image jerked him into motion. Yanking the keys from the ignition, he jumped from the truck. Hell, he should be glad Rianne had this streak of stubbornness. He should hoot and holler that she and her kids didn't need him.

Then why was he ticked?

Because you need her to need you. Just a little.

Dammit. It was true. Call it chauvinistic, macho, male. Call it Neanderthal. What he felt was protectiveness, pure and primal.

He opened her door. "Do we have a deal?" she asked.

"We have a deal," he groused, taking her elbow, assisting her down. Sun rays sank into her hair. "Just one thing. When we go out there'll be no discussion about who's paying."

She tossed him a wry look. "That a warning?"

"A promise," he said and ushered her toward the diner.

Inside, the smell of eggs, bacon and grits mantled the air. Rianne used the pay phone in the entrance to check on her kids.

"No problems?" he asked when she hung up.

"Sam got the lawn done. Emily weeded the pansies."

"There you go."

The ten o'clock coffee hounds had already gathered. Kat— a tray of bagels, muffins and glazed doughnuts in one hand, coffee carafe in the other—threw them a swift, friendly smile. She jutted her wrinkled chin toward a booth halfway down the street-side windows. The same one he, Seth and Luke sat in every Wednesday at six-fifteen, eating their eggs.

His brothers were there now.

"Hey, Jon Travis," Luke greeted as Jon and Rianne stopped beside the table. "We tried to call your house." He regarded Rianne. "Obviously you were busy."

"You both remember Rianne Worth?"

The men slid out of the booth. Seth offered a hand first. "Been a long time, Rianne. I remember when your hair was two feet long."

Luke chuckled. "And he's still smitten. How are you, Ms. Worth?" Gallantly, he held out a hand. "We've never met officially. I'm Luke, eldest Tucker brother."

"Please, call me Rianne. Formalities are for school. And, yes, Seth, it's been a very long time. The last time I saw you was on the field at Misty River High, chasing a football."

"Did we win?"

She laughed and slipped into the booth. "Yes, we did, as a matter of fact. It was the final game of the season." She named the year, when Jon had transferred from uniform to Drug Squad.

He watched Seth's eyes remembering and jealousy stuck out its tongue.

When they were seated, he beside Rianne, his brothers across the table, Kat offered coffee. Jon ordered multigrain bagels for Rianne and himself.

Seth inquired, "How's the house?"

"Getting there. Rianne picked out the wallpaper for Brittany's room this morning."

"Yeah?" Seth darted a look between him and Rianne.

Jon sipped his coffee, set down the mug. "I wanted another opinion."

Seth nodded sagely. "Sounds logical. Kids always want things that don't make sense." He elbowed Luke. "Right?"

"How should I know? You and Jon are the ones with kids."

The waitress brought a pair of steaming bagels.

Face set, Luke looked at Jon. "You given any more thought to that offer I mentioned last week?"

"No."

"Why not?"

"Already told you."

His brother grunted. "Town this size doesn't have the revenue for homemade furniture."

"Thanks for the vote of confidence."

"You'll go bonkers building furniture."

"And becoming Misty River's top lawman won't have the same effect?" *Not the time or place, Luke. Back off.* Jon watched Rianne's narrow hands break apart the bagel. His thigh pressed hers. She pressed back. A current hit his lower regions.

"Once a cop, always a cop," Luke said.

"Bull."

Seth scratched his jaw. "Town could use you, Jon."

"What is this, a conspiracy?"

"Come on, J.T.," Luke chided, voice low. "Misty River's going to hell in a big basket. We know it, you know it, the whole town knows it. Place needs someone who can do the job. Since there's no one else with the credentials you got within a hundred miles, you can't blame us for trying." He looked to the woman beside Jon. "Sorry, Rianne. We didn't mean for you to get in the middle of this."

"What is wrong with Misty River?" she asked.

"Nothing's wrong with Misty River," Jon told her.

"It's the police chief," Luke interrupted. He looked at Jon. "They caught Irving Meeks growing pot in his greenhouse. Did they charge him? Nope. Counseled him. Bet he's back at it. *You* would've done something."

Beside Jon, Rianne's eyes latched on to his brother's face while he belabored the issue of Pat Willard. "He's been in the position ten years too long. Every year arrests and charges decrease, but crime doesn't. Department's got this good ol' boy attitude. Jonny, here—"

"That's enough," Jon warned.

"—has experience up the yin yan. He could clean out the town in a heartbeat, but refuses to get involved."

"Dammit, Luke. Will you shut the hell up?"

His brother threw up his hands. "Fine. Go to waste."

"You know," Jon said, heart pounding, "you always were a long-winded SOB. No wonder you're a lawyer."

"Probably be mayor soon," Seth commented.

"Wouldn't doubt it," Jon agreed. He leaned back, laid a casual arm across the back of the bench, fingertips toying with the hair at Rianne's collar.

Seth grinned. "Wouldn't need to campaign."

Jon nodded. "Do it all himself."

"Yup. A one-man force paving truth and justice down the streets of Misty River."

"Laugh all you want," Luke grumped. "But you're the ones with kids. You want to see them dead or in juvie court one day, be my guest."

Stone silence.

"Aw, hell." Luke said. "My mouth's running away on me. I'm sorry, man, truly I am."

Jon hunched forward, pushed both thumbs up the belly of his mug. Pain splintered like a live thing through his body. "Forget it. I don't expect you to think about it all the time."

"But *you* do. I should've remembered that."

"Yeah, you should've," Seth conceded. "If you weren't my brother, I'd kick your—" He glanced at Rianne.

Luke fiddled with the knot in his tie.

Somewhere a group of men guffawed. Glassware clinked as Kat and another waitress cleaned tables across the narrow room.

"Forget it," Jon mumbled and nearly sighed with relief when Rianne's fingers settled on his leg.

Seth threw some bills on the table. "Ready?" he asked Luke.

They slid from the booth. Luke glanced at Jon. "Take care, J.T. Nice meeting you, Rianne."

When they left, she asked, "You okay?"

"Yeah." He'd deal with Luke later.

She withdrew her hand—its exit an ache—and picked up the last half of her bagel. "Will you take the position?"

"No."

She turned her head and looked at him for a heavy moment. Her dark eyes were as serious as he'd ever seen them. Fine lines graced the outer edges. "The night you thought a burglar prowled my backyard you were a cop, Jon."

"I acted like any heedful neighbor would."

"You acted like a cop."

Okay, he'd sneaked up on her like a damned predator. *Like a cop.* Every step, the kick of the chase singing in his blood.

No matter. If it killed him, he would live the next thirty years without the adrenaline. He didn't need it. Designing, creating, shaping wood was enough. Life, *his life,* had changed the second Nicky died. All he needed was a roof over his head, food in his belly, a job he could leave at five. If he got Brittany a few weeks a year his world would be complete. Chancing more involved commitments he could no longer handle. Chancing more meant responsibilities, obligations he'd cashed in sixteen months ago on a miserable January night.

Chancing more is Rianne.

He took in the line of her shoulders. The curve of her slender neck as she dusted her fingertips over her plate. She had delicate bones. The slant of cheek to chin smooth, finely structured.

A line from the nineteenth-century poet, John Keats, streamed through his brain: *A thing of beauty is a joy forever.*

No question how she'd feel beneath him. Soft, tiny, purely woman. He'd have to be gentle, careful. Manual labor had toughened his body.

Hell. If you need a woman that bad, drive to Portland for a night.

He didn't want a faceless bar pickup. He wanted Rianne.

Then be ready to take on the whole package.

Can't.

Coward.

"Anything else, you two?" Kat cut through his meandering like a saw through wood.

Jon shook his head and dug five bucks from his wallet; Rianne opened her purse. He kept his mouth shut. They walked out to his truck. What had started out as a perfectly fine day, his brother had turned into a perfectly rotten one.

Several hours later, Rianne stood in Video Views with Sam and Emily scanning the latest DVD releases. She wanted to reward the kids for their yard work. The lawn looked sleek as a golf course and not a weed competed with the flowers.

"Can we get this one, Mom?" Sam asked, shoving a Jim Carrey movie under her nose. "It's kinda old, but it's supposed to be really good, and we've never seen it. Emily wants it, too," he added as if his sister's fancies carried more weight.

Rianne skimmed the back blurb. She wasn't a Carrey fan, but knew his antics could make you laugh. After the week they'd had, her family was due.

"All right, get two," she said. "We'll watch one tonight and one tomorrow night."

Sam's eyes sparked. "Awesome! Hey, Em." He nudged his sister browsing through a cluster of Disney. "We can pick two. Why don't you get *Finding Nemo?* It's really good. I saw it with Joey last summer and it's not scary at all. Honest," he added when she frowned at the toothless grinning turtle on the cover.

Emily pushed her glasses up her button nose. "Okay."

A second later, she crowded Rianne.

"Hey, Kirby," a voice sneered behind them. "Gonna stay home with Mommy and baby sis tonight?"

Rianne turned to see a smirking Cody Huller. He still wore the remnants of Sam's knuckles along his right cheekbone.

A man, an older, beer-bellied version of the boy who had fought her son, stood several feet down the aisle. Brent Huller. Taking a slow, lewd scan of her body.

Too late now to wish she'd changed into baggy jeans and a sweatshirt when Jon had dropped her off at home.

Emily hid her face against Rianne's side; Sam glared at the belligerent teen. "Take a hike, Huller."

The father sauntered up. "Troubles, Cody?"

"Nah."

Turning Emily toward the cashier, Rianne said to Sam, "Let's pay for these."

She hurried the children toward the checkout counter

where several customers waited in line. To her disgust, Brent Huller moved in behind her. The odor of cheap whiskey struck her nose. "Your kid's got nerve."

Emily wrapped her arms around Rianne's waist, shivered, her doe eyes anxious. "Can we go, Mom?"

Rianne caught up her daughter's hair. "In a minute, baby." Thankfully a cashier came open. Rianne moved to the counter, quickly digging a twenty from her purse.

Outside, it was all she could do not to herd the kids at a run to the car. As it was, Emily, gripping Rianne's hand, trotted to keep up. They reached the car in fifteen seconds.

"What's your hurry, lady?"

For an overweight man, Huller Senior moved swifter than a snake. He and his son were upon them the instant Rianne shoved her key into the Toyota's door. *Click.* Thank God. Yesterday, it had taken three attempts to free the lock.

"Don't ignore me, teach," the man ordered. "I got something to say to you."

Rianne pushed Emily inside. The child scrambled across the seat. "Sorry, Mr. Huller, I don't have time to chat."

"'Sorry, Mr. Huller,'" he mimicked. "Ain't you prim and proper?"

"Leave my mom alone." Sam stepped between her and the oaf.

He laughed. "Well, well. I see what you mean, Cody. We got us a real live banty rooster. Wanna take my son on again, kid?"

Rianne breathed hard through her nose. The man taunted her son the way Duane had two years ago when the boy had dared to defy his father when he bellyached about reheated leftovers for supper. Duane had taken it out on her. She'd ended up in the hospital. The next day, swamped in humiliation, she'd started the extinction of her marriage.

She faced Brent Huller. "Get in the car, Sam." He budged

not an inch. Rianne clasped his thin shoulders, felt the vibrating anger. "Do as I ask, please."

"Then tell him to leave us alone!"

"Sam."

"We were minding our own business and—"

"*Sam.*" Their eyes held.

A frustrated tug and he moved to the rear door.

"Kid's got no manners," Huller commented, shoving beefy fingers into the waist of saggy jeans.

"Mr. Huller." She glared directly into his small, wormy eyes. "What happened between my son and yours is over. Belonguering it won't help. Cody and Sam will be back to school Monday. Hopefully they'll behave themselves there, and—" she stressed the word "—*anywhere* else for that matter."

"That so? Well, get this, teach. My boy don't take lectures from you. Your kid threw the first punch. Does it again? He'll deal with me."

And you with me, jackass. "Rest assured. Sam won't be speaking to Cody anymore. Good-bye, Mr. Huller."

"Just a minute." He reached for the top of the door, holding fast. "I'm not done yet."

"I am. Now back off." She got behind the wheel. Using both hands, she yanked the door free, instantly setting the All Lock button.

"Is he coming after us?" Emily squeaked, staring at the Hullers as Rianne started the car.

"Not in this life." She would drive to Minnesota before she'd let the jerk come near her kids again. She backed out carefully. She wouldn't put it past Huller to step deliberately into her path and scream blue murder.

He kept his distance. Trust went both ways. Driving through the parking lot, she kept an eye on the rearview mirror. When she turned onto the street, he was gone.

Precaution—a souvenir of living with a cop for more than a decade—had her driving up and down five streets, through the center of town before she turned back toward their dead-end cul-de-sac. When she saw Jon's pickup next door, she chanted a silent prayer of thanks.

As if reading her mind, Emily pointed, "Mr. Tucker's home, Mom! That man won't hurt us now."

Could she blame her kids for their apprehension? To them, Mom was easy prey. In contrast, Jon, with his large, powered presence, was a safe harbor. Despite her affection for Jon, the notion stung. She wanted her kids to look to her as their sanctuary, to feel sheltered under *her* wings.

She was still mulling it over when she crawled under the covers that night and reached for the journal her L.A. therapist encouraged her to keep.

Since last summer, her home had been secure, happy. In Misty River she sought for her children what she'd had living with her own widowed mother. Molly Worth had showered their home in love, laughter, joy—in spite of the loneliness she hid in her heart. Not until her mother lay dying did Rianne come to know of her melancholy.

"Don't be sad for me, baby," she had told a weeping Rianne one day. "I'm going home to my Jack, don't you see? I've missed him so much, so very much all these years. Let me go. I want to be with him again." She'd clasped Rianne's hand. "My beautiful, strong daughter. Be at peace for me. One day you'll find a man who'll fill your heart with love. You'll see."

Rianne had believed that man was Duane Kirby.

Two years later, bewildered and huddled in a corner with her first bruised eye, she'd realized Molly Worth was wrong. Utterly wrong. Rianne had found a man all right. But, he hadn't filled her heart with love or peace.

Now he was dead, gone—*amen to that*—and she was here. Survivor of more than life. Survivor of *self.*

Tucking an arm under her head, she stared at the moonlight through the lace-scalloped curtains. He would have hated this room with its frills; their Los Angeles house had mirrored a baser affluence. Here, her home fit her means. Cozy and embracing—reflecting her family's needs and her self-reliance. Reflecting her.

"Then tell him to leave us alone." Sam's statement had her fluffing the pillow.

Did her actions confuse the children? One minute Sam complained about her overprotection; next, he demanded it. And, Emily, sweet child, divined Jon as her white knight booming over hills of battle.

The way I did twenty years ago. Ah, Jon...

Where were they headed?

She didn't know. Truly didn't know.

After several long minutes, she picked up her pen and wrote:

He's changed. Unbelievably so. Yet...yet, there is a sameness, a kernel time and years haven't quite altered. It's hidden. Deep in his spirit. He keeps it screened from the world, and I wonder, in my heart of hearts, what it would take to bring out that kernel—bring *him*—into the light again. Can you believe I'd even think this about a man...?

She tossed back the comforter, padded to the window and pulled aside the curtain. Across the hedge, his house was dark. Had he watched her lights go out tonight?

If he became Misty River's police chief, then what? Would her children's image of him change if he resumed a career in law enforcement? Would hers?

He's not Duane.

She shut the drapes and slipped into bed.

It wasn't as if she was marrying Jon Tucker. They were simply neighbors.

She thought of his kisses, warm, wonderful. Different each time. "We're just neighbors," she said aloud. Like a pledge. But she lay awake a long while, wondering how he'd acted as a cop.

Chapter Eight

Sunday evening Jon stepped up to the front door and rang the bell of his childhood home. Shadows pulled at its corners and roofline. The place lay in shambles. If he hadn't looked twice at the off-kilter letters next to the door, he might have driven past this small bungalow he had escaped for two decades.

Looking around, words tagged his mind. Decay, rotten, blight. Words of ruin. The way his mother had ruined her life. And his childhood.

Sweat broke out across his forehead.

The inside latch scraped. The door squeaked open. His mother stood facing him.

She'd aged far past her sixty-one years. Hair once thick and ash blond, reclined in gray, permed curls around her skull. Lines mapped her face. A shawl draped her shoulders. Stains spotted her blouse, matching those on her cheap blue slacks and dirty, fuzzy slippers. In her most inebriated stupor, he recalled Maxine Tucker as a tall, attractive woman. *Young.*

Today, no vestige of that woman remained.

She simply stared, a puzzled look in her sunken gray eyes. He watched dawning come slowly. "Hi, Ma."

"Jonny," she whispered as if he were a vision from the dead. Maybe, to her, he was.

"It's been a while."

"Twenty-one years, ten months."

Surprise struck him. Had she cared, then? "How are you?"

"You know Seth and Luke still live in town?" Her voice told him of lungs suffering too much smoke.

"Yeah, I know."

"For years now. They come by maybe once, twice a year. Round my birthday, at Christmas. Seth's got a girl. 'Bout fourteen or so. Luke's got no kids."

"Ma, can I come in?" Jon asked.

"Whaddya want? 'T'ain't my birthday, and Christmas is long gone."

"I came to see how you were, and—" he kneaded his left shoulder "—to talk." Though he didn't know what about. She'd never been an approachable mother. Irrelevancies or heavy stuff, that had been his father's domain. His father, the listener. Out back, in the shed. Had its charred beams rotted into the earth?

"Well, now you've seen. You want to talk, then talk and get it over with."

Dropping his hand, he was suddenly sorry he'd come. A spur-of-the-moment thing. Thinking of Rianne. Thinking— his heart doing a big ol' drumbeat—about her in the wallpaper store, choosing patterns for Brittany. Thinking about them in the diner. About how good she felt at his side. How right.

How much he liked her kids. How much she filled the canyon of his soul.

Made him care again.

So here he stood.

He saw now the gesture was wrong. In the heart, where it counted, his mother hadn't changed. She nursed her grudges—and, no doubt, her hangovers—while he'd let his go…was trying to.

He moved to leave.

"How long you been in town?" she rasped.

"About a month. I bought the old MacDowall place."

"An' you're just now getting 'round to your old ma?"

He shifted his feet. Stuck his hands into his hip pockets. *Guilty as charged.* He'd put off coming here. Afraid of what he'd find. "I needed time. I didn't think you'd see me."

"What changed your mind?"

He pushed out a breath, looked down into her booze-eroded face. "You're my mother."

Something ghosted through her eyes. Sorrow?

"Mothers are supposed to forgive and forget, huh?"

"I don't expect you to forget, Ma. Not even forgive. Maybe I was hoping you'd lay it aside for a while, is all."

"Your daddy was dying, Jonny. He was dying in that hospital and you left anyway. Didn't even come by to say your fare-thee-wells. What kinda son does that?"

"Don't think I haven't paid for it a hundredfold." Luke had phoned him in Seattle the day their father's fire-seared lungs gave out. Two weeks after the shed's demise. And Jon's escape from Misty River. That night, with the news like a burn itself, he'd walked hours in pouring rain, envisioning his father trapped in that fire-engulfed shed where Maxine had tossed a careless cigarette into the wood shavings. No, Jon had never gone back. He couldn't face the woman before him now. Couldn't look in her eyes without setting blame at her feet.

Maxine took in his full height. "Heard you got yourself in the cop business up north."

"You might say." Seattle was as far as he'd dared run from Oregon. From a mother who had, by definition of negligence, killed his father. *What goes around comes around.*

"Gonna be a cop here, too?"

"No." He slapped at a mosquito on his arm.

"Why not?"

The question seemed entrenched in his family. "I'm through with police work."

"You married?"

"Divorced."

"Kids?"

He hesitated. "One. Brittany. She lives with her mother." One day he'd explain Nicky.

A lull ensued. Seemed she was set on talking in the doorway with him standing under the swaybacked porch roof. Uncomfortable with her scrutiny, Jon said, "Look, Ma. Maybe we should do this another time when it's not so late."

"It's only seven-thirty. But if you wanna run off, that's your business. I can't hold you here."

He tried again. "You could invite me in."

"I could. But what good would that do? You'd just look around and condemn me. You never liked living here—why would you want to come inside now? For old times' sake? See how many beer cases are stacked against the fridge?"

"Ma—"

"Well, there aren't any, just so you know. Been sober ten years now. Didn't know that, did you?"

"No. No, I didn't. That's great, Ma."

"Seth helped me. He's a good boy, my Seth."

"Yeah," Jon agreed, thinking of his quiet, serious brother. "He is." A good, *gentle* man.

"Luke never bothers. Too busy being a fancy lawyer. Too ashamed to bother with the likes of his disgusting mother. You'n him are a lot alike. 'Cept you look exactly like your daddy. Spitting image, truth be told. Hair's too long, though." She studied him intently. "You visit your daddy's grave?"

"Not yet." *Soon.* Closure with Travis Tucker. "I figured on doing it next week."

"I put flowers on it every Sunday. Seen that little Worth girl up there puttering around her mamma's resting place a time or two. Nice girl, that one. Always was pretty as a picture. They say she's widowed. Too bad, her having two kids and all."

He stared at his mother. "You've talked to Rianne?"

"Once I did. She was at the cemetery same as me. Helped me weed a bunch of wild mustard around your daddy's headstone. Even helped me to my car when it started to rain. Arthritis acts up all the time now." Maxine swiped a knuckle under her nose. "Yep, a real sweet girl."

He was stunned. Rianne and Maxine? Down on their knees, heads bent, weeding wild mustard...*together?* Two women, opposite as whiskey and Sprite?

Shaken, he stepped back, waded through the junk on the narrow porch, waded through emotion tangling in his chest. Gripping the flimsy railing, he looked past the house toward the rear yard. His father had died right where two charred walls still stood leaning like haunted sails in a sea of weeds, surrounded by lumps of scrap metal and wood, overgrown with moss and rotted leaves. Amazingly, within the nearest wall, the blackened door—he could hear its squawk as his father opened it—hung askew from a single, bent hinge.

Hey, Dad. Sure could use your ear now.

His gaze tracked back to an old wooden barrel, a flat tire, a rusted bed spring. A yard full of discarded life.

Maxine hated outside work. In contrast, Travis Tucker had loved it. And the shed, his haven from his booze-bombed wife, where he'd sat carving his wood.

For one frightening moment Jon loathed Maxine. For what she'd done to their family. To his dad.

He wanted her nowhere near Rianne. Didn't want his mother feeding off Rianne's moral goodness.

Rianne was clean. Maxine had never been clean.

A snake twisted inside him. Shame.

Behind him, the door groaned. His mother shuffled her way to his side. He smelt the mustiness of her lonely life.

"Whatcha lookin' at?"

"The yard needs work."

"I got a kid comes once a week to do it. He ain't much good, but he's all I can afford."

"What about Seth's girl? She's old enough."

She made a scoffing sound. "Don't want my granddaughter dirtying her hands on this place. Besides, Seth's ex-wife doesn't want me associating with her. Probably thinks I'll contaminate her. Probably right, too."

Jon turned his head, looked at his mother hugging a shawl around her, though the evening hung with the day's heat. She stared back. "You here to pass judgment?"

"I told you, I came to talk."

"So you did. You gonna come again?"

"If you want."

She gazed across the abandoned lot bordering her property where once a gas station had operated. Forty years ago, this section of town, cut off by a strip of railroad—a long-since forgotten part of the Simon Benson logging era of the early 1900s—had earned the legit title "other side of the tracks."

"Good," she wheezed. "I'll make us a pot of tea then."

Jon straightened. In a motion totally foreign to them both, he laid a hand on her frail shoulder. "You take care now, Ma."

She followed him to the edge of the steps and watched him climb into his truck. Once out of the driveway, he gave her a short wave. She didn't return it, simply stood clutching her shawl, a small, forlorn figure in the deepening dusk.

He stopped at the town library on his way home. The building closed at nine. Thirty minutes left. Perfect to find a couple of books to give him some down time after Maxine.

His mother. He hadn't expected her to look so old, so *shriveled*. Three decades of scorn had evaporated the instant she opened her door.

She couldn't hurt him anymore. Not her drunken stupors, her rages nor her vehement mouth. The hole inside him had begun to close on that miserable little porch. *Rianne weeding with Maxine.*

Rianne, who found solace in the earth and growing things.

Rianne, who helped a lonely old woman out of the rain.

Rianne, who stood ten feet down an aisle, a pair of half lenses perched on the tip of her pretty nose.

Jon jacked a shoulder against a shelf, and...drank her in.

A sight to behold, this woman who attracted him. Lemony-tinted blouse. Poet sleeves. Trim black slacks. Nifty little granny shoes. A long-strapped purse dangling off one shoulder.

"Definitely a night gardener," he said when patience died.

"Jon!" A smile. Not shy. Pleased. "Where'd you come from?"

"Been here, oh, five minutes." He grinned.

She set back one herb book and pulled another. "Nonsense. I've been right here all the time. You were nowhere around."

"Looking for me, were you?" He pushed off the shelf and sauntered forward.

"Of course not. It's a small library." She flipped a page.

"Uh-huh. Then how come you're reading *Victorian Houses?*"

"Ooh!" The nasty culprit slapped shut.

Casually, he slipped it from her fingers and laid it on the shelf. He skimmed a fingertip down her cheek. "I like this color."

"The blouse? Yellow's my favorite. Sunny."

"Mmm. I'm thinking this pink under your freckles here. And here." He lifted her glasses to her head then touched the end of her nose with the same finger. "Very classy."

That tiny loopy smile. "Are you trying to embarrass me further, Mr. Tucker?"

"Nope." Her dark eyes. He could bury himself in them. *In her.* Taking her hand, he tugged her toward the aisle's rear. Against the shelving's end, he braced his arms above her head. "I've wanted to do this all day," he muttered.

Her mouth was there, lifting, reaching. *Soft.*

They were breathing hard when he drew away and looked down into her flushed face. Her eyes were glazed. Tracing back a curl from her left eyebrow, he said, "That time by the gym, when Gene Hyde scared you? I wanted to kiss you then."

Her palms found her elbows.

Shy, he realized. After what they'd just shared she still felt shy around him. Amazing. Intriguing. It set him stone-hard.

He took the glasses off her hair and slipped them into her breast pocket. "You were so young. Sweet, young, so damned sexy."

Bowing her head, she murmured, "I've never been sexy."

Jon chuckled. "Oh, honey, trust me. Open an encyclopedia and you'll find a picture of you by the word."

For a moment she looked unsure, then she slipped from the cage of his body. "I have to go."

He caught her hand. "Rianne? Did I offend you?"

Her hair swung along her shoulders. "I need to go home. The kids are alone."

"They can wait an extra minute. What is it? Tell me." He peered into her face. And it struck him. "You don't believe me."

"No."

"Why?"

"Because." A sigh. "I don't do things right a lot of times."

"Like what?"

She studied a fingernail. "The way I am with a man."

His mouth itched to grin like a glad-happy dog. She was Venus, Aphrodite, didn't she know?

Her marriage history sobered him.

"Honey, if the way you are with me got any more perfect, we'd be doing the wild-wicked here on the library floor. Only reason we're not is because I don't want to embarrass old Mrs. Harkness out there." He let her absorb that. "You're sexy, Rianne. Through and through. Don't ever think otherwise." To drive home the point, he gave her a swift, smacking kiss that pierced the quiet. "Believe me."

She leveled her shoulders. "All right. I believe you."

He wasn't totally convinced, but it was a start.

The PA announced that the library closed in ten minutes.

"Any books you want to check out?" he asked.

"Two gardening ones."

He took her elbow. "Let's get them."

Three minutes later, Jon carried her books and *Victorian Houses*—for himself—through the doors into the warm night. On the sidewalk, he told her, "I visited my mother today. Thanks for helping her at the cemetery. She told me you once gave her a hand picking the weeds."

"When the soil is warming, it's important to go every few days. Maxine and I happened to be there one morning." She glanced up. "Your dad is in the row above my mother."

Somehow that bothered him, Rianne knowing where his father rested when his own son didn't. "I appreciate you helping her. Not many people would."

"Do you know that for sure?"

"My mother was the town drunk for thirty years. I doubt too many have forgotten."

"Oh, Jon." Rianne stopped and placed a cool palm on his tense arm. "If that's how they think, you don't want them as her friends."

"Personally, I don't care who she pals with. She's made her nest, as they say."

"You don't mean that."

"I do. Her boozing killed my father and made my brothers' lives at home hell. I can't forgive her for that." Sadness, vivid in her clear, brown eyes. He looked away. "Don't pity me, Rianne. I've made my choices."

"Okay," she said slowly. "However, if she and I meet again, don't expect me to turn away from her."

"I don't expect you to do anything you're not comfortable with." He pinned her eyes with his. "Not for me. Not for anyone."

She waited a moment. "I'd rather have your approval."

"Why?"

"Because she's your mother."

"And an adult. As you are. As I am."

"You're missing the point."

"Am I?" he asked quietly. He wanted to kiss her again, not talk about an old woman mired in self-destruction. "All right. Do what you think is best. If it concerns me and I disagree I'll tell you. Fair enough?"

They walked across the parking lot. Their vehicles were the last left, two lonely shadows under a pole lamp. He took her hand, wove their fingers and slowed his pace to a stroll. "Wish I'd had the nerve to do this twenty years ago."

"What's that?"

"Carry your books, walk you home."

Her laughter was a playful sound on the night. "It's not home, it's my car."

"A guy can pretend."

"I was too young then."

He swung their hands comfortably between them. "Didn't mean I couldn't fantasize."

"You weren't the only one."

"Oh?" He had an immediate craving to know her fantasies, her dreams of the Right Guy. "Who was yours?"

"Uh-uh, I'm not telling."

"Rory Morgan? I remember Seth complaining that all the ninth-grade girls were in love with Morgan."

"I wasn't."

"Who, then? Come on," he teased. "Fess up."

She giggled. "No way."

"Why not? It's been more than a couple decades. The guy's probably married with ten kids."

"He isn't."

"Gonna keep me in suspense, huh?"

"Mmm-hmm."

They'd reached her car. "Tell me it wasn't Seth," he said.

A covert smile. She dug for the keys in her purse. When the door opened, she took the books from his hand, tossed them onto the back seat, and slipped behind the wheel. Rolling down the window, she closed the door. The smile hadn't dimmed.

Jon propped an elbow on the car's roof. "Was it Seth?" His brother was her age. She'd watched him play football.

She started the ignition.

"Come on, Rianne—" *Dammit, who tempted your girlish heart?*

The car rolled backward. Secret delight in her eyes.

"It was Seth, wasn't it?" he called, standing in her headlights, hands to hips.

Swinging from the stall, she passed him slowly.

"Well?" he demanded.

"If you really must know…it was his brother." And with that, she left him to the empty lot.

The cordless phone on her night table rang an hour later. Marking the spot where she was reading about pests and diseases in *Your Backyard Herb Garden*, Rianne reached for the receiver.

"Hello?"

"I can't believe it's Luke."

She laughed. "You don't give up, do you? No wonder you were a policeman."

"This is important stuff," he groused.

"I gathered that." She felt warm to the tips of her toes.

"Oh, hell. Rianne, Luke was seven years older. Way too old."

"So were you."

"I was younger than him by a year."

"I know."

"Anyway, Luke was at college."

"I know."

Silence strummed through the line.

"Me?" Deep and dark was his voice. Like the night.

"If it wasn't Seth or Luke, which brother's left?"

Another heartbeat of silence. "This is crazy," he said, the words a little jagged.

She smiled. "You started it."

"I don't mean crazy tonight. I mean that we were both thinking about each other back then already."

She pushed up on the pillows, lifted away the heavy book, and took off her reading glasses. "It's not crazy. You rescued me in English. And from Gene Hyde. You were my teenage hero." Her poetic Heathcliff on the moors. She paused, heart thumping. "Now you're my adult hero."

More silence. "New-Agers would chalk the whole mess up to karma or past lives," he muttered.

"They may be right."

"Rianne?"

"Yes?"

"What were you doing when I called?"

"Reading."

"In bed?"

"Yes. Where are you?"

"On the back veranda. Waiting for your light to go out."

In her lower extremities, she felt a charge of electricity. "I'm glad," she whispered.

"Got a nightie on?"

She swallowed. "Yes. You?"

He chortled, the sound a sensual stroke up her spine. "No nightie. I sleep naked."

"You're outside without…?" The image— *Oh, my.*

Laughter, a low rumble. "No, I'm still dressed. Same tan shirt and jeans you saw tonight. Bare feet, though. Wish I could see your nightie."

"It's a plain thing. Nothing fancy."

"Tell me."

"Cotton…blue…has an eyelet lace hem…low front."

"How low?"

"Low enough."

He made a sound that stroked her veins. She visualized midnight eyes. "Jon?"

"Yeah?"

"I can stand in the window for you."

"No, honey. You stay warm."

Suddenly, more than anything, she wanted him to see her. "Wait there. I have a better idea." Carrying the phone, she slipped from her covers, out of the room, through the house, to the back door. The cool night air flowed through the thin fabric of her gown as she stepped onto the deck and tiptoed to the corner nearest his property. "Can you see me?" she asked quietly. Higher than the cottage, the Victorian loomed like a jagged wall in front of her. She waved a hand.

"Oh, yeah, I can see you, babe. Just barely, but… Hold on." She heard a scrape. Several seconds later, he said, "Look away from me" and then she was in the beam of his flashlight. "Beautiful," his voice murmured in her ear. "You're like an angel over there. Turn around."

She did. Beneath the cotton her skin warmed. She closed her eyes, imagining his hands, his touch. "Jon."

The light went out. "Sexy angel. What you do to me." She heard the intake of his breath. "Listen, go back inside. Can't tell what's prowling around in those woods."

She surveyed the dark stand of Douglas fir rimming their backyards and, for one foreign instant, was grateful he'd been a policeman. She hurried into the house, locked the door and slipped down the hall to the bedroom.

He asked, "Are you getting back under the covers?"

"Yes."

"I can hear it. Rianne?"

"Hmm?"

"I think about you. About what we'd do behind locked doors."

Her pulse rushed. *This is how it should be. The way relationships were meant.* Taking pride in her body, knowing it could excite a man. In a healthy way.

"You there?"

"I'm here."

"I'm hanging up now, okay?"

"Okay."

"Sweet dreams, peaches."

She smiled. "'Night."

The dial tone hummed in her ear. Carefully, she set back the receiver, put away her book and glasses and lay back. *Were you like this as a husband, Jon?*

Slumping in the old, cushiony chair in Mrs. Zeglen's office on Monday, Sam picked his thumbnail. The counselor was down the hall, talking in soft tones to another kid. He didn't mind waiting. Mrs. Zee's room was cluttered but cool. Not like the guy in L.A. That one was organized to the point of no return.

Sam hated organized. Organized reminded him of his dad in his spit-shined shoes, his spotless LAPD uniform with the creases so exact you could calculate a square root by them. Since he and Mom and Em had moved to Misty River, Sam had the most *un*organized room of all his friends. He loved it.

Mrs. Zeglen breezed in and closed the door. "Sorry I'm late, Sam." Rounding the desk, she flung herself into her beat-up chair.

"'S okay. I got nowhere to go right now."

She smiled over the glasses on her nose. "So. Where shall we start? Would you like to tell me about your long weekend?"

That was another thing about Mrs. Zee he liked. She never assumed you had a problem to discuss. Instead, she called his two-day suspension a long weekend.

Relaxing a little, he sat straighter.

He wanted to tell her everything. Starting from the second that old belt sander scraped the patch of skin clean off his leg to when old man Huller bullied his mom and how he wasn't afraid of the old fart. But he didn't want to stick out his chest. Not like that dweeb Cody. No, he'd start off casual, leave out a lot of the nifty stuff, give a quick rundown and end with him and his sis watching movies while his mom went to the library.

"How did you feel when Mr. Huller approached your mom at the video store?" Mrs. Zeglen asked when he finished.

"I wanted to break his nose," Sam said, anger rising again. "He was being a real jacka—jerk."

"Would that have helped, Sam?"

"I dunno. Probably not." He bounced a knee. "It would've made me feel better."

Mrs. Zee nodded, like she knew where he was coming from. "And now? Do you still feel the same?"

He caught himself latching onto his thumbnail again and set his hands on his thighs. "Nah. Mom handled it okay. She was pretty great, actually."

Mrs. Zee smiled. "And when you had time to think about it, how did you feel then?"

How *had* he felt? Sam looked around the room. Books and papers and junk everywhere. The walls, covered in big, flashy posters about teamwork and reaching the stars and making every second count. A guy jogging uphill on a lonely country road above the words: Success doesn't come to you. You go to it.

Sam liked to think that was him. Going for the big stuff.

Mrs. Zee's question packed big stuff. So…how *did* he feel? Good? Okay? No. More. "Proud, I guess. Mom's pretty strong in a lot of ways. Not, like, physically. Emotionally, y'know? I never…" He worked on his thumb again.

"You never what?"

"Guess I never figured her to be *that* strong. Like in here." He tapped his chest. "When my dad was alive she always jumped to his tune. He'd bark; she'd jump. It made me mad."

"Mad the way Cody made you mad last Wednesday?"

"Yeah."

"Have you seen him today?"

"Just in the hall once. I ignored him." He wished Joey would, too. But Joey was acting real weird these days. He and Sam didn't do the stuff they once had. Now all Joey did was act tough with Cody and his stupid friends. "Joey's such a dork now 'cause of Cody," he blurted.

Mrs. Zeglen shifted in her chair. She didn't speak for several moments. "You don't like Joey switching loyalties, do you? It hurts when that happens."

Damn. She knew. She knew what he suspected about Joey. More knee-bouncing. "Yeah. Joey should know better. Cody's an idiot."

"But maybe not in Joey's eyes. Maybe Joey feels Cody is a cool guy."

Sam pulled a face.

"I wonder…" Mrs. Zeglen said in that way of hers—like she was thinking things through real careful. "Maybe Cody reminds you of your dad. In your heart you believe Cody might hurt Joey one day, the way your dad did your mom, so you're feeling a little helpless right now."

Was that what he believed? Hearing her say it straight out, he knew she was right. Cody *was* a bad influence on his pal. Sam and Joey had shared a lot together. They were best friends. *Once.* Sam had told him all about his dad and the way his family used to be and Joey had shared tons about how his mom used to be a hooker. Until she'd met his stepfather eight years ago. Now, they were a normal family, just like Sam's.

Except Sam no longer had a dad. But that could change one day, too. If it did, he hoped his mom would pick somebody like Jon Tucker.

The thought made him smile. Jon as a stepdad. Yeah, that'd be cool. Jon was like Joey's dad. Real big. And strong. Not in a bad way, but in a quiet, *good* way.

He'd be someone Sam could talk to man-to-man. Tell things to. Like how he didn't want counseling anymore, and how he wanted his mom to stop worrying about him. Man stuff. Jon could teach him how to use all those wood tools and ride the Harley. Then his mom would see that Sam wasn't a boy. She'd let him share regular responsibilities around the house. Like the lawn-mowing.

Mrs. Zee was looking at him. She said, "If you'd rather not talk about your dad or Cody now, that's okay. We can deal with it whenever you're ready."

A breath of relief. His knee stopped jumping. "Okay, yeah. Maybe later."

She reached behind the desk for a round, fancy tin. "Want a macadamia-nut cookie for the road? I made them last night."

"Hey, my favorite." Yep, he definitely liked Mrs. Zee's kind of counseling. He reached in and took two.

She laughed. "You owe me for that, Sam Kirby. Be here Thursday or you're never getting another."

Grinning around a mouthful of delicious pastry, he sauntered out the door. "Sure I will, Mrs. Zee." And he would, too.

Whenever he decided to show up again.

Chapter Nine

"How did it go today with Mrs. Zeglen?" Rianne asked, watching her son wolf down his last piece of apple crumble. Supper was almost finished. Time to get to the point.

As expected, Sam shrugged. "Okay."

"Just okay?"

"Nothing special happened."

Rianne breathed easier. "Anything new at school?"

"Uh-uh." Sam shoved his plate aside and reached down for one of the kittens. Nuzzling its soft fur, he crooned, "Hey, Dude. You're getting bigger and bigger every day." The kitten mewled, purred and pulled itself with tiny claws up his shoulder.

Okay, Rianne thought. *Cody Huller didn't take precedence.* She watched her daughter dig into her dessert. Always a slow eater, Emily was gaining weight. No distress upsetting her tummy.

"And you, Em?"

"I handed in my science project today and I was *first*."

"Terrific, sweetie. I wasn't aware you'd finished it."

"Uh-huh. The other night when you were at the library."
Emily looked adoringly at her brother. "Sam helped me 'cause
I helped him mow the lawn. Sort of."

"You mowed the lawn?"

"She did not mow the lawn," Sam interjected, giving Emily
a narrowed look. "She helped hold the garbage bag open
while I threw the grass in."

"That's mowing," Emily insisted.

"Is not." Sam darted Rianne a look. "She didn't touch the
mower, Mom, honest."

"I believe you, Sam, and—" she tugged Emily's hair gently before the girl got her hackles up "—I'm proud you gave
your brother a hand with the bag."

"You are?"

Her heart rolled over. "Of course I am. I'm also proud that
Sam helped you with your homework."

Pushing aside her dessert, Emily caught one of the two remaining kittens and set it in her lap. The lone kit on the floor
squeaked softly, wobbling in and out of a labyrinth of chair
legs. Nearby, Sweetpea sat looking bored.

Rianne laughed. "Come here, wee lass." She picked up the
motley creature, the runt, and cradled it between her palms.

Emily grinned. "Now we each have one, right Mom?"

"When do we have to give them away, Mom?" This from
Sam.

"In about a month."

"No!" Emily cried. The kitten cowered under her arm.
"Don't give them away. Can't we keep them? Please, Mom?"

"We already have Sweetpea, pooch. We can't have four
cats."

"But can we keep Smokey?" she asked of the kit she cuddled.

Rianne sighed. "As it is, we need to watch Sweetpea when she goes outside. Think how much harder it would be with four."

"But I could watch Smokey, Sam could watch Dude and you could watch Sweetpea. Please, Mom."

"That wouldn't be fair to Squeak," Sam pointed out. Squeak was the runt Rianne held. "She'd be the only one adopted."

Good one, son. Rianne watched her daughter study Squeak. Emily's mouth turned down as Sam's logic hit home.

"Well…" the girl began. "If we have to give them away…" She brightened. "Can we pick who to?"

"Absolutely. Got someone in mind?"

Emily listed four of her classmates as maybes and one teacher as a good bet. Perking up, her daughter added, "Maybe Mr. Tucker's—Jon's—" the name came with a shy smile that told Rianne he'd clarified its use for her "—maybe we can give one to his daughter when she comes for the summer holidays."

Rianne set Squeak beside Sweetpea and began stacking the plates. She had explained Brittany to Emily the day she and Jon had gone on the wallpaper run. Giving the girl a kitten was generous and sweet, *pure Emily.* Jon was another matter. Rianne imagined him scowling for a week. Still…when he spoke of Brittany his heart lit his eyes. "We'll see, Em."

"It's okay, Mom." Emily wriggled in her chair. "He likes cats now. He even said so."

"Really? When?"

"Yesterday, when you went to gas the car. He came over to ask Sam if his leg was okay."

"He did?"

"Yeah, he—"

"I was almost finished scraping the deck," Sam cut in. "He asked how it was going. I said okay. Then he asked how my leg was and I said fine." The boy glanced at his sister. "Then Em came out with Smokey."

Emily nodded fervently. "And I showed Jon Smokey and he took him in his hands and looked at him eye-to-eye like this." Slipping off her chair, she modeled Jon's apparent stance, mooring her legs, holding the kit high in the air. "Then he stuck his nose in his fur like this." She buried her own pug-nose in the animal's neck. Emily giggled. "He said Smokey's hair felt like insect feet in his nostrils. Isn't that funny, Mom?"

Rianne smiled. That was Jon, offering nonsense. Teasing Emily. Making her laugh. He had a knack for that. He had a knack for a lot of things. Like calling Rianne sexy angel while she...

Blushing, she turned to clean the stove. A looney bug must have bitten her last night. What possessed her to twirl on a dark porch—in her nightie, no less!—for a man standing in the shadows like a peeping Tom?

No peeping Tom. Jon.

The man she wanted on her bed. On her. *I want to know. I want to know what it feels like to have his hands on my skin, his mouth on my belly, between my heart and my womb...*

She scrubbed the burners harder. *Quit it! Quit this incessant thinking about Jon, this silly romantic dreaming, do you hear? Just quit, quit, quit!*

"So, can we, Mom?" Emily broke Rianne's litany. "Can we ask his daughter if she wants a kitty when she comes?"

"We'll check with Jon first, Em."

The child kissed Smokey on the head and put him beside his sister. "Can I go ask now?"

"You need to finish your homework."

"I did it after school."

"And clean your room. I saw clothes on the floor."

"All done."

Rianne turned, raised a dubious brow. "Em?" Her voice slipped to her mother-knows tone.

"It is. Honest."

"Is not," Sam said. "I saw socks on your floor."

Emily scowled. "My room's still way cleaner than yours."

Rianne suppressed a grin. Sibling rivalry. Her children were making up for lost time. "Both of you, go check."

"Then can we go ask Mr.—Jon?" Emily persisted.

"We'll ask him closer to the time, honey."

Appeased, Emily headed for her bedroom.

"Sam," Rianne called after him.

He turned.

"Thanks. For reassuring Em about the kittens."

A teenager's shrug. "No big deal." But his eyes lit before he continued down the hall.

Shortly after lunch on Tuesday, Jon rolled the Harley out of the detached garage and pushed it around to the front of the house. Damn thing needed a tune-up but he wasn't in the mood to do it today. He just wanted to ride.

He'd spent all morning messing with Brittany's wallpaper. Wetting it, laying it on the drywall, rolling it to perfection. And still the stuff ended up with more bubbles than an Aero bar.

Then, at twelve-thirty Brittany had phoned. In tears. Colleen and Allan the Almighty were planning to move to Ireland for God-knew-how-long in two weeks, because Al-baby had taken a promotion and now his oil company needed him to assist in some fangdangled deep-sea exploration in the North Atlantic.

Jon wanted to knock the idjit's teeth out the back of his head. Ireland? Brittany across a continent *and* the Atlantic?

He clamped his jaw. Colleen should have put a stop to it. Hell, she'd screamed enough at him about *his* job turning their family upside down. Damn her for making his punkin-girl cry.

He'd wanted to talk to Colleen, but she'd been at work. Another thing that irked Jon. Ten was far too risky an age for Brittany to be a latchkey kid. He paid Colleen sound alimony. Every month. Extra *especially* for an after-school sitter. Didn't matter that it was only fifteen minutes before his ex got home. It was too long. Psychos needed less than five minutes.

Damn.

Now, Colleen wanted to take the last piece of his heart into another country. A historically restless country. One that appeared calm now, but who knew what could explode in the mind of some religious fanatic later?

He threw the Harley's kickstand and looked across his weedy yard at the cottage. He pictured Rianne inside, alone, baking bread or cookies. Throwing together a casserole for tonight. He saw her straightening the beds. Tossing in a load of laundry. Stopping to play with those dumb cats.

When Emily and Sam came through that door later today, Rianne would be there. No question. She'd always be there for her kids. Building a home with the tool of unconditional love. The way she had tried to mold her marriage.

His fists tightened. If hell existed he hoped her husband broiled for eternity.

He went back into the house, dug Nicky's helmet and jacket from a storage box and, tucking the articles under his arm, strode to Rianne's rear-porch door. Banging on the screen's wood framing, he peered into the kitchen. He'd imagined right. Two trays of brownies cooled on a towel. Their scent closed his eyes. When he opened them she stood on the other side of the mesh, staring at him. He stared back.

She had on a T-shirt that curved its logo, "Make My Day: Smile" around her breasts. Lower, she wore a pair of denim cutoffs, frayed at the edges. Her feet were bare.

"You busy?" he asked.

She took in his leather jacket, leather pants, the helmet.

"I'm going riding," he explained. "Want to come along?"

Pushing open the screen, she gifted him with her semi-smile. "Give me two minutes to change." She pointed at the counter. "Have a brownie. They're fresh from the oven." As she headed down the hallway, she asked, "What should I wear?"

Not a damned thing. "Jeans, a warm top, some boots."

He heard her rummage in the bedroom. "Excuse the mess in the kitchen. It's my cleaning day."

Jon looked around. Since he'd seen it last, pots of green things thrived on the windowsill. A leafy plant with white flowers sat in the center of the table. In a block of sunlight, the kittens played peekaboo while Sweetpea buffed her face.

Mess? Where? The place had the stamp of home. Warm, welcoming. *Loving.*

He looked out the screen door. He should have gone riding alone. His hand was on the door handle when she returned.

"Almost ready."

She dropped a pair of knee-high winter boots to the floor. Gray socks covered her bare feet with their cherry-red toenails and she'd changed into stonewashed jeans and a pink hoody.

He offered the jacket and helmet. "These should fit. They're Nick's."

Startled, she looked up. "I can wear Sam's winter bomber."

"Leather's the only thing that'll keep the wind from going through your bones."

Her mouth tugged a smile. "I'll feel like a Hells Angel."

Stepping forward, he caught her chin. "You are an angel. The best kind." He kissed her swift and hard.

They were on a country road with the wind slapping their faces and the roar of the bike in their wake. Heading for free and easy times. He took the bends slowly, smoothly, leaning in tune with the machine as it grabbed the road. The sun warmed their helmets. Trees whipped by. Rianne's arms hugged his waist, her cheek cuddled his shoulder, her breasts pressed his back. *Forget the memories, Jon. Just ride.*

At a junction, he halted and moored his boots. The bike thrashed under them. He flung up his visor, flung back a grin. "Want to go on?"

"Can we go to Franklin's Mill?" she asked, eyes sparkling, cheeks red.

"Remember that, do you?"

"Who doesn't? Every kid in town ended up there at one time or another."

He rubbed the side of his nose. "Who'd you go with?"

She laughed. "Not a boy. A group of us girls went down one Saturday to soak up the sun and do a little swimming."

He half turned on the seat. "Skinny-dipping?" The image of her naked in nature shot blood to his penis.

"Not me," she retorted.

"Too daring for you?"

She winked. "Not daring enough."

He chuckled. "Be still, my dirty mind." Releasing the clutch, he swung down an ill-used path shrouded by cotton-woods, oaks and Douglas fir.

All that existed of the old sawmill—built in 1925 by the Franklins in their logging heyday and shut down in the 1950s—was a broken-down waterwheel and mill house. The vertical-slab wood and roof were dark with moss and rot.

Across the ten-acre meadow stood a house, erected at the time of the mill's closure. Its windows were boarded and moss fed on its roof as well, while the wide, rambling porch tilted left like a wrenched hip. No one had lived in the house for as long as Jon could remember.

He cut the engine. Silence rang like a tolling bell. He kicked out the stand, unsnapped his helmet.

Rianne climbed off the seat. "It's lonelier than I remember," she said, looking around the meadow of the long-gone mill yard. Carefully, she removed Nicky's helmet then shook out her hair. The sun lacquered it.

"Someone still comes up here." He nodded toward the scorched remains of a campfire. Two dozen empty beer cans glinted among moldered stumps and purple loosestrife. "Probably still hoping to catch sight of Maggie Stuart's ghost."

"The woman who drowned forty-some years ago?"

Jon nodded. "The truly imaginative said she walked among the rocks of Misty River's beach when the moon was full."

"Wasn't she your mother's sister?"

"Twin sister. Drowned right after Luke was born." He studied the branch of water that gave the town its name. Once a frenetic source of rapids spilling into the Nehalem, the river now ran from the Cascade Range, placid as its name. "You believe the legend?"

"If I did, it wouldn't be with fear. My mom used to say Maggie Stuart was the gentlest of souls." Setting the helmet on the seat, she canted her face to the sky, took a long, deep breath. "Ahh, I love the smell of woods." Her lips bowed. "Let's look around."

Hand-in-hand they walked down to the rickety mill house set in a low trough that fed into the river. Jon placed a hand on Rianne's waist, guiding her over the rough terrain. When had he last felt this urge to protect a woman? When he and Colleen were young. In love.

"How's Sam doing at school this week?" he asked, forcing his mind away from feelings he no longer believed in.

"He and the Huller boy are avoiding each other."

They picked their way around moss-plagued humps—grave sites to the debris of logs and sawdust piles of a bygone era.

"And his leg?"

"Almost healed."

He felt enormous relief on both counts.

They stopped in front of the yawning hole of the ancient building, once the entrance to Franklin's sawmill. Somewhere inside the dark cavern, on the other side of the rusted-out steam boiler, water dripped in lethargic, rhythmic sequence. A rodent, likely a skunk from the faint smell, scratched in a dank corner.

Down along Misty River's treelined banks stood three cabins, relics of the 1960s, when the dwindling Franklin family had attempted to erect a small resort. The venture had failed miserably after the drowning. Jon wondered who owned the site and its thirty acres now, and he asked Rianne.

"That would still be Boone Franklin. He lives in Ohio and rents it to one of the local farmers." She scanned the forest. "I heard the man fenced off the clearing for fear Maggie's ghost would affect his beef prices. Stupid, isn't it?"

Jon grunted. "Small-town mentality."

It was something he'd have to get used to again. If Misty River became home. A thought jolted him. What if Rianne found the town and its mind-set too confining? What if, in a few months, a year, she decided to relocate? Take her kids back to the city where amenities ran rampant, where schools decreed lifestyles?

He caught her arm. "Stay," he said.

"We can't, Jon. The kids—"

"I mean in Misty River. Don't move away again."

Her eyes widened. "I wasn't planning to leave." She laid a palm on his cheek. The fear eased. "What made you think I would?"

"The town might get to you one day."

"Never. It's my home."

Covering her narrow hand with his own, he longed to shut down, drift on the sensation of skin on skin. Drift on the peace of this place. "What about Sam and Emily? What if things don't work out for them?"

She slipped her hand free. "What they had before Misty River wasn't home." Averting her eyes, she said, "It was…a sham."

Suddenly, he needed to know. "Tell me about him."

She turned, heading down an overgrown path, a long-ago logging trail. Here, under towering Douglas fir, the air lay cool, still, sweetened by sap and earth moisture. Beds of spongy needles quieted their footfalls. A second clearing—more narrow than the first, and fenced—beckoned sixty feet hence.

Jon saw only Rianne. Wooden stance, arms wrapping her waist, face upturned toward a canopy of prickly branches through which sunlight sprinkled like the mist that gave the town its name.

"Duane Kirby," she said, the words as hushed as the forest around them, "was with the LAPD."

"A cop?" *Ah, damn.*

"For twelve years. I met him through the wife of another officer. She and I taught at the same school. I was in the process of divorcing Duane when he died in a high-speed chase one rainy night. He hit a light standard at an intersection." She paused. "We'd been separated two months. It took that long," her voice sounded sore, "for the bruises to disappear and my rib to mend." Her eyes settled on Jon. Ice went down his spine. "My husband was an abuser. I let him hurt me for many years."

Hearing the words from Sam had torn his guts.

Hearing them from Rianne ripped his soul.

He wanted to tuck her against his heart.

For one desperate instant he wished the man still lived.

He kept his hands balled in his jacket. He knew if he touched her now, she'd shatter. She needed dignity more than his arms. He waited while she took two deep breaths and secured a willful strand of hair behind her ear with wobbly fingers.

Color returned to her cheeks; her lips lost their pinched appearance. In her eyes, defiance. "I know what he did was wrong. I know that staying with him was wrong. If you have a problem with that, then so be it. But, I won't be leaving Misty River. I won't be moving to another house. It may not be perfect—"

He had her against him, hand fisted in her hair, pressing her face into his chest. "Hush, just hush. I'm here."

He held her as if she might splinter. Insects whirred in the grass. A small breeze lifted the hair on his collar. High above the treetops, a hawk circled lazily.

"I don't need perfect, Jon," she murmured, her arms slipping around him. "But I do need a home where there's normalcy, love, peace. Sounds like an Alan Jackson song, but there it is."

"Shhh." He closed his eyes. The sun-warmed scent of her hair tumbled into him. His body trembled. His blood rushed. A man had hurt her. Marred her defenseless body. Put sadness in her eyes.

Those eyes locked on his face. "I'm okay," she said, as if to assure him. "Ever since I came back to Misty River. The proof is in telling you. Last summer I wouldn't have told a soul." She attempted a smile. "So, you see, the wound is closing."

"You shouldn't have had it in the first place."

"No, I should've walked away, but—"

He set a finger to her lips. "Duane Kirby was the wrongdoer," he said, astounded at his composure. "Not you."

She kissed him. Softly, sweetly. His veins sang.

He pulled her closer, and closer still, against his leaping heart. "Rianne." He unzipped her jacket, delved under the hem of her sweater to smooth skin. "Ah, Ri. Sweet woman."

Her hands gripped his wrists. "Jon, wait—"

The words were a cold-water dousing. "Aw, hell, Rianne, I'm sorry." He set his forehead to hers. "God, I could kick myself. Seems I'm always taking advantage when you're upset."

"It has nothing to do with advantage, Jon. It's me." Her eyes held a thousand secrets. She touched his face. "Only me."

Dazed he stared as she retreated through the evergreens, sunshine falling as fairy dust through the branches around her.

Rianne, he thought. A woman of class and decency. Of family. No matter what landed in her path, she climbed over it and trudged forward. A lesson he could learn. *Don't give up.* Because that's what he'd done when Nicky died. He'd given up on himself, believed he was better off alone, and in doing so had given up on his only remaining child.

You're a mess, Jon. A serious mess. His heart rushed in his chest. He paced up and down. Adjusted his breathing. Shoved his hands through his hair.

And stared straight at a crop of newly sprouted marijuana.

Scowling, Jon took the steps of the Misty River Police Department two at a time. He'd dropped Rianne off in time for her kids' arrival from school, then left because he needed to talk to Willard.

Now he regretted his hurry. He should have stayed. Talked to her instead of seeking the man he knew too well from his youth. Seawater churned in his gut.

Officer Duane Kirby. A lawman. Wearing a badge of honor. *Where was your honor, you SOB, when it came to your wife?*

The thought bore down on Jon as he stormed through the

doors of the police department. No wonder she'd queried him about taking on Willard's job.

Thank God he hadn't told her about the pot crop.

"Chief Willard around?" Jon asked the desk clerk, a blonde chewing gum with the same finesse as a freshly landed salmon gasping air.

"Who wants to know?"

"Jon Tucker."

"You got an appointment, Mr. Tucker?"

"No, but I think he'll want to hear what I have to say."

"What's that?"

"I'll discuss it with Chief Willard, if you don't mind."

"If you don't have an appointment—"

Jon and patience parted company. Planting his hands on her desk, he leaned down. "This is a real-time emergency," he gritted softly. "Now, where is he? Or should I check his office myself?"

Shock registered in the woman's eyes. She shoved back her chair. "Just a minute. I'll see."

"Thank you." He watched her clack off to the back of the room in chunky shoes. She disappeared into a corner office. Eight seconds. She reappeared and motioned him over, then scuttled away when he approached.

A small, rotund man pushing his seventh decade sat behind an absurdly large mahogany desk. "Jon Tucker, I presume?"

"You presume right, Chief Willard." Politely he held out a hand.

The old man met it with a surprisingly strong palm. "Sit down, boy. You one of Maxine and Travis's kids?"

"Their second."

The old man flicked a grin. "You boys didn't have that great a start, as I recall, but y'all did right fine over the years."

"We made do." *Not that it's any of your business.*

Willard leaned his chair back on two legs. "Did more than that. Luke's our best defense lawyer. Seth's got a helluva contractor's business going for himself."

Jon noted the man didn't include him in those "right fine" years. "Chief, you might be interested—"

"Heard you were a hotshot cop over to Seattle."

"I was in law enforcement for a while, yeah." The hotshot bit was something he'd rather not discuss—or consider.

Willard's eyes squinted. "How long a while?"

"Twenty years."

"How come you quit?"

"Got tired of it. Chief, about what I saw at the old—"

"A young, strapping boy like you got tired?" He laughed again, his Michelin belly jiggling. "What are you, thirty-five?"

"Forty-two."

Willard waved a pudgy hand. "Hell, just a kid. What're you planning to do back in Misty River? Heard you bought the old MacDowall place."

Pointedly, Jon checked his watch. "Look, Chief, I'd really like to sit and shoot the breeze, but I've got a few things to do yet before the stores close. About Franklin's Mill—"

The chief frowned. "I know all about what's going on up there. Don't you worry about it, son. We got it under control."

I'm not your son, you old fart. "Does Boone Franklin know about what's going on with his land?"

"Boone? Nah. He hasn't lived here in more'n thirty, forty years. Not since his parents died. Been renting the land to Larry Marshall. He grazes cows on it every summer."

"He's grazing more than cows, Chief. There's a nice little grow op there as well. Ten to one they're using the old house as storage." Which explained the skunklike odor. "Doesn't that property border town municipality? That makes it hellishly close to your jurisdiction. Aren't you worried how it'll affect the townsfolk?"

Willard dropped the chair back on all fours and leaned forward with his hands linked on the big splashy calendar that graced his desk. "Look, son. A lot of the locals saw bad times in the last few years what with floods, logging going sour and then beef prices hitting rock bottom. Plus spot fires. People here are just common folk trying to rub two nickels together. Know what I mean? I figure if they can scrape a few extra bucks here and there, who's to blame 'em? Besides, word is, a lot of seniors use it for medicinal purposes nowadays."

Jon forced himself to stay in his seat. Every muscle strained for action. "Where does he ship to?"

"Who's to say he is shipping? Far as I know, it's for private use."

"Where's Marshall live?"

"Why?" That fast, Willard's eyes cooled.

"Call it curiosity."

The chief scratched his head as if it made no difference what Jon surmised. "In town here. Works in construction most months, runs a few head of cows at Franklin's on the side."

And he probably had a lab in his basement; Jon wondered if it had been searched. He asked Willard.

The chief steepled his fingers under his jowly jaw and stared stonily at Jon. "I told you, we got it under control. Leave it there. I've made a note of your report right here." A nicotined fingertip tapped his left temple. "Right here," he repeated.

Jon rose. "I'll hold you to that, Chief Willard, or I'll be contacting the Oregon State Police." The memory of Nicky lying on that gurney, of Jon's own inability to see the signs of drug use, collected in his eyes.

The old man shifted. "You making a threat, boy?"

"I'm stating a fact. Thanks for your time." On a sharp heel, he left.

By the time he got to the Harley parked at the curb, anger had festered worse than a boil full of pus. It wasn't his business. Dammit, he was not a cop anymore.

Innocent people—possibly kids—could get involved.

Nicky died because of drugs.

Gripping the bike's handlebars, Jon waited for the nausea to slacken, the sweat to cool. *Brittany*, he thought. Merciful heaven, his peanut would be in Misty River soon.

"It's not perfect, Jon."

He snorted a laugh. If only Rianne knew how *imperfect* it was. Scouring both hands down his face, he looked around. A pickup and two cars crawled by. Another memory invaded: him as a youth walking down the block with his brothers. He and Luke teasing Seth. Teasing girls. Laughing, joking. Free and easy.

Until Willard brought Maxine home, drunk.

No, life hadn't been perfect in Misty River, but it was still *his* Misty River.

Jon cranked the ignition. The bike boomed awake. A trio of teens jabbed their thumbs in the air and shouted, "Sweet!"

Like Nicky had.

Like Sam would.

Jon charged from the curb, ghosts of past and present pinching his heels.

Home from school, Sam popped a half wheelie up his driveway at the same time Jon rolled up next door on his Harley. Man, that bike was something. Big, black, shiny. What he wouldn't give to ride it. For two minutes. Just down the block and back.

He shoved his mountain bike up against the house, dropped his knapsack and trotted across his neighbor's yard. "Hey, Jon."

"Sam."

He'd never seen Jon decked out all in leather. Shoot, it was awesome. He looked like some kind of bad guy, but not really. More like a rebel. A mad rebel, Sam saw as he walked closer. "You go for a ride just now?" he asked.

Jon did something to the bike, then grabbed his helmet off the seat. "Yep."

"Was it fun?"

"A regular riot." He headed for the steps of his house.

Sam followed. "When you going again?"

Jon didn't answer. He took the steps two at a time.

"Can I—"

"Not today, boy."

"How do you know what I was going to ask?"

At the top, the man turned. A little shiver went through Sam. The guy was taller than most men, but from this angle he looked like Wolverine of the *X-men.* "I figure you want a ride on my Harley."

"Yeah, I was kinda hoping—"

"I don't have time right now." He looked toward Sam's house. "Maybe you should consider doing your homework first, then we can talk." He went inside and closed the door.

Sam's fingers twitched. *"Get your homework done before you show your face in this room again."* He heard his dad's voice. Saw his dad's face.

He looked at Jon's door.

Humiliation scored his cheeks.

Guilt chewed his gut.

He wanted to run home, hide. From his dad, from Jon Tucker.

Anger pushed up and spewed out his mouth. "No!"

He backed away, flung up his hand, waved a brutal farewell and stormed back to his mountain bike. *Go to hell, Tucker. You're no different than he was. No different at all.*

Chapter Ten

"Hey, Claw-Man," Cody whispered between Sam and Joey as they scanned the candy shelf of Poppers Corner Grocery on Wednesday after supper. "Dare ya to snitch an Oh Henry."

"You mean steal it?"

"No, genius. I mean set it on fire. Whaddya think? Yeah, I mean steal it."

Sam shoved the bar back in place, all appetite for sweets gone. "Get a life, Huller."

"Chicken poop."

"Yeah, well, I'm not a thief."

Huller prodded Joey. "You a wimp like him or you got some in-tes-ti-nal pow-er?" He snickered at his own idiotic word usage like it was real clever or something.

Joey fingered the candy bar he'd chosen. "I dunno, Code." He glanced at the clerk behind the counter. She was busy with one of those word-puzzler books. Sam could see Joey waffling, torn between wanting to do something illegal to impress the punk with them and wanting to obey the law.

"Why are you doing this?" Sam asked Cody. "You want to get us in trouble?" He frowned at Joey. "Don't do it, man. If you get caught, he's not taking the blame."

"Take a hike, Kirby. Joey's a big boy."

Disgusted, Sam headed for the door. *Losers!*

Through the window he saw Jon's truck pull into a parking spot, and a grin tugged his mouth. Then he remembered. Jon.

Telling Sam to get lost.

Ordering him to go do his homework.

Like he was a little snot-nosed, in-the-way kid who had dirt for brains.

He spun around and quickly walked back to the two still in the candy aisle. Jon Tucker was no better than *Sergeant* Duane Kirby. Well, Sam'd had it with big shots and high-and-mighty attitudes telling him what he could and couldn't do.

He reached past Joey, grabbed an Oh Henry and slipped it into the deep pocket of his baggy Gap pants.

"All riiight," Cody hissed, a great grin on his wide face. "Put it there, dude." He gave Sam a knuckle and thumb handshake.

Sam looked at Joey. "You gonna?"

"Already did."

"Let's get outta here."

At the door he nearly bumped into Jon coming into the store. "Hey, Sam," his neighbor said. Mister Innocent.

"Hi." Sam pushed out the door and kept walking, Joey and Cody on his heels. He wished he'd said no when Joey called after school and suggested they head uptown to see what's shaking. But he'd been eager to do something with his pal again. It'd been a long while and, after the fight last week…well, Sam wanted to find out how Joey felt about things.

He hadn't expected to see Cody at Joey's house. Grinning

like a stupid monkey with his stupid gelled hair sticking up like stupid fork tines. Grinning, because he knew his presence ticked Sam off big-time.

He didn't get it. What was Joey trying to prove hanging out with Huller? *Such a dirtbag!* His old man, too. Kids at school said he was always unemployed, ripping off the welfare system.

One thing Sam knew for sure, Joey's mom didn't like the Hullers any more than his own mom did. He could tell that day in Mr. Kosky's office. Mrs. Fraser had glared at the Hullers like she wanted to kill them before she'd hauled Joey out of the room.

Now, here he and Joey were, stealing with Huller. *Stealing!* Sam's cheeks burned. If it weren't for Jon—

"Guess you ain't a gutless wonder after all, Claw-Man." Cody breasted him as they headed down the sidewalk.

"Shut your cakehole, Huller. I didn't do it for you."

"Yeah? I say you did. I say you want me'n Joe to be your friends so badly, you'll do anything."

"Yeah, right. Not."

Cody parked himself in front of both boys. "Prove it. Prove you ain't a little weasel scared of his own shadow."

That's the groundhog, dummy. Sam glanced at Joey. He looked redder than Sam's mom's nail polish. *Think I need you, Joe? Ha.*

Cody laughed softly, as if reading Sam's thoughts. "Go back in there and steal another."

"I'm not getting caught to prove anything to you." Sam turned and headed down the sidewalk, away from them. His left fingers fisted at his side; the no-good hand clenched in his pocket. The faces of his mom, Emily and Mrs. Zeglen hazed through his mind. Behind him, Huller laughed. *Dork.*

In Popper's parking lot Jon was getting into his truck.

Sam glanced back. Joey and Cody were sauntering off, best buds.

"Need a ride, son?" Jon called.

Get lost. "No." Sam broke into a trot, swerved down an alley and ran for home.

Fifteen minutes later he ignored his mother's call that supper would be ready shortly and walked straight to his bedroom and closed the door.

What had he done to make Joey not want to be his pal? He sat on the bed and scrutinized his right hand. He tried to think of the times he and Joey had hung with some of the guys at school. No one had treated him differently. Except Cody. The scum.

But Joey? *Geez.*

Flopping back on his bed, Sam stared at the ceiling with its black '65 Corvette and silver Lexus posters. He swiped a wrist under his nose. Did he even want Joey as a friend anymore?

And then there was Jon, acting like he was his friend one minute and his dad the next.

Well, he didn't need them. Either of them.

Two taps on his door. Softly his mom called, "Sam? Supper's on the table."

With the heels of his palms, he rubbed his eyes.

"Be right there."

Seconds later, he heard the clink of dishware in the kitchen. He swung off the bed, relieved. Mom sprouted eagle eyes and dog ears when it came to him.

He sneaked into the bathroom, flushed the candy bar down the toilet, then scrubbed the life-sucks look off his face.

Rianne stood in the same spot she had ten days earlier—in the darkened recess of Jon's back veranda, waiting for him to answer her knock. No fruity gifts this time. Just an apology.

He swung open the door, looming in the back light of his spacious kitchen.

For a moment, she hesitated. "Can we talk a minute?"

"Come in."

She went. At the butcher-block island she stopped and turned. He'd shut the door, but he hadn't moved. Good. Close proximity with him jumbled her thoughts. She needed to say what she came for without interference. Of any sort.

"I want to apologize for what happened a couple days ago, at Franklin's Mill after I told you about my husband. It had nothing to do with you. It's me. I'm still a little unsure of…" She looked around, trying to organize the words. Words she wanted him to understand.

"Men?"

"Yes. But not you." *Don't be afraid of honesty.* Hadn't she told her kids that a dozen times? "But sometimes, like tonight at the door when I couldn't see your face right away, I remember things." *Like when Duane came home from work.*

"I scared you."

"No. Yes. For a split second."

He said nothing.

"It's something I still need to work on. My therapist said anxiety is difficult to dissolve." She tugged her earlobe. "When it first started happening—the abuse—Duane was remorseful. He'd bring home bouquets or some small gift and everything would be good for a while. In the last years even that changed. He controlled every breath I took."

"Rianne, you don't need to tell me this."

"Yes, I do. I need you to know because of what I feel here." She pressed a fist to her chest. "I haven't felt this way for many years." She shook her head. "I've *never* felt this way."

Jon leaned against the doorjamb. His fingers found his

jeans pockets. "Does it make you warm, this feeling?" His eyes were black, intense.

"Yes. But it scares me. You're so…potent. Not just in a physical way, but emotionally. You're like an elixir. I can't seem to resist you, even when I know I should…because…" *I'm still healing.*

He stood silent. The sleeves of his gray-and-black shirt were loosely slung back, halving the wolf tattoo. But it was that white cotton triangle at his collarbone warming her femaleness.

He pushed off the door. "Can I come over there?"

Knight to the rescue. "In a minute. You need to understand—" her eyes held him "—there are things I have to deal with before I can get…involved."

"Involved. As in sex?"

She nodded then scanned the country kitchen. A woman's dream. "I'm just now getting my life, my kids back together. I can't let anything get in the way of that."

"Meaning me?" His indigo eyes burned. "I won't, Rianne. Just for the record? You had no part in his makeup. None at all. What he did was his fault, not yours. You're a sweet, caring person. He took advantage of that in a criminal way. He should've been shot. If he still lived, I'd use him for target practice."

A tear tracked down her cheek. "I let my kids live with it. Sam's in counseling. Emily still spooks when things don't go right. I need them to be whole—"

Three steps and he was before her, tucking a strand of hair behind her ear. "They will be, Rianne. *They will be.* Sam's a reliable young man. Emily giggles at my jokes." He offered a smile. "You're doing an A-1 job with them. You should be proud." He glanced toward the unadorned corner window facing her house. "How much time do you have?"

"I told the kids twenty minutes."

"I'd like you to see Brittany's room. I finished the wallpaper tonight."

The room was perfect. Jon had achieved the vision Rianne perceived in the store. He'd covered the closet wall and the one where sunlight would enhance the delicate design.

The remaining two walls he'd done in a muted cream that matched the background of the vines. What surprised her more were the three miniature John Waterhouse prints framed in rough bark: *The Lady of Shalott, The Shrine* and *Miranda the Tempest.* All her favorites. Harmonizing with the character of the house.

"It's absolutely beautiful, Jon. Brittany will love it."

"Think so?" His voice echoed vulnerability. He stood in the doorway, like a shy teenager come courting. Her heart tripped.

"I guarantee it. Em's going to be jealous when she sees it."

"I'd like that," he said. "Not the jealous part, but the seeing part. I'd like for Brit and Emily to be friends."

"Will Brittany be staying for a while?"

"The summer." He frowned. The tired lines she'd noticed before deepened. "Her mother's moving to Ireland with her fiancé. Brittany doesn't want to go. Frankly, I'm not partial to the idea."

"Was Ireland a sudden decision?"

He snorted. "You could say. I found out the other day. That's why I had to get out of here and ride." His eyes darkened. "I needed you." When she didn't move, merely stared back, he added, "I haven't needed anyone for a long, long time."

She went to him then. Stroked his Apache-straight hair. "What's happening to us, Jon?"

"Don't you know?"

She fastened on those navy eyes. "I know what I feel, but

my mind balks at it. Each day I convince myself it's fanciful thinking."

"Is it?"

"Not when my heart races and my tummy flutters and I get edgy inside whenever I see you. It's too real." She looked at his shirt pocket. Rising and falling, slowly, steadily.

"I can't give you anything beyond the physical, Rianne. Family picnics at the zoo, talking into the night, chocolates, flowers... Not gonna happen. Can you deal with that? Can you deal with nothing more than an affair, if it comes to that?"

Looking at him, she might have drowned. "Yes," she whispered. "If you can deal with a woman still on the mend."

He was silent so long she wondered if he'd changed his mind. Then he circled the shell of her ear with his callused carpenter's finger. "We're a regular duet, y'know?" He pulled her to him and she burrowed into his chest, savoring the scents of wood and paint and man. He set his mouth on her hair. "God, sometimes you scare the hell out of me." His body shuddered on a breath. "You deserve far better."

"You've given me what no man has."

"Not enough." He loosened his hold. "One day you'll meet a nice man—"

"*You're* a nice man."

He gave her a sexy grin. "Not sure if I like the sound of that. You know the old adage about nice guys finishing last."

On tiptoe, she kissed his cheek. "The room is lovely. You know your daughter's heart."

He looked around. "Yeah. Guess I do."

Slipping from his arms, she stepped back.

"Thanks, Rianne."

"For what?"

"For understanding."

A small nod, and she turned, went down the stairs and out of the house. *Will you know my heart one day, Jon?*

He worked all weekend on his house. He saw no one, spoke to no one—with a single exception. His Saturday evening call to his daughter.

By then he knew Rianne had gone somewhere with the kids for the Memorial Day weekend. He hadn't seen her leave, but the house looked deserted. The lawn needed cutting. Around four o'clock a strange car pulled into the carport, a tall woman walked around to the back, used a key and went into the house. Ten minutes later, she left.

Sunday night he sat on his veranda and smoked a rare cigar while the trees tucked in the sun and night sheathed the sky.

He slept for two hours.

Monday morning he rose at dawn, showered, had breakfast and made a point of riding to the old mill site again. The father in him wanted to destroy the crop and be done with it. He could do it easily. No one would be the wiser. The cop in him knew evidence was integral for sentencing. Demolishing this grow op would simply force them to move the operation, and Willard to turn a blind eye.

Still, he watched.

Waited.

Come on, creeps, show up.

Dammit, surveillance wasn't his job. That life had died with Nicky. This was Willard's town, his responsibility.

Not mine.

Frustrated, Jon stalked back into the old man's office.

"Larry Marshall lives in *your* town, Chief. He's *your* man. Do something before a kid gets hurt."

Ten minutes later, he stormed out, twice as angry and ten times as vexed. Willard had said he'd "dealt with the problem." Jon didn't trust the man. He could smell crooked cop the way he could a bandit. They bore a flat-out stench. He'd give the man another week, then call the state police.

Later that night, he was nursing a soda on the veranda when Rianne's old Toyota chugged up the drive. Car doors slammed. Emily's voice whined softly. Sam's grumbled. Rianne's sounded tired.

Jon stayed put for a half hour, then went to the end of the deck. Her bedroom window reflected the darkness of the entire property. Mentally relieved she was home, that she was safe, that she hadn't left town for good, he went to bed, his body succumbing to the sleep it craved after four restive nights.

Nicky stumbled toward him—calling, crying for help, arms reaching. And Jon struggled. Struggled to touch his son, unable to move because his feet were mired in a swamp of marijuana.

He woke Tuesday to a gray dawn feeling as if he'd slept in damp denim. He took a long cool shower and shaved three days of growth off his face. Human again, he prowled the house, watching until Sam and Emily left for school, then, Rianne's fruit bowl in hand, he knocked on her screen door.

She had on another T-shirt, this one with a shaggy mutt ripping up a shoe and the caption reading, Need a friend? Get a cat. Her own orange feline curled around her legs and meowed.

"I'm a bit overdue on this," he said through the screen and held up her dish.

A smile flickered. "I knew where it was."

He pulled open the door. A black ball of fur darted past his legs. "Hey!" He swooped up the kitten before it made the veranda steps. "Where do you think you're off to, pipsqueak?" He set the kit inside the door where it galloped off to pounce on a sibling.

On the welcome mat, Jon toed off his boots before stepping into the house and placing the bowl on the counter. The aroma of coffee and toast suffused the kitchen. He shut the door and, for a moment, watched Rianne fill two mugs.

He'd thought long and hard about the night he'd asked her to see Brit's room, and he'd come to the conclusion that, after all was said and done, Rianne didn't entirely trust him. She offered a bold, honest front, proving to the world she had won her own War of Independence, but he knew deep down she harbored an element of caution when it came to him and their relationship.

She set the mugs on the table. A white twisty thing held her hair. Loose strands hung along her temples.

"Where did you go for the weekend?" he asked.

"To the coast. I'd promised the kids a walk along the beach and some cheese at Tillamook."

"Have fun?"

"Had a ball. The kids loved going through the big cheese factory." Her head came up. "I should've asked you to come with us."

"You needed time with your family." He came to the table and curled his hands around the back of a chair. "Do you want that coffee?"

"I...no, actually I don't."

"Neither do I."

Her brown eyes held his.

"I'm sorry," he said, "I was an ass for suggesting an affair." *For making you feel you need to be a one-night stand.* "But I won't beat around the bush, Rianne. I want you. More, maybe, than I've ever wanted a woman. But there are things I need to work out, things you know nothing about."

"We all have closet skeletons. Recognizing them makes us strong."

His mouth tugged at a smile. "Ever been a psychologist?"

She walked to him and laid a hand on his arm. "Just human." Her eyes didn't waver. "I'd rather have an affair with you, Jon Tucker, than a lifetime of nothing. You make me feel again."

His groin leapt. "Last time I had sex was three years ago. Colleen and I—"

She set a finger to his lips. "Let's leave the past where it is. It's not part of us."

Not part of them together. Except that it made him who he was and her who she was.

"I trust you," she whispered, touching his face.

Trust him. Not to rush, but to go slow, be gentle, be tender. He could handle that. He could definitely handle that.

He met her eyes. First things first. Because he owed her. "Remember the date I said we'd have? Tomorrow. Right after the kids leave for school."

Delight lifted the corners of her mouth. "How did you know I'm taking tomorrow off?"

"Intuition," he said, straightening and kissing her forehead, "because where we're headed is gonna take all day."

Sam stared at the back of Joey's head. They were in math class and Mr. Sloane was droning on about principles, interests and percents. Joey slouched three desks up and across the aisle from Sam, doodling on the glossy page of his textbook. Probably drawing a beard on the guy buying a car in the picture.

Sam never defaced books. Not that he was a Goody Two-shoes; he just didn't like the idea of marking up things that didn't belong to him personally. Joey, obviously, stuck his loyalties elsewhere. Like dorkface Huller.

Unable to sit, Sam got up, sharpened his pencil at the back of the room. Someone behind him snickered.

He focused on the bright day outside the narrow window. If only he wasn't so confused. First Joey, then Jon...

Trouble was, he'd shared stuff with Joey. Private stuff. Joey'd had a hard life with his mom and the things she'd done, and his real dad landing in jail. Heck, they'd both had crappy lives. That's why things clicked between them. Why they'd shared dreams, hopes, wants.

Why they'd gone to the cemetery, sworn on Joey's great-grandfather's grave to be blood brothers.

How could Joey ignore that? How could he snub his Shoshone heritage and the sacred bond he and Sam had made?

How could he take up with a moron like Cody?

The bell rang for next class. Sam returned to his desk, shoved his books into his backpack and headed for the door.

In the hall, Joey fell in step beside him. "You tell anyone about Poppers?"

"No."

"Good, 'cause I'll say you stole, too, and helped me pick. That makes you guilty *and* an assistant."

"Accessory." *Thank you, Dad.*

"Whatever. I'll rat you out with me and Code."

They reached Sam's locker. Three turns of the lock's dial and it sprang apart. Sam crashed open the door. Tossing in the math text, he reached down, jerked out his English binder and slammed the locker shut. He turned to his former pal.

"I thought you were cool, dude. But you're not. You're a loser just like my old man was."

Joey straightened his lank shoulders. "Don't compare me to your wacko father. I'm nothing like him, *nothing.*"

For several beats they stared at each other.

Sam asked, "What'd I ever do to you, Joe? We were friends. *Best* friends. Blood brothers. Then one day you act like I'm scum or something. I don't get it. I thought we respected each other." Backpack shouldered, he took off down the hall.

Joey caught up. "That blood-brother stuff? All garbage."

"You didn't think so at the time." At the time the little ceremony had been sacred. It had set a deep peace in Sam's heart.

"That's the trouble with you, Kirby," Joey scoffed. "You take everything so serious. Stop being such a geek."

Sam stopped. Students V'd past them. Two, dashing to catch a friend, bumped into him. "A geek? I *shoplifted* with you."

"Shut up," Joey hissed, eyes shifting. "The whole school doesn't need to know."

Sam barked a laugh. "The whole school probably knows already. Huller's the biggest blabbermouth there is."

"He won't talk."

For a second, Sam felt sorry for Joey. The guy looked honestly worried. Then anger returned. "Right, Fraser. You believe it."

He walked on to English.

The light rap on the back door had Rianne hurrying down the hall. *Be calm, girl. This isn't the first time you've dressed up for a man.*

But he was the first man since Duane. And that had been long-ago history. During the final years of their marriage, her late husband hadn't wanted her dressed up. Ever. He'd picked out her clothes: lackluster and sedate for teaching, Wal-Mart specials or garage-sale pickups for casual. No heels. Her makeup had consisted of a pale lip gloss, which she used until her finger dried the jar's interior. After his death, she'd undergone weeks of therapy to shoulder slow, sound changes.

With the help of a teacher friend in L.A., Rianne had re-learned fashion. Burgundy lipsticks. Bangles. Pierced ears. Gap tank tops. Liz Claiborne skirts. Coldwater Creek sweaters.

The heavy gray drizzle outside didn't deter her mood. Jon had promised her a day. A full day. With no interruptions.

Her strappy stilettos clicked confidently against the floor. He wanted her highest pair; she wasn't about to let him down. Not in any way. This was as much for him as for her.

"Hey." His voice strolled over her when she opened the door.

"Hey, back."

Raindrops gilded his loose hair, patched his big shoulders. He looked incredible. Red-and-tan shirt, wide belt, soft black jeans, buffed boots.

The green jersey knit she wore had her wishing for sleek and elegant. His grin washed away her doubts.

"You wore it." Pure male praise charged the words. Ink eyes browsed the dress and more.

Amazing how ridiculously shy she felt. Like the girl who'd struggled over Walt Whitman's poetry in his pickup. Who'd jumped from Gene Hyde's hawking hands and fallen into Jon's gentle ones.

He stepped out of the damp. "It's raining," he commented unnecessarily. "Maybe you'd rather stay here."

"And miss showing you off?"

He grinned and took her cold fingers. "That was supposed to be my line. "God, looking at you…have I died and gone to heaven?"

His eyes made her bold, made her sultry. A woman with secret delights. "Let's find out."

Chapter Eleven

Jon suggested they eat at Bailey's Restaurant and Lounge in Clatskanie, eight miles northwest of Misty River. Away from knowing eyes and the gossip vine.

Rianne agreed. What she felt for the man sitting across the table, lingering over his coffee, was too new, too multifarious for the scrutiny of Misty River's townsfolk.

Today Jon was hers. And she his. Today, even her children existed on the periphery.

"I love spring rains." She watched the weather beat down on the brown waters of the narrow Clatskanie River. "They offer promise and hope."

His hands were on hers, warm, rough as bark, the knuckles thick and dusted with hair. A working man's hands.

He said, "When I was a kid, I walked in the rain every chance I got. It settled me inside."

Yes, she thought. In his heart, in his soul, he would have

had much to settle. "That day I was unloading my groceries? You looked like Neptune, the Roman god of the sea, but without the beard. Very dramatic, very….formidable."

His mouth worked into a smile. "Neptune had a lot of wives, but the one I liked best was Salacia, goddess of spring water. He wanted her so much he had a dolphin track her down and bring her to him. Good thing I don't need a dolphin."

Her cheeks warmed. She looked at their hands.

"Don't go bashful on me now, honey."

"I'm not good at this."

"At what?"

"Playing female innuendos."

"Is that what you think you have to do?"

"I haven't a clue what to do. This is—new for me."

He braided their fingers. "For me, too. I was married seventeen years. You're my first date since the divorce."

"I feel like a teenager. Like I'm playing hooky from school with my boyfriend."

"If we were back in high school, I guarantee we wouldn't be sitting here. We'd be in my old yellow pickup, necking."

Or more.

"Come on." He tugged her from the booth. "It's time."

Down deep her womb zinged.

He paid for the meal and they started back toward Misty River. The rain slicked the woods in verdant green. A passing rig sprayed the cab; Jon set the wipers on high for a moment.

"Rianne." Shadowed by the dim interior, he drove watching the wet road, hands curved on the wheel, jaw rigid. "What we do at my place will be different—" he looked at her then, the black fringe of his lashes darkening his eyes "—and very fine."

"Can I sit beside you?" She wanted his solidness.

He opened his arm. Her tension left. Her senses dined on his skin.

He drove through the rain, steadily, cautiously, saying little, an insular man with a fragile heart. For him she would wait. Forever.

A mile farther, he surprised her, turning his mouth to her forehead, pressing a kiss there. He kissed her again, and then again on the same spot, before pulling into his lane and shutting off the engine.

Rain tapped the truck's roof like a million pencil tips.

His arm cocooned her. "Ready?"

Suddenly, she was. As though she'd waited for this day, this moment, all her life. "Yes."

He said, "It'll go only as far as you want, Rianne." Then, umbrella aloft, he hustled them to the veranda.

Inside the foyer, he caught her hand. At the kitchen windows, in the afternoon's ashen light, he held her face. "Before we go upstairs, I want you to know this is not an easy decision for me nor do I take this lightly. You are—"

She put a palm over his mouth and gave him a secret. "I would not trade this day for all my marriage nights."

His eyes were the navy of sea storms.

"I'm not looking for returns, Jon."

Without another word, he led her out of the kitchen, up the stairs and past Brittany's room to his bedroom.

He carried her into a room with wood floors and a pair of wide, bay windows where a gust of wet wind smacked the pane. A king-sized brass bed covered in rusts and yellows throned the main wall. Gently he laid her against fat pillows before sitting at her hip and smoothing back her hair. In the soft dull light, on the big bed, she felt safe and warm and impossibly wanton.

"I promised I'd go slow and I will," he said. "Any time you want to stop, it's all you have to say. One word. Stop."

"I won't."

He didn't smile, but dug into the night table drawer and tossed two foil packets on top. "Starters." This time he hitched a smile. "I bought them yesterday."

"Me, too," she admitted. "In my purse, downstairs."

"We'll keep them for other times."

Yes, other times. *Many* other times.

His work-hardened finger touched her mouth. Traveled her jawline to her ear. A few strands of hair caught on his calluses. The contour of her neck seemed to fascinate him.

She held her breath. At her breast, he asked, "More?"

She nodded. The finger found the tiny nub nudging fabric and circled, circled, circled. *More?* his eyes asked.

Much more.

He journeyed lower, across her belly, down her hip. Slow, seductive, sensual. Memorizing. He was memorizing each facet of her body. It gladdened and saddened her. *Are you storing up for future dreams, Jon? When we're no longer a couple?*

Leaning down, he kissed the arch of her foot.

Oh...! She closed her eyes.

He said, "I want to look at you. Will you let me?"

She dipped her chin, unable to get beyond the searing in her throat. She wanted to tell him she loved him, except her heart pounded too fast.

"Open your eyes, Rianne. Watch what I do."

Barely a breath. Heat like wildfire.

He removed her clothing, then his. Slowly. Kissing here, kissing there.

Touches that burned. Jon's touches.

Hearts thrashing.

Would he think her thin? Breasts too freckled? Stretch marks too evident?

A touch to her navel. A shivery spot.

He said, "I've never seen a waist so small." Blue as distant hills, his eyes. "You're tiny, delicate. Very womanly."

She touched his jaw where beard stubble was beginning to eclipse skin. "No one's ever said."

"I've always thought it. Back then. Tell me what you want."

"I want you on top of me." *In me.* She clutched his loose hair. Ropes in rapids. She ran a sheaf between her lips, tasting his texture even there. "Kiss me. Kiss me when you do it."

"My body's almost twice your size."

She shook her head, dizzy with want. "I want you, Jon. *You.*"

He cradled her in his arms, kissing her. Waltzed his tongue with hers. Coaxing, whispering, discovering.

Damp skin to damp skin.

Seconds, minutes. Forever.

She reached for him, urgent.

Besieged, he mounted her. She adjusted her legs.

He crooned endearments, encouragement. Kissed her face. Stroked her hair. Smiled down at her.

She loved him.

The bed creaked.

She loved him with all that was her—past and present. And followed him into beauty and joy.

"You have a gorgeous home."

Rianne stood at the screened back door in one of Jon's black T-shirts and surveyed his yard. Trees in full leaf glistened and quivered under the ceaseless drizzle. A light gust brought in the smell of wet grass.

What she couldn't do with that yard. With this house.

Don't think of it. Hadn't they agreed? No commitments.

But a terrible emptiness crept in still.

She padded to a tall stool at the oak island.

"I don't know why I bought it," he said, turning down the

burner on the stove. A veggie stir fry simmered. "Too big for one person. But, the price was right and I liked the privacy."

"Until your neighbor's cat decided different," she teased.

He threw her a grin. "How's old Sweetpea?"

"Getting tired of breast-feeding."

He chuckled. "Kids got some families lined up?"

"Mmm-hmm. Em figures you'll need one for Brittany."

His amusement fled.

"Jon, it's okay. Maybe one of the other teachers…"

He scraped the steaming vegetables onto two plates and set them on the table. "It's not that. I'd like Brit to have a cat. Trouble is, she may not be coming here at all."

Oh, no. "Are they going to Ireland, then?"

He tossed the pan into the sink. Metal rang on metal. "Apparently. Colleen called Sunday and said they're getting the paperwork in order."

"How long?"

He shrugged, wearing a lost, forlorn expression. "Couple of years, maybe more. Come on, let's eat."

She went to him, banded her arms around his bare waist and slipped her fingers into his empty belt loops. His chest smelled of lovemaking. She didn't speak, just held on.

"Can she take your daughter away like that? Don't you have to sign something to allow Brittany to leave the country?"

She and Duane had been in the process of sorting through reams of fine print before he died. One had included no out-of-country relocation of the children. Duane had wanted no out-of-state relocation, and had been fighting for it when he died.

"She wants me to, yeah." Lines cut near his mouth.

"Don't do it, Jon. Fight to bring Brittany here."

Sighing, he stepped to the table. "She needs her mother."

"She needs a loving parent." Rianne drew a chair and a

plate around so she sat next to him. Selfishly, she wanted his warmth at her side and a clear view of the rain.

Jon picked up his fork. "She'll have that in Ireland. Colleen may be a lot of things, but she does love her kids—Brittany."

"So do you. How does Brittany feel about the move?"

"Scared."

Rianne's heart ached. Father and daughter separated by ten thousand miles. Father and son separated forever.

They ate in silence. Unable to hold back any longer, she said, "Please don't take this the wrong way, but if you let Brittany go, she might think you're abandoning her."

He tossed down his napkin. "Think I don't know that? It kills me to know it."

"Then don't let her leave, Jon," Rianne said. "She needs you." *And you need her. More than you know.*

His blue eyes pulled at her soul. "Do you need me, Rianne?"

A current ran through her. *Yes!* "That's not—"

He placed a hand on her naked thigh. "How much? More than *you'll* admit?"

"Jon, I—"

"Enough to do it right here?" His voice was dark and low as distant thunder. "With only the screen door between us and a wayward visitor?"

She caught her breath. *This is what it feels like to fall in love. To make love.*

"Do it your way, Rianne. Take what you need."

Take what you need. Oh, yes! Laughing aloud, she climbed into his lap, glorying in her newfound control.

"Rianne?"

"Hmm?"

"Where'd you get this?" he traced a soapy finger along a jagged, three-inch scar between her spine and her freckled shoulder blade. They were in his dual-nozzle shower stall, where he was shampooing her hair. In bed, the mark had gone unnoticed. He'd been too busy with other things.

"An accident."

"What kind of accident?"

"I fell against an open cabinet door."

"How?"

She leaned into the spray. "I need to rinse my hair."

Swallowing down the sting of her distrust, he waited until she was done. Opening the stall door, he snatched a towel. Carefully, he dried her before leading her out, a bundle in blue terrycloth.

Face-to-face, hands on her shoulders, he kept her still. "How'd you fall on that door, honey?"

Her eyes were steady. "It happened the day I was taken to the hospital. Duane had come home late from a shift and was upset I hadn't kept supper waiting. I explained that Sam had to be at the school for a drama rehearsal and couldn't wait. Duane hated drama. Real boys played football or soccer, not Shakespeare."

Jon clenched his jaw.

"I went to get a pan to make something for him. He didn't want leftovers. He—he grabbed my hair, and I fell."

That hair curled damply on her shoulders. Jon loved her hair. Loved the feel of it on his skin. A madman had used her beautiful hair as a weapon. Because she had mothered her son.

He wanted to kill. Rage pumped through his blood. Cautiously, he stepped back. His fingers flexed, fisted. He searched around, needing to ease the fury in his chest.

"Jon."

He turned.

Her face was cloud-white.

He shook his head, scattering the images, scattering the pain. Her warm, slender hands slipped to his face.

His throat hurt. "Ri—"

"That time is over and finished, do you hear?"

On the nightstand the phone rang, ending the moment.

It was Colleen. "Can you come up?" she asked. To Seattle.

Heart jarring, he caught Rianne's hand and pulled her on to the bed beside him. "Brit?"

"She's fighting Ireland. She wants to live with you."

His breathing leveled. "What did you tell her?"

"That we'd talk it over—in person."

"My house is in the middle of major renos right now."

"Are you living in it?"

"Yeah, but—"

"She won't mind the mess for a few months."

His heart banged his ribs. "Colleen, this—"

"Look, she refuses to relocate with us. I think a lot of it has to do with Allan and I getting married there. She's not completely…taken with him."

An understatement. But Allan could be Brittany's one chance at having a male role model. One she could look up to. "I'll talk to her. Is she there?"

"She's at a friend's till supper. Can you drive up now? We could talk while she's there."

"The answer would still be the same."

"I don't want—" Colleen's voice broke "—her running away."

"Has she threatened to?"

"Twice. Both times her knapsack was packed, ready to go."

Jon cursed silently. "And you didn't call me?"

"I didn't think she was serious."

Not serious? Our daughter preps to run away and you don't think it's serious? He beat down his outrage. How dare

Colleen slough off Brittany's problems like a speck of lint. She *knew* better. Seventeen years she'd lived with him, a cop.

"Will you come?" she asked. "Maybe if she sees you in person, talks to you…"

"I'll be there tonight." *When my daughter is home.*

"Thanks."

Jon hung up and scrubbed his cheeks. "What a mess."

"Is Colleen in favor of Brittany living with you?"

He pinched the bridge of his nose. "I don't know. Probably. *Dammit.*" He rose, paced the room. "I'm not a family man. I screwed up with one kid. I can't take the chance on Brit."

"Yes, you can," Rianne said, rising from the bed. "I've seen what you did in her room. What you've done for Sam. In here," she palmed his chest, "you're a first-class father."

He shook his head. "I lost Nicky because I was working fourteen-hour days chasing drug dealers." His smile wasn't a smile, he knew, but a mark of agony. "Ironic? You bet."

"I don't understand."

She wouldn't. She would never understand.

Fool, she has guilt of her own.

He said, "I…I loved the busts, the investigations." He hauled in a breath; his throat was a blister. "Colleen complained she couldn't handle Nick. He was stubborn, sassy, leaving the house at night, not coming home till all hours. I'd lay down rules, he'd break them."

He scrubbed his hands down his face again. "One night I came home late. The ambulance was there. Nick and two buddies had this little rock group and they'd practice in the garage. This night they practiced trying Ecstasy."

"Oh, Jon, no."

"Oh, yeah." His eyes stung. "Stuff reacted like a severe allergy. My boy…" He blew a breath, squeezed shut his eyes. "I knew every trafficker on the street, worked informants, could tell you the names of dealers' kids." Shame cloaked him like a woolen mackinaw. "But I didn't know about my own son. *I didn't know.*"

She held him, heart-to-heart.

"I can't go through that again, Rianne. Not for anyone."

"You're here." Colleen opened the door of the A-framed house Jon had bought a decade ago. "I thought you might chicken out."

She would.

"Daddy!" Brittany barreled past her mother and leapt into his arms as he stepped from the tiny, shadow-box porch into the foyer. "Mom said you were coming!"

"Hey, button-nose." He breathed in her child scent as she burrowed against his neck. "How's m'girl?"

"Great, now you're here. I've been waiting *all day.* It's been really *awful.*"

Ignoring Colleen's starched face, he kissed his daughter's blond head and set her on her feet. "Well, I'm here and I'm not leaving for a day or so."

"Yay!" she cheered. "Can we go to a movie and shopping and the park and—"

Jon laughed. It felt good. "Hold on, peanut. One thing at a time. First, I need to talk to your mom. Okay?"

The girl sobered. "I know." She clutched Jon's hand with both her own. "I don't want to go to Ireland, but Mom—" she glanced over "—won't listen."

"We'll both listen, Brit, I promise. But before we do, can you get me a glass of water?" He steered her toward the kitchen. "I'm thirsty as a cactus, eating those potato chips on the road."

When Brittany dashed off, Colleen griped, "You do that so well, don't you?"

"What?"

"Suck her into the Daddy's-home-so-everything's-fine routine."

Jon shoved his hands into the pockets of his tailored slacks. "Did you get me up here just to pick a fight, Colleen?"

She shook her head. "It's been a hairy day. Brit's been on pins and needles since she knew you were coming. I'm just worried this meeting won't go the way she's hoping."

Tall, slim, with a cap of Viking-blond hair, Colleen was a stunning woman. At the moment, she looked shaken; Jon empathized. Brittany wanted him instead of her mother. His mood loosened.

"I swear," Colleen went on. "I don't know what gets into her at times. She snivels. She's cranky. She stays in her bedroom all the time." Colleen sighed. "She and Allan…"

Jon cocked his head.

"All right. If you want to know, they don't get along."

"She's confused about Ireland," he said, trying to appease.

"Confused? I explained everything. She knows we won't be there that long. Twenty-four months at most."

He knew different. Overseas expeditions could last years. "To a ten-year-old two years is a hundred. She'll be entering puberty when she returns to the States."

"God, you make it sound like it's an exile."

"In her mind it is."

"She'll get used to it."

"You sure? She cries every second phone call."

Colleen's lips thinned. "These days she cries over everything. Over a spat with her friend, over a low math mark, if I won't let her sleep at Alison's. Last week she cried because I'd bought the wrong cereal. Myra Watson says it's prepubescent behavior. Both her girls went through it."

Jon knew the woman. A know-it-all whose kids were little hoodlums. "Brit's had a rough sixteen months since Nick."

Colleen straightened the cuff on her immaculate silk blouse. "She's not the only one."

No kidding.

"Anyway," Colleen continued, "you have to convince her to go with us, or take her back with you. God knows, I'd rather she come with us than go to that godforsaken town you hail from." She looked down the hall to where a tap was running and sighed again.

"I'm not promising anything." He slapped on a grin when Brittany came around the corner with a large glass. "Thanks, peanut. You remembered the ice." He drank deeply, pacifying the burn in his throat, though not the ache in his heart. "Arghh. Good."

"More, Dad?"

"No, love. That was great." He handed back the glass. "Put it in the dishwasher, okay?"

"'Kay."

He watched her dash off again. He'd bet his Harley the last few minutes were her happiest in a while. Turning to the woman in front of him, he said, "When should we do this, now or in the morning?" It was nearing eight.

"Now. I've got a full agenda tomorrow. Brit," she called. "Your father wants to talk to you."

"And with your mother." He gave Colleen a pointed look; she flashed one in return that said, "Can't you do this on your own?" and led him into the living room.

The house hadn't changed much in the year since their divorce. The carpet was the same dun color, the furniture the same dark oak. Pictures were different. Abstract art. Everywhere faces and bodies collapsed and crashed.

Jon sat on the couch opposite his ex, the coffee table between them. Brittany cuddled beside him, her small hands impounding one of his, her head against his arm.

"What happened to the marine paintings?" he asked. He'd always liked seascapes and underwater life. Whales, fishing trawlers, rain-pelted seas. Men in rubber boots and slickers, scraping out an honest day's work from the deep.

"I sold them. Allan likes modernistic impressionism." Colleen lifted her chin. "He's a modern man. Doesn't sit in ruts."

Unlike him.

He refused her goading. What did it matter when time ran only on pain?

And now?

Now he was a man who gave little and expected nothing.

Kind of like you're doing with your daughter.

He shifted under his guilt.

And Rianne? No give-and-take there?

He rubbed his tired eyes, felt another chunk of his cement wall collapse and looked down at his daughter. Could he do this one thing right?

"Mom says you want to live with me in Misty River."

"Yeah," she said in a small, cautious voice.

"I think you should go with Mom to Ireland."

She shook her head. "Uh-uh. No. It's too far away from you, and then you'll be sad."

His heart pitched. "In Misty River you'll be an all-day plane trip away from Mom in Ireland. Which will make *her* sad."

"I know, but Mom'll have Allan to keep her company. You won't have anybody."

Uh-oh. "Honey, I'm doing okay." Sort of. Rianne had done that, patched some of the holes in his life where the wind blew cold. No doubt she'd insulate him completely— if he let her. "We can still see each other summers. And at Christmas and spring break." He hauled her onto his lap. "You'll always be able to visit. We'll talk hours on the phone. I promise."

She began to sniff. "It won't be like here. I won't know anybody and school'll be different. And you can't see me play soccer there."

"Mom will make videos, Brit."

Tears came in earnest; she pressed her face into his shirt. "I don't want to go. Please, Daddy. Let me live with you."

His throat burned. "Punkin, your place is with Mom and—"

"Why can't you move with us? Don't you love Mom anymore?"

He looked at Colleen. "I do, baby, but as a friend."

"Is that how you love me?" Brittany muffled in his neck.

He closed his eyes. Emotion teemed through his blood, stung his heart. "Brit, I love you more than life."

She scrambled off his lap. "That's not true. If you did, you'd take me with you!" Whirling, she ran from the room. Her feet drummed up the stairs. A door slammed. Muted sobs streamed clean through to the soles of his feet.

He dropped his head back on the sofa. "Dammit to hell."

"You've got to take her, that's all there is to it."

"I *can't.*"

"Why? You haven't given me one decent reason."

He got up and went to the window. In the front yard, the magnolia flaunted its white blooms like fat stars in the night. He'd always loved the tree for that reason. His welcome-home beacon each spring, when he turned off Roosevelt onto Ninety-sixth Street, exhausted, his mind cabled to criminals and crime.

A movement caught his eye. Across the street, a tall teenager shot hoops by the light of the garage. *Dustin.* Nick's pal. Did he miss the fun they'd had?

Jon turned from the memories. Misty River was a better place to be. Nick had never set foot there.

Colleen said, "You can't refuse her, Jon. You're her idol. You always were. To both kids."

"You are, too, Colleen."

"Yeah." A sour laugh escaped. "That's why she wants to live in that godforsaken hole-in-the-wall down in Oregon." She looked at him askance. "Are you a cop there as well?"

"I'll be making furniture." In spite of his resolve, the statement sounded empty, without promise.

"That's a new twist, you a carpenter."

He shrugged. Her opinions no longer mattered. Even at the start of their marriage, Colleen had done her own thing, shaving her life from his with each passing year until she seemed more roommate than wife.

Can you blame her when work always came first?

He regarded the woman on the sofa. The hem of her costly green skirt lay chastely over her knees. The shade didn't suit her. Green matched sunrise hair, chestnut eyes. Earth colors. Fertile colors.

Rianne's colors.

You're losing it, Jon.

He looked toward the stairs. He should go up, see Brittany. Rianne would. Rianne wouldn't leave her behind.

Rianne with her battered body and her scarred heart would die fighting for her children. *Had* almost died.

Colleen hauled him back to the present. "Will making furniture guarantee a decent income?"

"My finances are healthy, as you know."

For the first time she blushed.

A headache chewed in his left temple. He knew what he had to do. Oh, yeah, he knew exactly. For his baby girl. It had his heart bonging worse than an alcoholic's faced with the promise of a two-day drunk. He stood, moved to the stairs. "I'll tell her."

"Jon?"

He stopped, his foot on the bottom step.

His ex-wife's eyes glistened. "Don't be afraid to set the rules for her down there in Podunk, okay?" she said softly.

Chapter Twelve

Sam hated Fridays. They meant the weekend loomed around the corner like a black hole. He couldn't really call Joey anymore, or Jon… Sam sure wasn't going over there. Especially now that Jon had his daughter hanging around. Besides, Sam's mom made it clear they shouldn't bother their neighbor. He needed time with his kid.

Something splintered inside Sam. He wished he *could* go over to Jon's. He knew Jon was wondering why Sam never talked to him anymore. He wished things were the same between them. He wished that Jon was the same. That Sam could ask him about finishing the porch.

He kicked a stone. Jon was better than his dad. Duane Kirby would never have let his son peel and paint their house. *Rotten jerk. I'm glad you're dead.* Well, not really, he just wished that his dad had been different. Sort of like Jon.

Yesterday Sam had seen the man crouch down to fix the zipper on his daughter's jacket and give her hair a playful tug.

Yeah, stuff like that. It would've made him remember his dad in a decent way. Would have let him love Duane Kirby. Instead, watching Jon made him resent Joey his stepdad, and the new girl—

He booted the stone again. Man, sometimes he was so confused! If only there was somebody he could talk to. Not Mrs. Zeglen. Not a counselor, but somebody who really, well, *knew.*

A cool wind, leftover from the dreary weather earlier in the week, brushed his cheeks. He didn't want to think about his dad, Joey, Mrs. Zee or Jon.

"Hey, Claw-Man!"

Sam flung a look at Huller and Joey crossing the street toward him. A small thread of distrust spun down his arms. Where had they come from?

"Where ya goin'?" Huller asked, falling in step beside him.

"Home—where else?"

"Wanna come for a ride with me and Joe later?"

"Where to?"

"Around."

"Who's driving?"

"Jared. He's got this rod…"

Sam tuned out. Cody's seventeen-year-old brother didn't interest him. The guy had a record with the cops for drunk driving and street racing.

"So, you wanna?" Huller asked.

"I'll see."

"What else you got to do, Kirby? Baby-sit Em-i-ly?"

Sam glanced at Joey flanking his right side. His former buddy hadn't said a word. He wasn't meeting Sam's eye either. His mouth was clamped shut, and red stained his brown cheeks. Sam noticed the hair Joey had once kept short now reached his jacket collar. And, it seemed he'd grown another three inches. Huge, these changes between them.

A motorcycle rumbled up the street. Jon, on his Harley, with his daughter sticking to his waist like a tree frog. The man didn't look their way. He was too busy talking over his shoulder to his kid.

"Suhweeet." This from Cody, staring after the bike.

"Faaat." Joey was practically drooling.

"When you guys going?" Sam snapped.

Cody's grin was sly. His nose ring blinked in a beam of sunlight. "Eight, nine. Gonna be ready?"

"Maybe."

They stopped at Joey's driveway. Cody smirked. "You know where to find us."

Sam scanned the Fraser house, then looked straight at Joey who was studying a potted plant in his front yard.

"Yeah," Sam replied. "I'll know where to find you."

He headed on down the sidewalk.

Jon took Brittany's hand as they waited on the back porch of Rianne's cottage Sunday evening. How many times had he stood here since that day with the kittens?

Tonight was different. Tonight their families would mesh in a small way. Tonight he wanted friendship between his daughter and Rianne's. He wanted Brittany to like Misty River. To be happy here, with him.

She'd cried leaving her mother. Yet, she insisted on living here, not Ireland, the determined little mite.

"You'll like Emily," he said. "Sam and Ms. Worth, too. They're a nice family, peanut."

"What if they don't like me, Dad?" She chewed her cheek and looked up at him with such worry in her round, hazel eyes he almost said to hell with it and jogged her home.

Rianne stood framed in the doorway. He hadn't seen her in four days. Not since they'd had sex—*love not sex*—on that rainy morning and Colleen had called him back to Seattle.

Her semismile. God, he'd missed it.

Then, her eyes widened at Brit. He set his hands on his daughter's shoulders. "This is Brittany. My baby."

"Da-ad," she whispered up at him.

Without hesitation, Rianne bent and took his child's hand. "Hello, sweetie. I'm so glad to meet you. Do you like chocolate chip cookies? I just made some. Emily," she called, "come see who's here."

And that was that. Nothing to worry about.

Jon watched the two girls disappear into Emily's bedroom, a plate of four cookies between them, kittens in their arms. Girlish giggles echoing down the hall.

He couldn't have been more pleased. The children needed each other, albeit for different reasons. Even Sam had galloped up from the rec room to introduce himself. For the first time, Jon saw his punkin get red-cheeked at the sight of a young boy. He understood now what Colleen had meant about girls in the prepubescent stage and wondered how he'd handle it a couple years down the road. Thank God Rianne lived next door.

And, while you help me out, be sure to keep your distance.

Stuff it, Jon.

"Want a cookie?" she asked.

His smile faltered. She seemed distant. Not unfriendly, but not completely at ease.

"I'd rather have you," he said, attempting a little humor.

"That wouldn't be a good idea."

"Nice fantasy, though," he continued to tease.

She didn't smile. She just looked at him from where she stood by the stove. She said, "Brittany's a sweetheart."

"She is that. What's wrong, Rianne?"

"Us."

There it was. Front and center. *Us.*

From a wire-mesh bowl, she plucked an apple and curved her fingers around the fruit. "What we had was beautiful. Wonderful." Her russet eyes spoke details. "It's never been that way for me."

"But?"

"You mentioned fantasy. We had it, and it was lovely. Now comes reality. You and Brittany need to establish a life, and I—we, in this house, need to get on with ours."

He rubbed his forehead. "What I said the other day, about not wanting family life again? I hurt you." After she'd left his house he'd gone downstairs to his weight room, strapped on the gloves, punched the bag for an hour.

Her eyes were bottomless. "What I feel is incidental to—"

"The hell it is."

"—to what you must be going through. I can only imagine it. If one of my kids…" She inhaled, set the apple back without a bite. "What I'm trying to say is I'm willing to wait. Two years, ten, as long as it takes for you to heal, Jon."

He stepped forward; she held up a hand. "I care too much to smear what's in here—" a touch to her heart "—with casual sex."

"Can I at least hold you?" His throat was a fresh bruise.

She didn't hesitate. She walked into his arms and he, pressing his face to hair sweetened by the scent of peaches, tucked her into his heart.

"Let's start again," he wanted to say.

In the end, he simply set his lips to her brow and let her go. Two minutes later, he stood alone in his big, echoing house.

The moonless night enveloped her like a dark, secret blanket. She went to the other side of the house this time—where he wouldn't see the flashlight flicker—and knelt on the cool earth. The petunias and pansies planted two weeks ago needed deadheading. What *she* needed was a solution to get over Jon. Tonight, when he'd introduced Brittany...such love—staggering, greedy—rushed through Rianne.

With the heel of her hand, she mopped her teary cheeks. How hard it had been not to call him back, not to give in, to say, "Yes, let's go on without ever moving forward."

But she'd meant what she said.

A cool lonely wind swatted her face, an omen of the weeks to come. Well, so be it.

Brittany turned big eyes on Jon from across the cab of his truck and asked, "Do you think she'll want to see me?"

His heart lurched. This was the first time his daughter would meet her paternal grandmother. The severance he'd executed twenty years ago had had its cost. Nicky would never have the chance. Nor would the woman living in that tatty house have the chance to know her grandson.

"She'll love seeing you." He pulled up along the curb and shut off the motor. "Not getting second thoughts, are you?"

Brittany stared at the house, worry riding her brow. "No, but it looks so *old*."

"It is old," he said, seeing the weathered, beaten wood once again. "It's where I grew up with my brothers—your uncles—a long, long time ago. We tattled on each other as kids here, fought to defend our private space, played football in the backyard. We argued, laughed, dreamed in that house."

Brittany clutched the supermarket carnations they'd bought. "Grandma's yard looks bad. Maybe I could help fix it up."

He leaned over and kissed her hair. "Thanks, darlin'." In one week, she had slipped like sunshine into his house, into his life. Turning the first into a place for laughter and smiles, giving the second a reason simply to enjoy the moment.

God, he hoped one day she'd love and respect him without regret. "Let's see if your grandma's home."

He should have called first; though he wasn't sure he could have handled it if Maxine had refused to see his child.

They walked along the weed-infested flower beds, up the decayed steps of the porch.

Through the screened door, music marched.

John Philip Sousa.

Jon pulled open the door and stepped into the familiar, drab front room. In contrast, a spanking new Sony pelted out *The Stars and Stripes Forever*. He walked over and shut it off. "Ma?"

She shuffled around the corner from the kitchen. "What'd you go'n do that for?" she demanded. Then she saw Brittany. "*Ohhh.*" Her gnarled hands lifted slowly, curled as one under her chin. Aged gray eyes blinked.

"Ma, my daughter, Brittany. Brit, your Grandma Tucker."

"Jonny…oh! You brought her to see me." She moved across the tiny room and ran a leathery palm down Brittany's thick, soft hair. "She's *beautiful.*"

Around the twinge in his chest, Jon said, "Tell her, Brit, why you're here."

"My mom's going to Ireland for a couple of years with her fiancé. I'm going to live with my dad while she's there."

"You'll be here? In Misty River?"

"Uh-huh." She held out the flowers. "For you."

Taking them, Maxine's eyes watered. "Want to come check the cake I'm baking? It's chocolate. You like chocolate?"

Brittany zeroed a look on Jon. He nodded. She took her grandmother's hand. Maxine said to him, "I got tea if you want."

He managed a smile. "Why not?"

Forty minutes later, he pulled from the curb while his mother, faded shawl wrapped around her bony shoulders, watched. Beside him, Brittany held a round plastic tub of cake. She waved until maples and firs cut off the house.

"Can we invite her over for supper one night, Dad?"

"Once you're a little more settled, honey."

"She's different from Nana Nielsen."

"Yeah." Fastidious Grace Nielsen. "She is."

"But I like her. She's…um, don't tell Mom this, but I think Gramma Tucker is more like a grandma should be. Nana Nielsen never baked, and she's always worried about her house getting messed up. I mean I love her and stuff, but Gramma Tucker doesn't care about messes. Her whole house is sorta messy and her clothes are kinda sloppy and she doesn't talk to me like I'm a kid, y'know? Plus, she thinks I'm beautiful. Nana Nielsen thinks I'm only pretty. Alison says there's a very big difference between beautiful and pretty."

Jon's lips twitched as Brittany spun out her kid chatter. He hadn't realized how much he'd missed it.

He wanted the days to go slowly; the year he and Colleen had agreed on never to end. Still, if Brittany changed her mind, he'd take her to Ireland personally.

He dreaded the thought.

Six weeks ago he was a dead man wandering the cryptic, silent halls of an old Victorian. Now, his munchkin nattered off his ear. And he loved it.

"I really like it here, Dad. This is way better'n Seattle."

"Think so, huh?"

"Uh-huh. I got a grandma who bakes chocolate cakes and likes to give hugs and a *huuuge* room—which I love, love, *lo-ove*—and my very own *phone* and *bathroom* and I'm already friends with Emily. It's so neat she lives next door. We can go to school together and she has *kittens!* Oh, Dad, can we get one? Emily and Sam said I could pick whatever one I wanted. I love the little gray one best. He's sooo furry and *cute*. And Ms. Worth said…"

She prattled on.

Ah, Rianne…

How could he let her go?

How could he not?

Brittany had Colleen to fall back on if he screwed up. Who would Rianne and her kids have if he offered forever and failed?

He swung the truck up his drive. The cottage was quiet—no sign of kids. The Toyota sat in its carport.

"Can I go over to Emily's?" Brittany broke off her latest ramble about her friend Alison acting snooty because she once got a hundred on a math test.

"Why don't you phone Emily, invite her to see your room?" Jon suggested. He shut off the engine and handed her the house key. He liked the idea of the girls playing where he could hear them.

"O-*kay!*" She leapt from the truck and, dodging shingles, sawhorses and wood, raced to the door.

Resting his arms on the steering wheel, he watched her scamper inside, leaving the door wide open. His heart did a slow, thick tumble. He was goofy about his kid.

He looked next door. Tiny and weather-beaten, the house could stand a complete overhaul. He pictured himself repairing the carport roof, the steps, realigning shutters.

The images ebbed. Another man took his place. A man Rianne didn't need to wait for.

Grabbing up his mother's cake, he slammed out of the cab and stalked into his house. "Brittany!"

Her feet thundered to the top of the stairs. "Yeah, Dad?"

"Tell Emily if she wants to stay for supper she's welcome. And tell her dessert is your grandmother's chocolate cake."

"Yippee!"

Rolling up his sleeves, he strode into the kitchen. Be damned if he'd let another guy out-father him.

A week later, Sam stood again on Joey's front porch and rang the doorbell. Eight-thirty. Apart from the lit patches of pavement below the pole lamps, darkness swathed the street. A small rush of wind shook the shrubbery alongside the house.

The door swung open. Huller grinned slyly. "Claw-Man. Thought you'd chicken out."

"Up yours, Huller. Where's Joey?"

"Here," the boy in question answered, pushing past Huller and tripping down the steps.

"Joey," Mrs. Fraser called from inside. "I want you home no later than ten-thirty."

"Aw, Mom… It's Friday."

"You heard your mother." Mr. Fraser came to the door, his face stern. He looked straight at Joey.

"Yes, sir."

"Hi, Sam." The man smiled. "Miss you coming around here."

"Been doing some work on the house, painting the back porch and stuff." *And fighting with Joey.*

"Good for you. Well, you guys have fun." Again, his eyes spoke the unspoken to Joey. "See you later, son."

They headed down the sidewalk.

"Why d'you put up with that junk?" Huller asked Joey. "He's not your old man. Tell him to take a hike."

"He's great to my mom," Joey said. "Only guy who was."

"Oh, yeah. Forgot. Your old lady was a ho, right?"

Joey swung to a stop, cheeks afire. "Take that back, Cody. Take it back right this minute."

Cody held up his palms. "Sor-*ry*. You don't hafta chew my head off."

Joey started walking again, fast. Sam lengthened his stride to keep up. Something inside him thawed. Joey wasn't immune to Huller's meanness.

Half a block down the street, Sam asked Cody, "Your brother busy again tonight?" Last week when Cody bragged about riding with him, the guy had suddenly been "tied up."

"Yeah, what of it?"

Sam shrugged. He'd rather walk anyway. Walking with a guy like Cody meant less trouble. Sam wasn't sure if he would've ridden with the older Huller at the wheel.

It took twenty minutes to reach downtown. They browsed past shops, through car and truck lots, hit the video store, scanned new releases. At Poppers, they bought slushies; this time he and Joey paid for their candy bars.

Shortly after nine, they wandered down an alley, cutting from Main to First. Cody veered into the back parking lot of a small office building.

"Hey, willya look at this." He ran his hands over the hood of a sleek, black '85 Trans-Am, the only vehicle in the lot. The owner had backed in the car, leaving its nose convenient. On the driver's side, Huller pulled a screwdriver from his jacket.

"What're you doing?" Sam asked. He glanced at the office building. On the third floor a light burned.

"What's it look like I'm doing? I'm gonna rod this bird and we're taking a fast trip to funland."

"Not me." Sam backed away. "No way."

Huller jimmied the lock. Damn, Sam thought. Cody had planned this all along. Two clicks; it was done. He slid into the seat, jammed the screwdriver into the ignition. The car roared.

"Get in!" Huller barked, unlocking the passenger door. He revved the motor, laughing like an idiot.

On the third floor, a man came to the window. He waved a fist, then wheeled out of sight.

"The guy's coming!" Joey called, dancing on the spot. "Geez, Code, the owner's coming!"

Sam's heart vaulted into his throat. "I say let's run for it." He dashed toward the alley, bounced to a stop, and looked back at his pal. "C'mon, Joe, run!"

Joey sprinted toward him.

Huller gunned the car from its stall and screeched to a halt at the lot's entrance. Out his window, he barked, "C'mon, morons! He's probably called the cops. Let's go! We can ditch this puppy before they get here. *C'mon!*"

The mention of cops settled it for Joey. He jumped into the passenger side as the owner barreled through the door on a dead run. Camouflaged by dark and distance, the guy favored King Kong.

Sam dove into the back seat. Huller hit the gas. The Trans-Am rocketed down the alley.

"Whooo-hooo! That was close!" Cody laughed and slapped the wheel. "Yeah! We are partying to-*niiight!*"

Sam watched businesses flash by. He tried to keep himself in one spot long enough to get his seat belt on. Huller drove Mach-100, careening around corners, blasting through intersections. A truck, its signal blinking right, was stopped at the town outskirts. The Trans-Am veered to the left and missed the vehicle by the width of its paint job.

Sam's heart nearly stopped.

Joey gripped the dash.

Huller would kill them all.

"Let me out," Sam demanded.

"You nuts?" Huller laughed. "If I stop now the pigs are gonna be on my butt. We're outta here, man."

He jabbed the accelerator, pushing seventy. The car shot down the blacktop. Houses whipped past. Soon they hit the open road flanked by fields and woods.

Sam shoved his face between the two riding up front. "Stop the car, Cody. We're a mile out and I gotta be home by ten."

"'I gotta be home by ten,'" the boy mocked. "Well, get this, Claw-Man. I'm driving. *I* say when you get out."

Joey said, "Slow down, Code. If the pigs are parked on a side road, they'll make us for sure." His fingers, attached to the dash, were pale in the function lights.

"Huh," Cody sneered. "Like to see 'em catch this baby."

To Sam's amazement he slowed enough to turn onto a dirt road. Its ruts had them all jouncing. The headlights zapped trees every which way. Sam smacked his head on the roof. At last the trail spit them out into an open area where a full white moon perched above the tree line.

Cody opened his window and stuck out his head.

"Yeeehaaa! Come get me now, Willard, you old fatso!" Howling with laughter, he cut a doughnut. Sam's insides hung on the bumper.

Ramming the brake, the boy threw open the door and leapt out. "Was that fun, or was that *fuuun!*"

Sam worked his rubbery legs and climbed from the vehicle. His heart beat like an elephant drum. "Geez, Huller! Are you nuts?" He looked around a small dark field. "Where are we?"

"Franklin's Mill. 'Fraid old Maggie's ghostie's gonna get you, Claw-Man?"

"There's no ghost up here," Joey cut in. He leaned on his open door. "That's all bull and you know it, Cody."

"Wetting your undies, Fraser? Like in the car? Afraid your Indian medicine man will jump out of the bushes?"

"Shut your mouth," Joey snapped. He headed for the trail. "C'mon, Sam. We don't need this crap."

Oh, now I'm your friend? But Sam wasn't hanging with Huller. He jogged after Joey.

"Wait," Cody called. "Where you going?"

"Home," Joey snapped.

"Home? But we just got started."

Joey flew Huller the bird. "And we're ending it."

"But—you can't leave now! I mean—what about the car?"

Sam and Joey kept walking.

"Hey, wait! Don't you want to see where I work?"

Joey stopped. "Work?"

"Yeah. Got a job. Right here." Huller set his hands on his skinny hips, stuck out his turkey chest. He sauntered over. "Been doing it for a couple weeks now. Over behind those trees."

"Right. You're just scared to be by yourself up here in the dark," Joey said. He and Sam started off again.

"Come see! It's true. I run a big irrigation system."

"Sure you do, Huller."

"No, really. Larry Marshall and my dad hired me."

Joey hesitated. "You jerking me?"

"No, c'mon." Cody waved them back.

Sam didn't want to look. He had a creepy feeling about Huller and his work. Joey followed the other boy across the clearing and into the trees. Trotting after them, Sam thought, *Be just like Huller to get us into the forest then disappear.* The idea unnerved him. They were at least a mile from town, and it was less than an hour from his curfew. He could imagine his mother pacing the floor, waiting for him. Calling the cops.

They broke from the trees. Another clearing.

"There," Huller pointed proudly.

Moonlight silvered foot-tall plants growing in an area the size of three backyards.

"What is this?" Joey scoffed. "Tomatoes?"

Huller bent double laughing. He yanked out a seedling. "Weed, man. Earliest stage."

"Marijuana?" In unison, Sam and Joey gaped at him.

Joey took the plant, stared at it; rolled it between his fingers. "Marshall and your dad are into dope?"

"What of it?" Huller sneered.

"It's illegal that's what, twit. If the cops—"

"What'll they do? I'm a minor. They can't touch me."

"Oh, that's smart," Sam put in. "You're a regular rocket scientist, Huller."

"What do you know, Kirby? You're just a little chicken fart." He stuck his hands under his arms, danced around. "Cluck, foop! Cluck, foop!"

A flush crept up Sam's neck.

"Got some stuff stashed 'round here?" Joey asked. Darkness screened his face, but excitement glinted in his eyes.

Huller's teeth winked in the moonlight. "Over at one of them shacks by the river." He headed back through the woods. Joey followed.

They were going to smoke pot. Sam knew it. Part of him wanted to smoke, too, an excited, anxious part, but another part of him wanted to run right down that dark path and all the way home. His mind blocked visions of his mom's sad eyes, of Emily's shocked expression, of Jon Tucker's disappointed look. His mom and Emily would never find out and if Jon did, well, who cared? He was nobody to Sam. Just a grouchy old neighbor.

Liar.

"Wait up," he called and ran after Joey.

In less than two minutes they reached the first of three old, abandoned cabins the Trans-Am's headlights had caught upon entering the clearing. Cody crawled through a shuttered window while Sam and Joey waited among scrubby bushes and listened to an owl hoot and the river gurgle along its tree-lined banks.

Huller came back out, a small plastic bag in hand. "Time to get gooned, dudes."

Laughing, he squatted on the ground and dug into the bag. From his shirt pocket he took out a package of cigarette paper and matches. Deftly, he rolled some weed, lit it, took a deep drag, then held the joint out to Joey.

Sam's heart whacked his ribs. In three seconds he'd be one of millions since the Sixties to smoke weed. Joey blew out a stream of smoke, coughed and passed the cigarette over.

Huller laughed as Sam sucked gingerly. "C'mon, Kirby, sippin' it ain't gonna do nothing."

Sam sucked harder. Smoke scorched his windpipe. Tears sprang to his eyes. Bending at the waist, he coughed until he thought his insides would rip apart. Huller rolled on the ground, laughing his idiot head off. Joey slapped Sam's back and chortled. "You don't snort the stuff, Sambone, you *smoke* it."

Sam sat back on his rump and wiped his eyes. His head felt like a crane was lifting it off his neck. His mouth tasted of ash. But Joey was grinning at him. The old Joey.

Sam held out his hand. "Gimme that thing."

Chapter Thirteen

She wanted distance, needed it. To give him time to settle in with Brittany, to give herself time to sort out her emotions.

At school she cluttered her mind with students, with teaching, with discussing year-end projects. She grinned at the kids and welcomed them into the library as always. The grin didn't reach her heart. There, the dull pang that was Jon lingered like an inflamed thorn.

Thank goodness the day was over. She checked the clock. Twenty minutes before final bell. Then home to abandon her peppy, pasted-on face.

At the counter behind her workstation, she began encasing eight new novels in clear plastic jackets. She wanted them done before Emily and Brittany bounded into the room. A smile tugged Rianne's mouth. Brittany. With each new day she loved the child more. Almost overnight, she'd become Emily's best friend.

Finally, *finally,* the wonder of girlish chatter and spirited giggles echoed in her home. For that alone Rianne would love Jon's daughter forever. Sparkly as a Christmas star, bubbly as a ten-soda punch, Brittany loved her father fiercely.

Yesterday, the girl had dashed from the Toyota, flinging into her father's arms. He'd laughed, his blue eyes on Rianne while his daughter chirped about school before he carried her into his house.

"Hi, Mom." A breathless voice said beside her.

"Hey, baby." Rianne righted the glasses on Em's nose. "You're three minutes early."

"Mrs. Baker let me go 'cause I cleaned my desk first."

"Good girl." Rianne nodded at the cart. "Want to shelve those easy readers?"

Emily towed the cart away and set to work. The bell rang. "Mom, can we have pizza tonight?"

"We can, and if you're inviting Brittany she'll have to ask her daddy. He might have other plans for them."

"Great! Hey, Brit…" Emily called to the girl coming through the library doors. "Guess what? Mom's making pizza tonight. Want to come over?"

Brittany's face fell. "Can't, Em. I promised my dad I'd stay home with him. We're watching a movie."

Emily patted Brittany's shoulder. "You can invite him over, too. Mom won't mind."

"You mean it, Ms. Worth?" The child's eyes widened.

And see Jon again? "Sure, honey. If you like, you can call him from here." She pointed to the phone in her office behind the main counter. "Press eight for an outside line."

The girl made her call. Moments later, she came out. "Ms. Worth? He wants to talk to you."

Ah, well. He probably had the next month planned for his daughter. Could she blame him? She had told him to stay clear.

She took up the receiver. Through the office window, she watched the girls carry books across the library. "Hi."

"I hear my kid and I are invited for pizza." His voice rumbled through the line.

"Homemade. Mushrooms, pineapple, green peppers, ham, bacon."

"Deluxe, huh? My favorite."

"You'll come, then?"

"I've got a bunch of stuff to do tonight."

Disappointment fell, quick, sharp. "Would you do it if Brittany ate at home?"

A pause. "Probably not."

"I see. I'd like you to come, Jon. As a friend."

"A friend."

"Yes."

Silence stretched.

He said, "All right. I'll bring a video for the kids."

She shut her eyes. "See you at six."

"Six it is."

She hung up.

Her fingers pulsed from their wrenching grip on the phone.

He brought wine as well—a riesling blended with Oregon sunshine, apricots and peaches. When she asked how he'd guessed, he said it suited her. Looking into those blue, blue eyes while listening to the yammer of three kids around the table, she hoped her pizza suited him.

He wore a blue striped shirt and stone-washed jeans that made her eyes loiter. Secured by a leather band, his black hair caught the light. He'd shaved. And she wished she'd donned a skirt instead of crop pants.

When the meal was done, Sam said to her, "I'm going over to Joey's tonight."

Rianne sipped her wine. "Don't be late like you were last Friday."

"It was ten-thirty. Only a half hour over."

"Ten-forty."

Her son darted a look at Jon. "What's a few minutes?"

"A lot when you're the one waiting and worrying. Nine-thirty tonight, Sam. Not a minute more. Otherwise, you're grounded for two weeks."

"Two weeks! That's not fair."

"Neither is anxiety," Rianne said mildly.

Jon watched her son with a frown between his eyes.

"Anyway, can I go?" Sam checked the sunflower clock. "I promised Joey seven-fifteen and it's almost seven-thirty."

"Will Cody Huller be there tonight?"

Sam made a face. "Nah. Just me and Joe."

"Joe and I," she corrected. "All right. But first, put your plate in the dishwasher."

He leapt from the table. "Thanks, Mom."

"Have a good time."

"Yep."

The instant he was gone, Emily asked, "Can we go watch the movie now, Mom?"

"Sure. Why not?" She looked at Jon. So much for family dinners. So much for optimistic plans and relaxation. By rights, she couldn't complain. The girls had laughed. Talk had centered around school, her work, Jon's renovations. "Sorry," she told him. "We're not usually this scattered. I try to have our evening meals..." Giving up, she sagged back in her chair.

"Family-focused?"

She gave him a smile. "Yeah."

He reached across the table, covered her hand. "It was a fine meal, Rianne. I haven't enjoyed one as much in years."

"I should've planned something more nutritious."

"Pizza is highly nutritious. Think of all those food groups in one delicious four-inch slice. You're a terrific cook."

Esteem for the heart. "It's the company," she murmured.

He drew away to top off her glass. She wanted a return of his strong, warm hand.

"Cody Huller," Jon remarked. "He the boy Sam fought with?"

"Yes." She looked over her shoulder then whispered, "Except, I thought Sam and Joey were at odds, too. Seems to have worked out, though. Sam's been upbeat all week."

Jon winked. "Got a girl, I bet."

She sputtered. "I hope not."

"Now, Mama. Can't stop those hormones. How's the leg?"

"Great. He's hoping for a scar."

They both laughed. How she had missed this. Missed Jon.

"I want to thank you for driving Brit home from school this week, and for making her feel welcome. She thinks your kids are the best thing since buttered bread. It's—" he scratched a black brow "—it's made the adjustment damn smooth."

And you, Jon? How are you adjusting? Do you realize you're a good father, after all? A sincere, generous man? She rose, picked up their plates, and took them to the dishwasher.

"Rianne."

He'd come up behind her to set his hands on her shoulders.

"Don't," she said. Blood hurried at the feel of him on her skin. "Let's keep this night the way it started, fun and without any pressure." It's what he wanted, wasn't it?

"Hell." He sighed, resting his forehead on her hair. "I miss you. I miss talking with you. Touching you. This…" His mouth found her temple.

She stepped out of his hands. Her own trembled. "The dishes need to be loaded," she said, and set about doing just that.

They stored leftovers in the fridge, wheeled the portable dishwasher to the sink, hooked the machine's hose to the faucet, turned it on. Rianne reached for the coffeepot. Water burst like a geyser from the sink, and caught her full in the chest.

"Omigod! Ohh!"

Jon shoved her out of the way, rammed a towel into the blowhole where the faucet had been. Holding down the fabric, he shut off the tap.

"What—" she took a breath "—happened?"

He removed the soaked towel and peered into the decapitated spout. "Worn washer, I'd guess." Digging into the narrow barrel, he retrieved a small black ring. "Yep, completely ratched." He tossed it onto the counter. "You're soaked."

She looked down at her blue top clinging like a bedraggled shower cap, the capris sporting big, wet flecks. "Great. I'm a sight for sore eyes."

His lips hitched. "Won't disagree there."

"Look who's talking." She eyed his splattered clothes. Within seconds they were laughing.

"Talk about unforgettable meals," Rianne said, heading for the mop in the broom closet. "This one was an absolute blast."

He caught her waist. Planted a quick kiss on her mouth. "Enough puns from the peanut gallery."

"Jon," she said, softly. "I *am* glad you're here."

His eyes darkened. "Me, too."

They stepped apart, subdued.

Soon, the kitchen looked normal again. He changed the washer with an extra she had in a junk drawer; she changed into fresh pants and a sweater. While she mopped the floor, he put on coffee. Simple, shared companionship. That family thing again.

She wouldn't think about it.

When the dishwasher chugged normally, she suggested

they take their mugs outside. The coffee was hot, strong, superb for quiet evenings.

With Jon.

She sat on the cushioned wicker bench along the wall of the house. Sweetpea, escaping her brood, hopped to Rianne's lap. Jon lowered himself beside her, hunching forward, cup cradled between his hands. She observed the line of his shoulders. Compelling shoulders. Authoritative. At his ear the silver stud glinted. A star. She recalled mouthing lobe and all when…

Stop.

Dusk fell fast. "How's Brittany like Chinook?" she asked.

"Loves it. She loves all of Misty River." He looked into his coffee. "I took her to see my mother."

Rianne had figured as much when the girl had asked Emily to share Maxine's cake. "How'd it go?"

"Ma's pleased as punch. Brit thinks she's the ideal grandma." He hiked a big shoulder. "Probably a novelty."

"Possibly. Though kids are funny that way. They sense things we, with our adult logic, no longer can."

"Guess time will tell. I want so much for her. Things I didn't do for Nicky."

"I can tell you this," Rianne said. "Brittany loves you—and her new home."

Snorting softly, he gazed at the Victorian. "Home. Is that what it is? All those empty rooms?" He slanted her a look. "We should trade houses. You'd fill them better than me."

We'd fill them better together. In his eyes, sadness. She said, "Brittany will make it a home."

His mouth kicked up at the corner. "She's already begun. Tells me I need new curtains and pictures. And more plants."

She returned the smile. "There you go."

"Huh." After a while, he said, "You have great kids. Special."

"Yes. They are. I'd always hoped for four." It seemed right, letting him see this dream she had cached for a lifetime. "Two boys, two girls." *With the right man.*

"Me, too. I figured a family of six around the supper table would've been perfect."

They sipped in silence. Light faded to charcoal, smudging shadows and shapes. Among her flowers, an insect chafed. Beyond the hedges, a nightbird trilled. The crisp evening air was fraught with lilac blossoms, juniper, earth. She could have tarried here for an eternity. With him. Under the stars.

Before fixing the faucet, he had rolled back his sleeves. She touched the wolf tattoo, intrigued. "When did you get this?"

"About two years after I joined the force."

"What's it stand for?"

"A nickname I got in high school."

"Which is?"

"Wolf." Over his shoulder, she caught his amusement. "Nothing too complex."

"Why Wolf?"

"I was good at chasing down the opponent in football. And later in crime."

"I never heard a thing that night in the garden." Warm skin. The tip of her finger tingled. "I like you watching over me."

"And I like watching over you." He was doing it now. Watching her. "I like your home, too. I feel comfortable in it. It may be old, but it's cozy."

"It's not the house, Jon."

Leaning back, he stretched his long legs. "I know." He rolled his head toward her. "It's you. And your kids."

Bronze slashed the angles of his face. His Byronic mouth hovered close. She could feel its heat. Taste breath spiced with coffee. His eyes reflected night and intimacy. Shoving off the cat, she went to the railing. A susurrus breeze sifted through the dark trees beyond.

"It won't go away, Rianne, this wanting between us."

Setting her cup on the railing, she faced him. For all the world, he looked relaxed, unconcerned. Maybe he was. "Yes," she said. "It will go away. It'll have to. I told you before, I won't make this some kind of—of charade."

He pushed slowly to his feet. "No one's asking you to." The words were hushed, like the night. "I was merely stating a fact."

"One neither of us needs reminding of." Exasperated, she pressed three fingers to her forehead. "Look, Jon. Let it go, okay? We've each made our choices so just…leave it be."

He lifted a hand to her hair. "I'm sorry."

"No." She jerked away and rushed down the steps. If her heart ached before, now it stung. What they'd shared that rainy morning encompassed dignity, joy. Not apology.

Her feet whispered over the grass. Blindly wiping at her silly, watery eyes, she reached the fringe of her yard. The woods welcomed her; his hand closing on her elbow stopped her.

"Let me go."

"Never." His arms closed around her. "Dammit, Rianne." Against her temple she felt warm puffs of air. He'd run.

"I can't deal with this, Jon. You make it too difficult."

"I know." His voice was rough as burlap. "I'll try harder."

"Trying allows mistakes. I don't want us to be a—" His mouth took hers.

Sensation. It streamed through her blood. She cupped his shoulders, raised on her toes, recognized his hardness.

He found her breast. Cool air swam up her skin. She might have shivered if not for his energetic mouth, his active fingers.

The tree pressed her back; its bark scraped the fabric of her clothes. His hands were in her waistband.

"Here," he grated. "Right here."

The words cleared mist.

She pushed at his shoulders. "Stop, Jon."

Instant release.

"God, Ri, I didn't mean…" Chest heaving.

She righted her slacks. "It's not that."

"Then what?"

"Trust."

He was silent. Their eyes held. "You don't trust me."

Oh, the hurt in his voice. "You know I do. I've always trusted you. In this. In everything. But you don't trust *me*."

"That's ridiculous."

"Is it? Jon, unless you open the door and let me in, let *us* heal each other's warts and scars, all we're doing is dancing around the issue."

He looked away.

"It's not enough for me anymore," she said quietly. "I'll bring Brittany home when the movie is done."

"You sure we should do this?" Sam asked Joey when they stood at the edge of the riverbank, surveying the broken down cabin. "What if old man Marshall or Cody's dad catches us?"

"They won't," Joey assured him. Last night, he and Joey had talked it through in his friend's bedroom. Simple plan: They would bike to Franklin's Mill, sneak through the window of the cabin and snitch a couple small bags of grass for themselves. Joey figured they should bring their knapsacks loaded with textbooks as if they were going to the library to study. It had fooled both their mothers. Now, they stood in front of the paneless window.

What if Huller's dad *did* catch them? Sam recalled the jerk hassling his mother at the video store. A has-been wrestler smelling like last week's roadkill.

His mother—who Sam himself outstretched these days by a good four inches—had taken him on. She'd stood toe-to-toe with the revolting worm and not backed down. The courage he'd seen in her eyes was something else. Huller's dad had taken a back seat that day, the pig. The memory almost turned Sam away.

"It's three o'clock, Samson," Joey interrupted. Dropping his knapsack, he swung a leg over the window ledge. "On a Thursday old man Huller's probably in the welfare line again. 'Sides Code said we could get some anytime we wanted."

"Right." Sam watched his pal disappear into the house. He glanced over his shoulder. Nothing disturbed the quiet of the day. Leaning through the window, he called out, "Heard the cops found the Trans-Am in a ditch ten miles this side of Portland." He wondered if the cops were dusting the vehicle for fingerprints this minute. He tried not to panic. Kids didn't go to jail. And who'd recognize his prints anyway?

Something banged against the wall inside the house. Joey reappeared holding two tiny plastic bags. "Voila."

Sam took his share and rammed it into his bookpack. "Think old man Huller'll miss it?"

"If he does, Code'll explain for us."

Sam didn't trust Cody. Heck, he didn't trust *being* here, doing this dope scene. If it wasn't for Joey… And where was Cody? Since last week he hadn't been around. Sam chewed the corner of his lip. "My mom found out? I'd be grounded for life."

"Me, too." Joey grinned and shrugged. "Except they're never gonna find out, so no sweat, right?"

Sam hoped. Saying nothing, he climbed on his bike. All the way home he envisioned old man Huller's hot-dog-sized fingers curling over the edge of the car door and his mom in the driver's seat, her face inches away.

Under the blankets the next night, Sam listened to the dark settle around him. He should go across the hall, into the sewing room and tell his mom about the Trans-Am.

He shuddered at the thought of the consequences. What would happen if people found out he tattled? Would his mom tell Joey's parents? Geez, Joey would freak. Cody would go ballistic. And then the whole school would be looking at Sam like he was a freak *and* a ratter.

But, man, if he didn't tell someone, he'd go crazy. Already he'd lost a week's sleep thinking about fingerprints and drug-sniffing dogs and jail. *Could* they send him to jail? A juvie center for sure. He'd heard stories about those places.

Shivering, he pulled the blanket to his chin, scared worse than when his dad had been alive.

He had to tell his mom. There was no one else. No one who'd be on his side the way Mom would. She'd hate what he'd done, but she'd stick by him, that much he knew. And she'd know what to do.

Throwing back the covers, he planted his feet on the lino-leum. Through the dark, the door of his bedroom beckoned. *Do it.*

He stood, padded over and wrapped his hand around the cool metal of the doorknob.

He had to chance it.

Because, no matter what Joey said, Sam didn't trust Cody to keep his mouth shut.

Rianne gaped at her pajama-clad son, standing in her sewing room. "You did what?"

"I said—"

"I heard what you said, Sam. A week ago you broke into a car, then went…*joyriding all over town?* My God, what on earth were you *thinking?* You could have been arrested. *Killed.* That Huller boy could have crashed the car into a tree. You could've…could've…"

She was shaking. Her hands clamped the sewing table

where she'd been mending after Sam had come home and gone to bed, *this* Friday night.

Images rolled through her mind. Sam and the Fraser boy. Spending most of this week together. What else had they done? Where did they go after school? Had the Huller boy been with them? Thank goodness, Emily had fallen asleep over an hour ago.

"I thought you didn't like the Huller boy." She observed her son's hound-dog eyes.

"I don't."

"Then why—"

"I don't *know*," he wailed. "It was stupid. Going with Cody was wrong. 'Specially after the fight." He looked up, eyes pained. "But Joey kept hanging out with him and I didn't know why and, well, I—I wanted Joey to be my friend again."

She softened. "So you figured it was easier to tag along than to give Joey up completely. Oh, Sam, that's not what friendships are about."

"I know, but I couldn't help it." He palmed his nose. "Joey's been my best friend since we moved here. And—and it's hard making friends in new places. Most kids who don't know me—" He looked away. "I see them staring."

"Oh, baby." She went to him and took the very hand that had caused him such angst in his short life. "You're a wonderful boy, Sam. A mother couldn't ask for better. However, going along with Cody in a stolen car was also against the law."

"I know. I'm sorry."

She took his face in her hands so there was no mistaking the nature of her words. "Tomorrow morning we're going down to the police department. You'll explain what happened."

"Mo-*om!*"

She held fast. "And apologize to the owner of that car."

Distress bleached his face. "What if they throw me in jail?"

"They won't. Technically you didn't steal the car, but you were an accessory to the crime." She pushed a stray strand off his brow. "Likely you'll do some community service for it."

"Mom, I'm scared. Please don't do this. I promise I'll never, ever talk to Cody again. I'll never, ever come *near* anyone's car again except our own. I'll take *years* of counseling. Ground me till I graduate. Please, please. Don't *do* this."

Rianne pulled her son's forehead to hers. Exhaustion. In her spine. In her soul. "Honey, I can't ignore what you've done. It involves the law."

"But if I go to the police, it'll mean bringing Joey's name in." His brown eyes despaired. "He'll hate me forever after this. We're just, y'know, getting to be close again."

She kissed his still-smooth cheek and let him go. "He may surprise you."

"He'll kill me."

"No, he won't, and if he holds it against you, then he was never your friend to begin with. Now, get some sleep. We'll talk more tomorrow."

He shuffled to the doorway.

"Sam?" *Why did you tell me?*

He turned. Dark hair skirted his chin. Rianne's breath caught. *He's becoming a man,* she thought with a small pang. "I'm proud of you for coming forward."

"Don't tell Jon, okay?"

She hesitated. "He might be able to help us. As a former policeman he'd know—"

"No! He'll just start raving, like Dad used to."

Jon? Raving? "Sam, I think—"

"Mom, trust me in this. He's not what you think. I *know.*"

She came forward, a chill on her spine. "What do you know, Sam?"

"Nuthin'."

"Samuel."

"Okay." He flung up his head. His look didn't waver. "He's a bully. He likes ordering people around and squashing them under his boot like they're…they're dirt."

This was not the Jon she knew. But then Duane hadn't been the man she'd known before they married, either.

"Look," Sam said, when he saw she wasn't convinced. "I don't want to talk about it, okay? Just promise you won't tell him."

They regarded each other for a long moment. She'd get to the bottom of this if it took her all night. "All right," she said. "We'll table it for now. But you are still going to the police tomorrow."

Nodding, he slipped from the room.

Rianne went back to her sewing table and sank onto the chair. Stolen cars? Joyriding? Jon a bully? What was going on? Was she losing it as a mother? Couldn't keep track of the whats, wheres, whens of her children?

She pressed her fingers to her eyes. She'd come here for a new start. Well, rocky or bumpy, she wasn't giving it up. Home meant Misty River. Home meant happiness and love. Protection.

Tonight the car situation could wait.

Jon could not.

She hadn't seen him since their pizza night. She imagined his reaction to Sam's escapade. He'd be disappointed, but for the life of her she couldn't see him ranting or shouting or humiliating Sam. No, Jon would insist on driving them downtown, to the police station. Standing by their side. Offering support in every way. And possibly talking to Sam about the right and wrong sides of the law—a lesson, it seemed, she'd missed somewhere along the way.

She picked up the phone.

* * *

Stretched out on the couch in his living room and slumbering through NBC's late-night news, Jon grabbed up the phone on its first ring. "H'lo."

"It's me," she said.

He drew up and off the cushions. "Hey."

"Sorry to wake you."

"You didn't. I was watching TV." *And dreaming of you.*

"Jon, I'm not sure how to ask this, but did something happen between you and Sam? Like an argument?"

He came completely alert. "No, why?"

Her sigh came softly into his ear. "I had a chat with him tonight about something and he gave me the impression you two aren't…on speaking terms."

"First I knew of it. What did he say?"

"He's clamming up. I thought you might know more. When was the last time you talked to him?"

Jon palmed his face. "At your house, I think. The night Brit and I were over. But Sam and I never really talked. He…" Had given Jon a brush-off. The boy hadn't responded to one question without mumbling a monosyllabic answer and he hadn't looked Jon in the eye during the entire meal. "I think Sam might have been a little jealous of Brittany and was giving me the cold shoulder because of it. Don't worry about it. He'll come around."

"I don't think that's it." Stress made her words ragged.

Jon stood. "What exactly did he say, Rianne?" Her pause had cold fingers tripping up his back.

"That you're a bully. That you like ordering people around."

He stared at the TV, not registering a word of its babble.

"He… He was very serious."

Into the kitchen Jon went, and out the back door. In the darkness he breathed a little easier. A light glowed from her sewing room. He wondered if she sat there. "Do you think he saw us in the woods that night, when we…when I…" *Rammed you against a tree.*

"No," she assured him quickly. "He'd gone to Joey's by then."

A cricket sang a monotone melody. The Big Dipper poured stars. He wanted to ask her to come over, or open the curtain.

"Jon?"

"Yeah?"

"You didn't do anything wrong that night."

"I broke your heart, Rianne."

"I'll get over it. G'night."

The phone clicked in his ear.

He sat on the porch steps until the cold drove him inside.

Chapter Fourteen

Jon took his first sip of morning coffee and scowled when the liquid seared his tongue. Terrific. The weekend was beginning the way the week had ended. Foul.

Got only yourself to blame. He rubbed his unshaven cheeks and padded barefoot to the window. Dawn shrouded Rianne's cottage in a foggy, mellow pink. Her bedroom window remained dark. He imagined her there, warm and soft in sleep.

He turned from the promise of day.

All night he'd thought of her call. Her worry about Sam and her sign-off ran a maze in his head until he'd tossed back the covers an hour ago and realized it all was for the best. Sam refusing his friendship, Rianne closing their relationship.

No strings. No chance for screw-ups.

Except he hadn't factored in his feelings, this need.

Rianne. Friend, lover.

He wanted to share life with her. He wanted to divide and

conquer worries and doubts with her, exalt in joys and hopes with her. He wanted secrets with her. Dreams. Soul-deep stirrings.

To build routines, habits. Who cooked supper tonight? Who got the groceries Saturday? Who helped the kids with their homework Thursday?

Rianne. His heart would savor her smile until he died.

He pushed from the counter, sloshing coffee onto his hand. He cursed the burn. What kind of man mooned over a woman, then held her at arm's length?

His gaze fell on a sheet of loose-leaf paper on the table. Brittany's summary of *A Wrinkle in Time*.

"Check my spelling, Dad," she'd said last night. He set down the mug, picked up the page. A glance told him she'd already completed the corrections.

Kid was committed.

He tossed his coffee down the sink. He could learn from her.

"Let me get this straight." Chief Willard leaned back in his chair and jammed his thick, bristly eyebrows together. "You stole Pete Rolston's car and drove it to Franklin's Mill?"

"No!" Sam countered. Rianne knotted her hands in her lap, curtailing the need to touch his arm. Bill Fraser, who'd taken this Monday morning off work, sat grim-faced beside Joey. "I mean," Sam continued, "Joey and I didn't steal the car. Cody Huller did. He hot-wired it. He drove it off the parking lot."

"That's when you jumped in with him," Willard pressed.

"Yeah. The owner started running after us and we—we got scared." Sam glanced at Joey sitting rock-still. Rianne knew the boy blamed her son for breaking a trust, albeit an illicit one, between them.

The chief snorted. "I imagine you did. Go on."

"We tried telling Cody not to steal it, but he…" another look at Joey "…well, he wouldn't listen."

"But you went along anyway."

Sam hung his head. "Yeah," he whispered.

"Where'd you guys drive to?"

"The old mill. We…um, just drove around there, then came back to town." Rianne saw Joey and Sam exchange a look. A niggle ran under her skin. "Cody wanted to drive to Portland but Joey and I… We'd get in trouble if we weren't home on time, so he dropped us off at the high school. We walked home from there."

"So you don't know what happened to the car after that?"

"No, sir."

"Why did you guys go to Franklin's Mill?"

Joey glared at the man behind the desk. "We didn't do anything wrong."

Willard narrowed his eyes. "Was I talking to you, boy?"

"No, but you're grilling Sam like he did something wrong."

"Ah, you think car stealing is okay."

Bill Fraser shifted in his seat. "Of course he doesn't, Chief." He stared hard at Joey. "What Joey meant was he didn't do anything destructive at the mill."

"We were just having some fun," Joey mumbled, slouching in the chair, cheeks red.

"Well," Willard huffed. "We'll see if jail's fun."

"Now, Chief—" Bill began.

Oh, God. What a mess. Rianne envisioned months of court time, piles of legal expenses they couldn't afford. Their name a scandal throughout the community and schools. Emily would revert to sleeping with her blankey and Sam would begin hiding his hand again, all to ward off the whispers, the pitying looks, the well-meaning comments. She knew the routine. And hated it.

What was Willard saying? "…costing the department a bushel of time and money, so I don't want you kids going anywhere—*anywhere,* you hear?" He rose. "Now, go sit on that bench in the hall. I need to speak with your folks."

Sam sat on one end, Joey on the other while their parents got the works: *rotten little weasels, bad boys, no-accounts, thugs, dirt-for-brains.* Like Sam's dad, Willard wore the same uniform. Geez, when the kids at school heard about this…

Sam wished he could crawl in a closet and never come out. He wished he'd never told his mother. He wished he could turn back time so he had the chance to change his mind about going to Joey's house, about telling him what he'd done and seeing the betrayal in his friend's eyes and the disgust that followed. He wished for a thousand things, none of them possible.

"Rat," Joey spat. *Here it comes.* "Why'd you tattle? Know what you started? Cody's gonna get hauled in, tell everything and then we'll be dead meat."

Sam looked at Joey, and, for the first time, thanked his dad for having been a policeman. "Are you stupid? You think they wouldn't have fingerprinted the car? I'd rather be up front and admit it, than have the cops thinking we had something to hide. Think they're ticked now? Picture them after wasting three months investigating and *then* catching us?"

Their eyes held. Sam could tell his logic was churning wheels in his friend's mind. Joey covered his face with his hands. "Geez, I wish we'd never gone up town that night."

Sam breathed easier. "Me either."

"Thanks for not saying anything about…you know…" Joey whispered.

"I'm not a complete idiot, Fraser."

They leaned against the wall in silence.

Sam said, "I want to take it back, but I'm grounded for two months."

"Yeah," Joey replied. "Same here."

Sam hoped no one found out. That would be the worst, everyone in school knowing. Voices behind Willard's closed door murmured nonstop. He wondered if his mom was taking a back seat to the chief or giving him the what-for.

The door opened and Sam's mother stalked through. A storm-faced Mr. Fraser followed.

"What is it?" Sam asked, rushing after his mom and out into the sunshine. Her face said it'd been a no-win situation in there.

"We need a lawyer."

"A lawyer? Mom, we can't afford a lawyer!" Panic, pure and deep ran through Sam's chest. "What did the chief say?"

Mr. Fraser unlocked the passenger door of his car. Mom's eyes calmed a little. "Willard wants charges against you boys."

"What?" they cried.

Mr. Fraser held open the door. "For theft and destruction of property. The car has three thousand dollars in damage."

"But…" Joey stammered. "It was fine when we left Cody."

"Not when the police found it the next morning." His father's tone ended all protests. "It's a wonder your *pal* didn't split his head open."

Jon rode the Harley out to Franklin's Mill ten minutes after he dropped Brittany and Emily off at school. Rain had fallen during the night and the trail through the woods lay wet and gooey. A flock of crows hit the sky in a flap of wings when he rumbled into the clearing. He cut the engine. The silence stung. Walking swiftly, he crossed to the path leading to the second, smaller clearing beyond the stand of evergreens. The crop sparkled, an emerald jewel, in sunshine and raindrops.

Inside the cabin he found the stash. Sacks of it. In the cellar, he found crates. He opened three. Guns. Rugers. AK-47s. Glocks. M-16s. He rode home in a rage.

Sergeant Lowe of the Oregon State Police Drug Enforcement and Arson/Explosive Sections wrote down every word Jon spoke, then thanked him for the information.

Two days later, the clatter of a bike falling to the ground in Rianne's backyard caught his attention. Sam home for lunch? A little unusual considering it was one of Rianne's work days. When she taught, the kids never came home at noon.

Unless it was an emergency.

Don't think about it.

Taking another swig of his bottled water, Jon stretched his legs where he sat, taking a break, on the top step of his back porch. A breeze rattled the leaves and cooled his sweaty skin.

A door slammed.

Quick lunch.

Feet drummed across wood. Or had Sam forgotten something? Jon contemplated intercepting the boy just to get a read on him. What had the kid meant telling his mother Jon was a bully?

Metal clanked in the garden shed. A lot of metal.

What was he up to?

Setting the water aside, Jon debated, then slid from the steps. He'd go see if the boy needed some help. Maybe he required tools for a school project.

The garden shed stood open. He headed for the little building. "Sam?"

No answer. Where had the kid gone so fast?

Jon scanned the yard, the woods. A patch of white slipped among the trees and vanished. He strode toward it and entered the cool shaded path on silent feet. Instinct told him not to startle the boy, or let him know he wasn't alone.

Rianne's property line stopped at a small creek that wound a trickle of water through alders, birch and several firs. Jon watched as Sam, a small spade in one hand, checked his surroundings, then skipped over to the other side. Ten feet from the creek, the boy dug the shovel into the spongy earth. With each toss of loam, another hair rose on Jon's neck. The kid was about to lay something down.

Please, don't let it be what I think. Heart two-stepping on his ribs, he watched Sam reach into his pocket, pull out a small bundle and drop it into the hole at his feet.

Twenty feet separated them. Jon calculated the distance to the next rise. Without a sound, he stepped away from the shield of trees and walked across the creek bed.

Sam's head whipped around. His jaw fell. In the next instant, Jon had him by the shoulder. "Digging for gold, Sam?"

The kid struggled. "Let me go! You're trespassing!"

Without releasing his grip, Jon bent and snatched the packet out of the hole. "First off, we're standing on *my* property. Second, possession of an illegal substance is an offense."

"I'm not keeping it," Sam said, eyes hot. "I'm trashing it."

"Uh-huh. That's what they all say."

"It's true!"

"Where'd you get it?"

"None of your business."

Jon pushed back his ball cap and ignored a wave of frustration at Sam's belligerence. *Shades of Nicky.* "Anything on my property, Sam, *is* my business."

"I can't tell. I'll…I'll get in trouble."

"You're in trouble now, boy. Pot's illegal."

Sam rolled his eyes. "I'm not stupid."

Jon tossed the bag gently in his hand. Couple grams. "No? Then what's this? Smart? What do you think your mom's going to say when she finds out her son does drugs."

"I don't! And…" Tears glimmered. "And she's not gonna find out. I told you I'm getting rid of it."

Jon contemplated arguing; he'd done that with Nicky. It hadn't gotten him anywhere. Now, for some reason, this son of Rianne's had gone to the same dark side. Sweat tickled his temples. "All right," he said slowly. "I'll give you the benefit of the doubt. But you will tell your mother about this."

"No, she'll—" He stared at his feet.

Jon studied the teenager's white face. "Sam," Jon said. "What's going on here?"

"I stole a car, okay? I mean, *I* didn't, Cody did and then Joey and I took these bags and the police are gonna charge us for damaging the car and now my mom needs a lawyer we can't afford and I need to get rid—"

"Hold it. Slow down and start from the beginning."

The boy did.

All this in ten days, Jon thought when Sam had finished. Nicky had died in less than thirty minutes. Life-then-death minutes.

"So," he said, feeling his pulse in his throat, "you thought smoking pot would win friends?"

The boy shrugged.

The forest settled around them. Long ago, Jon had learned waiting provided better results than prodding.

Sam scuffed a toe in the dirt. "You acted like my father. I didn't like it."

Jon's breath shallowed. Quietly, he said, "I've never laid an angry hand on you."

"You ordered me to do my homework like I was…was scum or something."

Orders. Again. "When?"

"Couple of weeks ago."

"Get to the point, lad. A lot's happened since then." He'd brought Brit home. Stalemated with Rianne. Lost his heart.

Sam raised his head. Defiance and tears glossed his eyes. "I came over to ask if I could ride on your Harley."

Jon listened, his mind trekking back through the minutes the boy described. Had he been *that* blunt, that unfeeling? *"He doesn't take well to commands."* Rianne's words at the hospital.

It all fit now. A handful of words, flying from the mouth. Routinely, he told Brit to do her homework. And clean up her room. Take out the trash. Help with the dishes. Was that...ordering?

Except, Brit wasn't Sam. She'd never felt or seen what Sam had. Jon's tone, his words, wouldn't have the same effect on her.

The boy's eyes told him again about Duane Kirby's abuse.

Staring at Sam's pinched face, Jon understood. In a way he'd betrayed the kid and the boy had retaliated. Gotten even for a past over which Jon had no control.

"I'm sorry, Sam, for making you think I was brushing you off, but this—" he held out the packet "—this is not how you deal with anger." *Or hurt feelings.* Nicky had spent years warding off the emotional morass of having a father yoked to his work, a father remarkable at brush-offs.

"Tonight, after school, you'll tell your mother." He held up a hand at Sam's stutter. "She's a strong woman. She won't cave. And I'll wager my Harley she'd rather know and help, son, than not know and see you flounder."

He turned and walked back to his house where he flushed the marijuana down the toilet.

Fifteen minutes later, Jon opened the door to Luke. Another down-and-dirty moment. They were piling up about as fast as the laundry in his hamper.

"Soup's on," he said, gesturing toward the kitchen.

"Already ate." Luke strode past. "This better be important, J.T. I cancelled a hundred-dollar appointment to come over here."

Jon closed the door. *Okay.*

In the kitchen, Luke lifted the lid of the tureen. "Vegetable, right?"

"Chicken vegetable."

"Huh. Maybe I will have some."

Jon got out two bowls, two spoons.

Luke ate leaning against the counter. Jon talked.

"I should have taken care of it right then," he said when he was done telling all Sam had relayed, all he, himself, had done. "Should've called the OSP when Willard shrugged it off." But he'd wanted to get the facts straight and organize a setup to catch Marshall and Huller in the act so he'd have proof. He'd sat in those woods four mornings last week, after Brittany had left for school. Watching. Doing what the state troopers, had they known, would have done.

But no.

He'd couldn't resist the rush. Pro-active stress, they called it. A policeman's high. Hell. Law enforcement wasn't his gig anymore. *Not-a-Cop.* It couldn't get any clearer.

Luke set aside the bowl and gripped the edges of the counter. The posture splayed the panels of his expensive navy jacket and exposed the stark, white shirt beneath. He looked what he was—a man confident in his own right, in his own skin.

It struck Jon that here, too, was more than he'd confessed: a deep abiding love for this brother.

"Wasn't your fault," Luke told him.

Jon sighed. *If you say so.* "I called the OSP Monday." Had he done it ten minutes after his first session with Willard, Sam might have been spared temptation.

Dammit to hell.

Rianne, Sam, Brittany, Emily. He'd let them all down. He swore, brutal enough to make Luke's eyebrows curve high.

"Take it easy, J.T. It's in the hands of the OSP now. Marshall and Huller live in town, but the state troopers will be looking at Willard. It's the job of the Misty River Police Department to check the residences of suspects."

Nothing new to Jon. So was Willard skimming a cut? The question had tripped through his mind more than once.

Dammit, his brothers were right. Misty River needed a new chief. Maybe he should give the position honest thought. He had a mess more investigatory experience than anyone in Willard's office.

He said, "What can you do for Rianne and her boy?"

"I'll talk to the Deputy DA. Sam and the Fraser boy likely will get some community service hours plus a curfew. Willard can threaten all he wants. Bottom line is Sam and Fraser weren't involved in the damage of the car. No juvie judge will send them to a detention facility for joyriding." He looked square at Jon. "You've got my word on it."

"And the dope?" Jon held his brother's eyes.

"Where's the evidence?"

Jon nodded. "Thanks, man."

"Just keep the kid on the straight and narrow," Luke said.

He could do that. Already an idea had rooted. "What about the Huller boy?" That one was bad news all around.

Luke shrugged. "Can't say. This is his fourth offense. Priors indicate shoplifting, tire-slashing, arson in a Dumpster." He pursed his lips. "Could end up at Tillamook YAC."

Youth Accountability Camp. A boot camp. Good place for the kid. Jon's shoulders slumped with relief. He jotted Rianne's number on a slip of paper and handed it to Luke. "Call her. If you need cash, let me know, but keep it between us."

He'd fork over next year's pension quota to help Rianne and her kids. Hell, he'd sell this house to keep her in the black.

"It'll be pro bono," Luke said, slipping the paper into a pocket. He regarded Jon. "You really care for her."

"Yeah. Yeah, I do."

"Going to do something about it?"

He hunched a shoulder. He'd messed up with Rianne and Sam same as with Colleen and Nicky. "We've come to an agreement."

"I'll bet. She stays on her side of the fence, you on yours. That about it?"

Tension slid back. "Let it lie."

"Good way to keep the sheets cold," Luke continued.

"I said butt out."

Luke pushed off the counter. Jon waited for his snappy retort, but his brother set the bowl in the sink and headed for the door. "See you Saturday."

Saturday. He'd nearly forgotten. He'd invited Luke, Seth and his daughter, Hallie, for a pot of chili so Brittany could meet the family. He was picking up Maxine as well. Brittany's directive. The kid had more machinations up her sleeve than an alligator had teeth. In the upcoming months he'd be on his toes.

"Good. Brit's expecting you," he said with a father's pride.

Luke stopped, hand on the doorknob. "How's she fitting in with the Misty River kids?"

"Like toast and jam."

"Sounds perfect."

"She is."

"You missed her."

"More than I can say."

"You're a better man for moving her here, J.T."

"We'll see."

His brother pulled open the door.

"Luke? Thanks."

Luke clapped Jon's shoulder. "We'll get those bastards."

When the door closed, Jon regarded his silent living room. The giant lone fern, the barrenness.

"It's not the house, Jon."

She was right, of course. It was him. Always had been.

Through the afternoon, he tore off old clapboard and hammered up new. Another week for the exterior walls. Next was the roof. Then Seth excavating the driveway. Before summer bled into fall, the house would stand completed.

Ruthlessly, he kept thoughts of Rianne and her kids at bay. Remorse had no place while he was working his wood. Tools could claim a finger in a blink. *Sam,* he thought. *How are you, boy?*

A flash of red caught his eye. Rianne drove into her carport. Doors slammed. Brittany skipped into his yard.

"Hi, Dad!"

"Hey, punkin."

Hands on her hips, she looked up at him. "Whatcha doin'?"

"Re-siding the house. How was school?"

"Okay. I'm starving. Is there anything good to eat?"

"Check the fridge for some of that blueberry loaf we bought the other day."

"Want some, too?"

"Sure. I'll be down in a couple minutes."

She disappeared around the back of the house. Moments later, the radio blared rock. His baby. Ten and barreling into hormonal sixteen by the second.

Fleetingly, he caught sight of Rianne crossing her back deck. A rust-colored jumper did wonders to her pale arms, her copper hair. He returned to his work.

A white pickup turned up her lane and parked. *Now what?* Two men got out. One was pig-bellied, the other scarecrow skinny. Guys who flossed with mouse tails.

The old Victorian sat back fifteen feet farther than Rianne's cottage. Jon moved not a muscle. His cop's eye clicked into focus. That they were up to no good was a guarantee.

They stared at the cottage, talking low. Pig-belly spat on the ground, laughed softly. Scarecrow hunched his shoulders and started toward the carport. Jon tracked their voices past the Toyota and into the backyard.

There was Sam scooting up the driveway on his bike, tires skidding on the crushed gravel.

"Well, well," one man sneered. "Look who's come home just in time to catch the fun."

Stealthily, Jon moved across the scaffolding. A small V of winterkill at the top of the hedge's foliage allowed him to see the men in the yard. Sam was staring at them.

Scarecrow glanced at Pig. "Thought he'd be bigger."

"Naw, he's just a runt. A runt, a weasel an' a thief." Eyes beady, Pig stepped forward. "Ain'tcha, Claw-Man? You're nothing but a crippled little weasel."

Sam backed toward the hedge. "What do you want?"

"Gonna get even for what you did to my boy Cody."

Jon's eyes narrowed. Cody. This was his father?

"Gonna have us a nice little talk, right, Larry?"

Larry Marshall. Willard's protected. Were the OSP setting up surveillance at Franklin's Mill this minute?

"Yup, just a private little tea party." Marshall jerked his head toward the lane. "Get in the truck, kid."

"No way." Sam shook his head. "I'm not leaving here."

"Oh, yes, you are."

Quietly, Jon started down the scaffolding.

"Sam? What's going on?" Rianne called. "Mr. Huller?"

"Well, well. If it ain't mama bear. You know your kid's a dirty little rat and a thief? 'Course you do."

"Excuse me?"

"You deaf, lady? I said your kid ratted on my son and then he stole from us." Huller shoved two fingers in Sam's face. "Pay-up time, runt."

Marshall grabbed Sam. "Let's take it out of his hide."

"Don't you touch my son!" Rianne tripped down the steps as Jon came through the hedge's gap. "I mean it! Leave him alone."

Laughing, Huller caught her around the waist. "Now, ain't you just the itsy-bitsy hellcat. You always get this fired up around a man?"

"Get your hands off her," Jon said. *"Now."*

"Who're you?" Huller demanded. "You got no business here."

"Get your goddamn hands off her."

Huller shoved Rianne away, hard. She stumbled forward, into Jon. "You okay?" he asked, steadying her.

"I'm fine," she said, eyes enormous, face egg-pale.

Logic fled, a beast from its hunter. *"Leave."* The word hissed through Jon's teeth.

Marshall lifted his anvil-shaped chin. "Butt out, neighbor. We got dealings with the kid."

"You got nothing." The slime had touched Rianne and Sam.

Huller took a step toward him. "What's it gonna be, big man? Two against one?"

"If necessary."

"Take off your tool belt."

"You're on." Jon undid the buckle, flung the weighted girdle to the ground. After the week he'd had, he was ripe for a fight.

"Jon." Rianne clasped his arm. "It's not worth it."

"Stay back, Ri." His world held two men. One had put filthy hands on his woman and revived her poisoned memories.

Suddenly Marshall whipped down, grabbed up the belt and slung it at Jon. Wrenches, pliers, screwdrivers and two hammer heads met flesh and bone. He staggered under the onslaught.

"Daddy!" Brittany's voice cut through a stinging haze. "You're hurting my daddy!"

"Go back inside, peanut." Jon clutched his ribs.

Huller's fist connected with his jaw. Snapped his head back.

"Stop it!" Rianne rushed between the men.

"Not so tough now, are ya?" Huller taunted.

Blood in his mouth. Emily, crouching by the rails, chewing her pinky. Violence beat Jon's temples. "Move aside, Rianne."

"No! This has to stop." She pushed his chest and held up a hand, warding off his opponent. "Go home, Mr. Huller. Please."

The swine laughed. "Look at that, Larry. Got a woman fighting his battles. Yessir, a hellcat, all right. You want a real man, you come looking for me, little lady."

"Shut up." Sam barged in. "Leave my mom alone."

"No, you shut up, Claw-Kid." A meaty hand wrenched Sam's shoulder. The boy cried out.

That's it. Time's up. Jon slammed a vicious fist into Huller's face, another into his gut. The man toppled like an oil drum. Between his fingers, blood seeped from his nose.

Breath serrating his lungs, Jon loomed over Huller. He wanted to kill the son of a bitch. Mash him into pulp. Put him where he'd never set eyes on Rianne or her kids again.

Fisting a hand in the man's shirt, he hauled Brent Huller up so they were nose to broken nose. "Get off this property," he said softly. "If I ever see you within a hundred miles of this family or this house, *we'll* be talking. You and me. Got that?"

The man wheezed.

Jon thrust him away. "You, too." He jerked his head at Marshall, who jumped to the aid of his partner. Moments later, their truck roared away.

Rianne tended Sam's shoulder.

Jon asked, "You all right, son?"

"Yeah."

"Have Mom put some ice on that." He gathered up his tool belt. His rib cage creaked with pain. "Brit, do me a favor and run a warm bath for me, okay?"

The girl dashed off.

Rianne murmured to Sam; the boy nodded and took a solemn-faced Emily into the house. Jon limped toward the hedge.

"Jon, wait." Rianne hurried to where he stood. "Thank you for helping Sam. I think you've just become his superhero for life."

Jon's mouth twisted. "Don't have him looking up to me. I liked hitting that idiot. It soothed my ego."

"Your ego?"

"I found out about their little grow op the day I took you up to Franklin's. I saw it after you went back to the Harley." Self-disgust. It soured his mouth.

She stared at him. "But you reported it. Luke told me."

He shook his head. "Doesn't matter."

"Jon, you did what any man down the street would've done."

Not soon enough. "And it damned near got Sam hurt today," he exploded. "It damned near got *you* hurt."

"This had nothing to do with you, why can't you see that?" Tears in her russet eyes.

"Talk to your son. He has something to tell you." Turning, he limped through the hedge to his house.

In the shadows of her bedroom, Rianne leaned against the window frame and stared at the dark house next door. It was after 1:00 a.m. She had yet to sleep.

Jon and Sam. The two men in her life. Both strong, both vulnerable. One at a crossroads over his son, the other at a crossroads over his father. She'd done as Jon said. She'd talked to Sam tonight and he'd spilled the truth about what he had done.

"I smoked weed, Mom. I stole it and tried to bury it in Jon's backyard."

She hadn't cried. But tears rained in her heart. Sammy, her little boy no longer, but a young man she scarcely recognized. They had talked on his bed until ten minutes ago. Talked about Duane and Joey and Jon. In the end, Sam had cried and she'd held him, stroking his hair, channeling love from her heart to his. He was her baby, her child. This mistake, his choices, were forever lessons. She had Jon to thank for that.

Jon.

She saw him again as he'd been today. Black ponytail. Warrior's shoulders. His big body limping away.

Jon, vigilantly protective of her little family.

Resisting his own worth as a man and a father.

She moved from the window. He had taught her to believe in herself. To trust.

She crawled into bed.

Twenty years he'd been in her heart. An eternity in her soul. They were meant for each other.

But she could not tell him, could not help him with what he had to discover alone.

Chapter Fifteen

Jon collapsed into one of the Adirondack chairs he'd built for the back deck. Soft and warm, the air lay muted. A paint-stroke of moon colored the wall of night above the hills and Venus broke over the tip of a fir.

Perfect night. Perfect to sit back. Empty the mind.

Right. As if that'll ever happen. He took out his second cigar of the year.

For two weeks he'd tried voiding her from his head. Where had it got him? Sleep taxed with memories. Days rife with sightings of her and the kids. How was Sam taking his 8:00 p.m. curfew, his penalty? Luke had relayed the court's pro-ceedings to Jon moments after they had occurred. Judge Orly, the area's juvenile judge, had slapped Sam with four months of probation and three hours a week of community service, washing graffiti from businesses, picking up trash on Main Street and at the rec center, as well as plucking weeds from the flower beds of the Courthouse. Jobs no kid relished. Violating the penalty, Orly had warned, could land Sam in a detention center for six months. Rianne, Luke said, had gone white at that.

Jon blew a stream of acrid smoke. He had to sell the property. Move to the other side of town.

Wimp.

Dammit, breaking away is for her protection.

Wuss.

She deserves a man who can stand by her.

Cursing, he shot to his feet, pelted the cigar to the deck slats, and ground it out with the heel of his boot.

"Daddy?"

He lurched around. Brittany stood on the other side of the screen door. Tiny elf in baby-blue pajamas. "Hey, sweetheart. You about ready for bed?"

She stepped outside, letting the door squawk shut. "Can I sit out here with you for a bit? Tomorrow's Saturday…" Her voice trailed on a soft whine.

Though he was a stickler about her 9:00 p.m. bedtime, she had a point. "All right then. Get a blanket from the hall closet and put on your slippers. It's a bit chilly." He sat again. Maybe the evening wouldn't dawdle tonight.

Thirty seconds later, she crawled into his lap, snuggled her head under his chin. He tucked the blanket around her bony little shoulders, enfolded her feet, slippers and all. She felt wonderful in his arms. Small, fragile, *his.*

"Why are you sitting out here in the dark?" Her voice was muffled against the thick woolen fabric.

"Porch light attracts bugs."

"But why here? Why aren't you watching TV?"

"Guess I needed some quiet time."

"Do I make too much noise?"

He gave her a brief, tight hug. "Never. The house was too quiet before you came. Now it's home again."

"I want to live here forever, Daddy. I don't want to live with Allan and Mom."

"I want you to stay, too, honey, but we'll talk about that closer to the time, okay?"

"'Kay."

They absorbed the quiet, the night and its creature sounds. Brittany stirred. "Are you going to be police chief?"

His gut tightened. "Would it bother you if I did?"

"Are those men going to jail?"

After five days of investigation and surveillance, the OSP had arrested Marshall and Huller. They were scheduled for court Monday. "Already on the way, pint."

He hoped for a "hanging judge." Running dope and weapons warranted pen time.

Brittany raised her head. "I want you to be the chief, Dad. I liked it when you were a policeman before."

"You did?"

"Uh-huh. Nicky always said you were the best policeman in the whole world."

Astonishment. "He did?"

Brittany nestled her head back under his jaw, yawned mightily. "Didn't you know that?"

No, he hadn't. He'd believed his son resented the force for taking his father away so many nights.

She said, "He wanted to be a policeman, too."

"Now, Brit…"

"He did, Dad." She sat up. "Nicky always watched *Cops*. Ask Mom. She used to hate it, but he'd watch it, anyway. And he used to read cop books. He'd hide them in the back of his sock drawer because Mom would get mad if she knew. She didn't want him to be a policeman, ever."

Suddenly, Brittany scrambled from his knees. "Wait here, 'kay?" She ran into the house, blanket flying like a cape.

Two minutes later, she was back curled on him again, flashlight and paper in hand. "Read this."

He turned on the light. Shone it on the page covered with roundish handwriting. It was a poem. About him.

He read:

<u>My Dad the Cop</u>
by Nick Tucker
I am a cop.
I have hope.
I see things others don't.
I am a cop.
My world is hard.
But with simplest regard,
I make matters clear
And lessen furies people fear.
I am a cop.

Jon stared into the darkness. Heart thundering. Eyes stinging. His son. His Nicky. Willful dark hair. Lanky frame. Quick grin. Jon closed his eyes. *Oh, God, son. I didn't know.*

So… Why…? *Why?*

Brittany folded the page, put it into his pocket. "I found it in his sock drawer. You keep it, Dad."

Jon cleared his throat. "He really wrote this?"

"Uh-huh. He read it instead of a story one time. We talked lots when he read me stories." Down under his chin she went.

"About what?" Brother and sister. Hoarding little secrets.

"Like why he stayed out late. He wanted to see what the bad guys did at night. He was scared to tell you 'cause he thought you wanted him to be a doctor or something."

Or something. "Brit, you do know how he died, right?"

"Uh-huh. He took some stuff and got allergic." Again, she straightened, pixie brows scrunched. "Why'd he do that, Dad?"

"It's a puzzle to me, too, peanut. That's why—" he touched the shirt where the poem warmed his heart "—this is difficult for me to understand."

"No, it's not. Not really. Nicky loved cop stuff." Her eyes went blank for a moment as if she was sorting through an invisible, loaded file. "Maybe…" she said, "maybe he wanted to see what it felt like being a bad guy."

He went very still. *Nooo… Aw, please, God, no…* Of all the possibilities Jon had considered, this would have been the most hideous. His son dying because of a horribly cruel experiment?

"Brittany." His voice was ragged in his ears. "Do you know if Nick took drugs before that night?"

She shook her head, distress in her dear eyes.

Jon stroked her cheek. "It's okay, punkin, I'm not mad." His fingers drifted over her hair. "I just need to know, okay?"

"He never told me," she whispered. "I don't know, Daddy. Can we talk about something else now?"

"Sure." He pulled her down to his chest, held her close. "What did you and Emily do today?"

"Nuthin' much. Just listened to Avril Lavigne CDs and braided each other's hair. We're making friendship bracelets. She's making me a pink and purple and orange one. I'm making her a red and white and yellow one."

"Sounds pretty."

"Mmm. I wish Emily was my little sister."

His body jerked a little. "You do?"

"Uh-huh. It'd be fun 'cause we could talk about stuff, and we wouldn't have to have sleepovers 'cause we'd be right in the same house all the time."

"What if you had a disagreement?"

"You mean fight? Uh-uh. We never fight."

"You might."

Brittany tunneled deeper into him. "She doesn't like fighting. She said her dad used to do it with her mom. All the time. It was really bad sometimes."

He would not go there. What Emily told Brittany he'd leave between them. Simpler that way. "What about Sam?"

"Sam?"

"Sam comes with Emily."

"Mmm, he's okay, I guess. Emily says he's really a nice brother, and a brain in math. Maybe he could help me sometimes, like Nicky did."

A long-forgotten recollection. A smile surrounded his heart. "Yes, he could."

For several minutes they listened to the night. An owl hooted. In some far-off gully, a coyote yapped. Down the street, a car drove into a driveway. Next door, the cottage windows framed cozy amber. He envisioned it… Cats and kids stretched out on rug and sofa. Homework scattered. *You and me, Rianne, recounting the day over a quiet coffee on the glider I built Sunday—*

"Dad?"

"Yeah, honey."

"How come you never talk to Rianne no more?"

The name had him closing his eyes. "I talk to her."

"No, you don't. That day when those bad men came? You sort of got mad at her. How come?"

"I wasn't mad, honey."

"But it sounded like you didn't want to see her anymore and Rianne sounded like she was going to cry. I wanted to help, but… Don't you like her?"

He expelled a long sigh. "Yes. Yes, I do. Very, very much." *I'm crazy about her.*

Suddenly, something inside him bent. And he knew without a doubt he loved Rianne more than he'd loved any one being—kids aside—in his life. All their talk of affairs and non-commitments evanesced with that one fact. *Ah, Rianne.*

Brittany scratched his chin absently with a finger. "Then you should marry her."

"I…" The frankness of her logic stunned him. "If it was that simple, I would."

"You should. Anyways, our house is bigger than theirs." Eagerness lifted her voice. "We could all live together here and then Emily really would be my sister."

"Aw, honey…"

She cupped his cheeks in her small hands. "You could be Emily and Sam's daddy 'cause theirs is dead and you're such a cool dad and Ms. Worth could sorta be my pretend mom 'cause I already have one and—"

"Brit—"

"No, listen, Daddy. It'd be great. You won't have to be a half dad no more. Instead, you'd be a full dad again."

Half dad? Full dad? "Peanut, what are you taking about?"

"Sam and Emily."

"Sam and Emily?" he echoed, dumbfounded.

"Uh-huh. When Nicky was alive you were a full dad. But then he died, so you were a half dad, just like Mom is a half mom. But she's going to marry Allan and have babies with him, so she'll be a full mom again. If you marry Rianne you'll be a full dad again, too, 'cause Emily and Sam can be your kids." Grinning ear-to-ear, utterly pleased with herself, she bounced on his lap. "See?"

Not really. But he was trying.

"And anyways," his daughter went on, "you're already a great dad, so it'd be easy for you." She gave him a slapdash kiss on the mouth. "Isn't it awesome I'm so smart?"

* * *

Jon focused on aligning the wood to the saw's teeth. Its bite squealed into the hot, late-afternoon air.

You're already a great dad.

Lord, was Brit right?

Great dads got involved with their children.

He hadn't always been. Nicky's dreams told him that. Dreams his son hadn't shared with Jon. But somewhere along the line Nicky *had* idolized him, *had* wanted to be like him.

Somewhere along the line, Jon realized with a small shock, he had made a difference with his boy.

The saw whined on a second piece of wood as he remembered chucking the ball with Nicky, helping him assemble science projects, taking him to see a Seahawks game. And—grinning now—listening to Nicky beat those drums in the garage until Jon thought his ears might rupture.

Quality time, not quantity. Damn psychologists. They were right.

He laid the measured board between the sawhorses and scored a corner. *You're such a cool dad.* His hands shook. His gut dived. Rose-colored glasses or not, Brittany loved him and was committed to making him happy.

Committed. A charged contention. He'd argued it enough with Rianne, hadn't he?

Sweat tracked down his temples. He hoisted the plank to his shoulder, made his way to the scaffolding, climbed to the spot where he worked. Layer by layer his house was transforming into one he could live in for the rest of his life. If Brittany stayed, he might one day see grandchildren scampering up and down its stairs and chasing through the backyard.

Committed. The word grabbed and clung. Well, damn it, he *was* committed! To the house, to Brittany, to his life here. In the past, he'd been committed to his job, yes, but also to his marriage. To teaching Nicky right from wrong, loving his children, making a home where they could grow, be nourished, find their own wings. Good or bad, he'd given it his best shot.

Rianne was right. He'd done what any man would do, given the circumstances. He'd erred, but he'd also succeeded. Brittany was proof. She was his triumph, his victory. She was what made life valuable, significant. He could succeed with Sam, too, and Emily; he'd help them grow into loving, dependable adults able to meet whatever left turn the roads of tomorrow flung out.

He stood quiet, hammer half raised above a nail.

Slowly he turned, looked toward the cottage. Toward Rianne.

Commitment. Ongoing success. Home. Love. A thousand and one tomorrows.

She embraced it all. The full-meal deal.

Carefully, he leaned the plank against the house and, tool belt clunking on his hips, paced across the veranda, to his kitchen door. A soft meow whipped his head around.

Sweetpea—white paws curled under her chest—crouched where he had chucked his sweatshirt over the railing after lunch. His police-academy sweatshirt.

Jon shook his head, laughed. From the get-go, the cat claimed more sense than him.

"Oh, no, you found her on your property again?" Rianne looked from the man to the cat in his arms.

"Back porch, on my shirt."

"Jon, I'm so sorry. She must have slipped out with Sam when he went to Joey's." Rianne pushed open the screen door and reached for the feline, only to have Jon back away.

"Can we talk?"

Sam? Had something happened to Sam again? She looked toward the corner of the house.

"It's not Sam," he said, reading her worry clearly. "Come out here for a minute. Please."

She closed the door with a snick and stared up at him. Out in the sunlight, she saw it. The difference. "What happened…?"

He shifted his feet. "I woke up and smelled the coffee."

She covered her grin at his little-boy self-consciousness. "Oh, Jon." The striking knife-straight locks were gone, replaced by a frugal, styled-back cut that at once toughened and rejuvenated his face.

"Yeah, I know." He ran a hand around his shorn nape. "Can't help the farmer's tan."

She pinched her lips. "You'll definitely need sun block for a while."

"Huh." He looked at the Victorian. "Should've cut it long ago." Back to her. "Should've done a lot of things long ago."

"You weren't ready."

"Suppose not." He scratched Sweetpea's chin. "I've come to some decisions. I'd like your feelings on them."

"Sure." She shoved her chilled hands into her cotton hoody. "Shoot."

"First." He took two slips of paper from his pocket—her torn two-hundred-dollar check—and set them on the railing.

"I thought you…"

"Would cash it?" A slanted smile. Dazzling her. "If you did, you don't know me very well, Rianne." The smile faded. "Okay. Here's the deal." His Adam's apple shuffled. He checked the purring cat. Looked at the door, at her.

He was nervous, she realized. Unduly nervous. "What is it?" Her own heart bounded, a small caged creature.

"Willard has been asked to retire forthwith and I'm thinking of applying for the job. Brit and I had a long talk last night about Nicky and I know I can get this town back on the right track. I've already talked to Luke and Seth. They'll write recommendations if necessary." He plucked at his naked ear. "Misty River isn't the big city. The pace will be slower, and that's fine. Working twenty-four-seven isn't what I want anymore." His eyes pinned her. "What do you say?"

Is this what had him so worried? "You don't need my permission for what you want to do, Jon."

"Not permission, support. I'll need it if the second decision is to work."

"Second decision?"

"Do I have your support?"

"Of course," she said softly. "You would've had it with my heart's blessings, regardless. You'll be a wonderful police chief." She meant every word. Jon was an honorable man. Misty River would do well with him at its protective prow.

"Phew. Okay." A sheepish grin. "I wasn't altogether sure."

"Because of Duane."

"Something like that."

Unable to stay separated any longer, she closed the distance between them and laid her hand on his rough cheek. "At times, Jon Tucker, I'd like to rattle your teeth. I'll say this one last time for both of us, then it's done. You and my late husband are solar systems apart in behavior, in looks, in caring, in ten million subtle and not-so-subtle ways. There is *no* comparison."

His beloved eyes fastened on her face. "Good, that's good. I had to hear you say it." He stroked Sweetpea.

There was more, she could see. "Jon?"

"Next week I'd like to take Sam to a youth rehab center in Seattle. Have him talk to some of the kids there who've been serious drug users. I think if he hears their stories and what they had to overcome to gain back their lives, it'll help him make better choices in the future."

"Would you be willing to take Joey Fraser, as well?"

"If his parents agree, he's in."

"They will."

"Okay. All right. That's settled then." Tickling Sweetpea's chin, he continued, "Um…one more thing…"

"Yes?"

He massaged the back of his neck. "It's like this. If your cat likes to sleep at my place, I was thinking you might, too."

Her heart sank. "We've been through that."

"No, I mean legally."

"Legally?"

He stepped around her, opened the screen, tossed in the cat. His eyes were warm tropical seas. "I'm asking you to marry me, Rianne. I want us living in that old Victorian together, with our kids around the table at supper. I want to put my head on your pillow and you to put yours on mine. I want to share the shower and homemade pizza with you. Towels. The TV. The couch. Rainy days. Sunny days. And, God willing, one day our grandchildren." A tenuous smile. "What do you say?"

"I…"

He had her face in his rough, woodworker's hands. "I'm so in love with you. So, so much." He kissed her. A sweet gift. "I should've known what we have comes only once. Forgive me?"

Her heart bloomed, lush and beautiful, a peony in her chest. "There is nothing to forgive, Jon."

"Will you?"

The wobble in his voice sent her arms around his neck, her face against his throat. Ah, the flavor of his skin. Wind and sun and Jon. His mouth. His taste. *Her* Jon.

They drew apart. His hard-hewn face, so cherished she could barely stand it.

"I take that to be a yes," he said gruffly.

"With a big fat *Y.*"

He laid a palm to her womb, and whispered, "Will you have my baby, Ri? Make us a family of six around that table?"

Too profound, too wonderful. She began to cry.

"Aw, sweetheart…" He gathered her close. "I should've waited to give you more time before asking."

She pressed her face into his shirt. "A baby…oh, love…"

The door squeaked open.

"Mommy?" Emily's voice quavered. "What's wrong?"

"What happened to Rianne, Dad?" Behind Emily, Brittany.

Sam zipped around the corner of the house on his bike. Dropping it on the grass, he leaped up the steps. "Mom?"

"It's all right, kids." Against her ear, Jon's voice shook. "Your mom and I are just having the best day we've had in a long, long while."

Rianne lifted her head, looked into those never-forgotten ink-blue eyes. Her heart beat a pure note of happiness.

The absolute best.

* * * * *

SPECIAL EDITION™

This month, Silhouette Special Edition
brings you the newest
Montana Mavericks story

ALL HE EVER WANTED
(SE #1664)

by reader favorite

Allison Leigh

When young Erik Stevenson fell down an abandoned
mine shaft, he was lucky to be saved by a brave—and
beautiful—rescue worker, Faith Taylor. She was struck by
the feelings that Erik's handsome father, Cameron, awoke
in her scarred heart and soul. But Cameron's heart had
barely recovered from the shock of losing his wife some
time ago. Would he be able to put the past aside—and
find happiness with Faith in his future?

GOLD RUSH GROOMS

Lucky in love—and striking it rich—
beneath the big skies of Montana!

**Don't miss this emotional story—
only from Silhouette Books.**

Available at your favorite retail outlet.

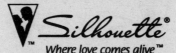

Where love comes alive™

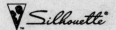

SPECIAL EDITION™

**Don't miss a brand-new miniseries
coming to Silhouette Special Edition**

THE FORTUNES OF TEXAS: Reunion

HER GOOD FORTUNE
by Marie Ferrarella

Available February 2005
Silhouette Special Edition #1665

Gloria Mendoza had returned to Texas for a
fresh start, and was determined not to get involved
with men. But when bank heir Jack Fortune was
assigned to help with her business affairs and
passion ignited between them, she realized some
vows were meant to be broken....

**Fortunes of Texas: Reunion—
The power of family.**

Available at your favorite retail outlet.

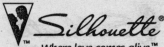

Where love comes alive™

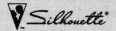

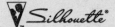

SPECIAL EDITION™

Discover why readers love
Judy Duarte!

From bad boys to heroes...
through the love of a good woman.

The tow-headed son of stunning socialite Kristin Reynolds had to be his. Because, once upon a time, fireman Joe Davenport and Kristin had been lovers, but were pulled apart by her family. Now, they were both adults. Surely Joe could handle parenthood without reigniting his old flame for the woman who tempted him to want the family—and the wife—he could never have.

THEIR SECRET SON
by Judy Duarte
Silhouette Special Edition #1667
On sale February 2005

Meet more Bayside Bachelors later this year!
WORTH FIGHTING FOR—Available May 2005
THE MATCHMAKER'S DADDY—Available June 2005

Only from Silhouette Books!

Where love comes alive™